AUTHOR	CLASS F
HOCKLEY, C.	
TITLE	
Steel ghost	

Chris Hockley was born in 1950 in Suffolk. He earned an honours degree in sociology, psychology and marketing from Manchester University's Institute of Science and Technology. He became a journalist, working on newspapers in Sussex, Bristol, West London, Sydney and Fleet Street. He is currently a sub-editor on the *Sun* and lives in London with his wife and two sons.

CHRIS HOCKLEY

Steel Ghost

GRAFTON BOOKS
A Division of the Collins Publishing Group

LONDON GLASGOW
TORONTO SYDNEY AUCKLAND

For Annelise, of course . . .

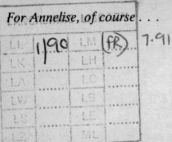

04091323

Grafton Books
A Division of the Collins Publishing Group
8 Grafton Street, London W1X 3LA

A Grafton Paperback Original 1989

Copyright © Chris Hockley 1989

ISBN 0-586-20593-4

Printed and bound in Great Britain by
Collins, Glasgow

Set in Times

1

Aleksandra closed her eyes and tried to forget what was happening. Above her, a sweating, blubbery man called Grigori Golikov huffed and puffed as he set about his business. Aleksandra felt nothing but his awesome weight bearing down on her – and prayed her old wooden bed would stand the strain, as she could not afford another.

Her mind worked in place of her body. Everything had its price, she thought. The bed, the dowdy acrylic clothes she sold over her counter at the department store. Toothbrushes, hair-grips, beetroot, tea. Everything. What she wanted above all was a flat in Moscow. And she had found her currency in sex and Grigori Golikov. He was a cumbersome, vain, loathsome oaf. But he was a Moscow Man. A high-up in the Party. A Russian sent in to make sure the Kazakhs did not get too carried away by their Muslim heritage. He had promised to see what he could do for her in Moscow in return for her favours in Alma-Ata.

Golikov despised Kazakhstan and could not wait to return to the capital. In that respect, at least, Aleksandra was with him. She had never understood why her parents had chosen to move from Moscow to a remote, forgotten homestead in country where exiles and other no-hopers were sent as a punishment. To her, too, it was a prison. But she had completed Stage One of her breakout by running away to Alma-Ata – and meeting someone like Golikov was Stage Two.

5

He was reaching his climax – mercifully, it had not taken long – and Aleksandra broke off from her thoughts to concentrate on making the right noises to please him. There was a sudden rush of cold air as the door was opened. Golikov stopped in mid-thrust and looked over his shoulder. A man in a thick navy greatcoat appeared from nowhere and stood at the foot of the bed, a pistol in his hand and a look of contempt on his face.

He was short, but powerfully built like a bull terrier. The dark blue of his coat emphasized his anaemic complexion, the sign of a hard-working man who spent too long in the office. His fair hair was a co-ordinate to his skin. Cut short and brushed back, it had been treated with some sort of cream or gel, causing tufts on his crown to stand up in spikes. His hard, piercing eyes shone like ice in moonlight, boring into Aleksandra until she felt she would be frozen on the spot.

It was an uncompromising, wicked glare, one which Aleksandra had experienced many times before and one which made her struggle for breath.

The intruder fired the gun immediately. Golikov was hit in the buttocks and cried out in pain. The gunman laughed, but kept the pistol raised and his aim steady. Golikov twisted off Aleksandra and fell to the floor, tangled in a straitjacket of sheets. The gunman fired again. His bullet entered Golikov's head through the bridge of his nose and burst out through the base of his skull.

Fine jets of blood squirted on to the sheets. Golikov's limbs flapped for a moment and then he was still.

Aleksandra wanted to scream, but her larynx was paralysed and she could only utter stunted guttural sounds as if someone had tied a ligature round her throat. Golikov had pulled off all the bedclothes, and she was left naked and exposed. She sat up and drew her knees under her chin so her legs formed the basis of a protective shield. The gunman stood where he had fired, staring at her, waiting for her to speak. She summoned all her resolve and managed to croak: 'You . . . why?'

'Because he was here, that's all.' The gunman was direct, his harsh voice and impatient manner making Aleksandra feel as if she had somehow asked a ridiculous question to which she already knew the answer.

'What now?' she asked, her voice thicker but trembling. 'Are you going to rape me?'

'No. I have no interest.'

'What then?' Aleksandra felt her stomach churning with fear. 'Why kill Golikov? Has he done something?'

'Who?'

Aleksandra looked at the corpse below her, a scarlet stain spreading on the sheets behind his head.

'Grigori Golikov. That was his name.'

'Really? I didn't know.' The gunman looked casually around the room. Freshly whitewashed walls holding shelves brimming with books, wooden figurines of peasant women, several bottles of perfume, a modest collection of records and a Japanese hi-fi procured by Golikov.

'Rather smaller than I expected,' he said. 'But neat and tidy. Excellent taste with a leaning towards luxury, just as always,' he said.

'As always? What do you mean?'

The man's eyes picked out the small table pushed into one corner of the room, where Aleksandra had wined and dined Golikov by candlelight. Two clean casseroles bore testimony to a fine meal of thinly sliced Julienne chicken.

The gunman chuckled.

'Always the perfect hostess,' he said.

'There you go again,' Aleksandra said. 'Always?

Always? I had not seen you before you began watching me. Do I know you? Should I know you?'

'Just as I have known you for many years,' the man replied.

Aleksandra studied him. She was certain she had never encountered him before the previous month, when he first followed her to the department store.

'Just as everything that happens tonight will be reciprocal,' he said, his face hardening. 'You tried to kill me. At last, I have come to repay the compliment. Only I, of course, will succeed where you failed.'

'What!' Aleksandra dug her heels into the bed and pushed back. But there was nowhere to go. She was pinned against the wall by the unwavering barrel of his pistol.

'Such treachery,' he said. 'I always knew you were capable of it. Plotting. Scheming. Throwing up a facade of being the devoted Party servant.'

Aleksandra gasped.

'You're mad,' she said, almost in a whisper. 'I have never joined the Party. Golikov is the closest I have come to it. Now you have killed him.'

'I did not come here to kill him. I came to kill you.'

'No! No!'

'Why so surprised?' the gunman said. 'You frequently made me feel at home as a guest in your house. You treated me with respect. Once, I remember, you even kissed me. Yet all the time you were weaving your murderous tapestry to destroy me.'

Aleksandra was panic-stricken and became hysterical.

'I don't know you!' she shouted. 'I have never met you before!'

'You, the Colonel and Lydia.'

'Who are they? I don't know them either! Why are you

doing this to me? Don't you realize? It's a mistake. A mistake! A mistake!'

'No mistake,' the gunman said calmly. 'I do not make mistakes. You really must accept your death more nobly, my dear, as befits a woman of your rank. You can expect nothing more, surely . . .'

Aleksandra leaped from the bed and ran blindly towards the door. The gunman got there first and kicked it shut. Aleksandra turned to face him, her eyes begging for mercy.

He knew what she wanted – and shook his head slowly.

He pressed his gun on her left breast and shot her once through the heart. She crashed back against the door before sliding down like a wet rag. She did not understand. Her mouth was still wide open with astonishment when she died.

The gunman bent to check she was not breathing. Before he left, he kicked her side. Brutally, repeatedly, until he broke her ribs.

'You cannot destroy me,' he snarled. 'I am indestructible.'

A village east of Kishtwar, in Kashmir.

The night was relentless in its saturating humidity, the visions relentless inside Quester's pounding head.

Two men marooned in a lonely cabin. The suicide of a beautiful woman. The bloody fight to save a city. An assassination attempt foiled by a spy. A bomb exploding under a bed in the middle of the night. A passionate and cherished love. A raging man's chill vow of revenge.

Where did they come from? What did they mean? Why did they return, night after night, to haunt him? They were so vivid . . . so real.

Quester woke with a start, panting and covered in

clinging sweat. It took him a moment to register where he was, to convince himself he was no longer where he had just been.

Gradually his surroundings, illuminated by a placid moon, came into focus. A crumbling room in the ramshackle home of a goatherd. Mud walls encasing a floor of chipped wooden slats. By the door, a straw charm the size and shape of a mongoose to ward off venomous snakes.

Quester tried to throw his mind back to the dreams, to put names and faces to the vaporous figures he had witnessed in his sleep. But, as ever, it was impossible. So near and yet so far, like trying to grasp a strand of chiffon as it is wafted up and away by a current of hot air. Quester lost the remnants of his patience and rammed a frustrated fist into his pillow.

He had even been to a psychiatrist to demand an explanation. It had been two years ago, back in London, but it could have been two minutes.

'How old?' the psychiatrist asked him.

'Forty something,' Quester answered.

'And how long have you been having these dreams?'

'As long as I can remember.'

'With what frequency?'

'Three or four nights in a row, two or three times a year.'

The psychiatrist looked him up and down.

'You look a powerful fellow,' he observed. 'With a powerful imagination.'

'Imagination? That's all?'

'You had an unusual childhood. In an orphanage, according to your records. It is certainly not rare that a child who is left to grow alone, without the parental guidance given to most youngsters, will develop a highly

10

sophisticated imagination flying off at all sorts of tangents. You have no history of illness. You have a happy marriage. What else can it be? Imagination. Ah yes, a strange and wonderful entity . . .'

'There must be more!' Quester exclaimed in frustration. 'There must be a reason!'

The psychiatrist frowned, shrugged his shoulders and mumbled a few words like perception, cognition and relevant learning experiences. He was clearly not inspired by Quester's plight.

'You're too healthy, too self-sufficient and, frankly, far too cynical to be helped by someone like me,' he said.

'But it's your job, damn it. What the hell am I paying you for?'

'There will be no charge for this initial consultation.'

'Put me under hypnosis. Take me back into my past. Unlock the skeletons in my cupboard. For Christ's sake, man, do something!'

'It would be a waste of time. Your time – and my time. I am fifty-six years old, Mr Quester. I have been in practice for thirty-five of them. Give me credit for my experience. I know immediately when a task is futile. Success begins with certain parameters. Certain types of people. Trust, patience, co-operation.'

Quester's trust, patience and co-operation evaporated – and he resorted to anger and hostility.

'You mean you would rather concentrate on conning little old ladies with pocketfuls of Valium and banknotes,' he shouted. 'More cost-effective than unravelling a real mystery, wouldn't you say, *doctor*?'

'Your insults are well-timed,' the psychiatrist responded unswervingly. 'I rest my case.'

Quester called him a pompous quack and walked out.

If only Rosanne was still alive. She used to talk him

through the dreams. She would use his chest as a pillow, her arms as a protective cocoon. She would let her flaming red hair flow over his shoulders while she reassured him, comforted him and helped him to forget. Now she was dead – strangled by a cancer which crept upon her so slowly, but killed her so quickly – and he had to face his cloud-cuckoo land alone.

He sighed with resignation and eased himself slowly from the bed. He was naked and had left the window wide open, snakes or no snakes. But it made no difference. The air was an enveloping mist of glue droplets. He felt a stab of pain in his right thigh. He rubbed it, but it would not go away. Cramp? Fatigue? Or had he strained a muscle when he slipped on a rock earlier in the day?

'You're a bloody wreck,' he muttered to himself. 'A physical and mental bloody wreck.'

Quester checked his watch, a state-of-the-art, computerized piece that was an anachronism in this place, where time had stood still for centuries. Three-thirty already. Damn! He began to worry about going into the day with a heavy head and clogged reflexes. He knew he would need all his concentration and all his skill. He had to blow up a mountain – and the smallest miscalculation could both kill himself and send an avalanche of granite hurtling on to the eggshell roofs of the village in which he was standing.

He smoked a cheroot and wondered if he really was mad. Enough people had told him so.

He preferred to believe in their misinterpretation of his loathing of authority. It fashioned his life. Made him what he was. A man who relied on his skill at his job to see him through. There were no fortunes to be made, but neither were there orders to take. As long as he carried on without mistakes, people would hire him to blow

12

things up and let him get on with it. Maybe they had reservations about his stability, but that was their problem.

He stared at the crystal night sky over Kashmir for half an hour before trying to sleep again. As his eyes finally closed, his mind embraced a dream that took its place alongside all the others in the backwaters of his soul.

The father beating the boy . . . and the boy throwing a knife at the father.

No. 10 Cathedral Street, Gori, Georgia. 1888.

Vissarion's hand flashed again across Joseph's cheek, landing with such force that five red finger marks appeared instantly on the boy's listless face.

The father was drunk, and staggered blindly into a wooden bowl placed on the brick floor to catch drips from a leaking roof. The steel rim of the bowl cracked him on the shins. And though he was wearing leather jackboots, the pain made him wince and heightened his rage.

He stamped on Joseph's bare feet and hit him again, this time in the stomach, before pinning the winded boy against the wall with a single loutish hand. Joseph felt the damp seeping on to his back through a tear in his shirt. He lifted a hand to his smarting face and ran it slowly across the peaks and troughs of a skin left pockmarked by smallpox. It was an untimely reminder of his wretched physical condition. Born with a web-like fusion of the second and third toes of his left foot, and nursing a left arm bent forever when he fell under a carriage, nature had still seen fit to give him smallpox. It had all but killed him – and now perhaps his father would finish the job.

Vissarion shouted: 'I'll teach you to have respect, you little runt! Once and for all, I'll teach you.'

Joseph couldn't see him clearly. A storm had blackened

the day and the shack's two small windows, battered by pearl-sized raindrops, could do nothing to lift the gloom. The only glow came from Vissarion's menacing eyes, the more savage through their setting in lavish eyebrow, moustache and beard. Vissarion came close and renewed his yelling. His stench of wine-contaminated breath and urine-soaked clothes swept into Joseph's nostrils.

'How many times have I told you? How many times? You are eight years old. You have had all that time to learn. Yet *still* you answer me back as if I was a common swineherd. I ask you, is that any way for a son of Georgia to behave? Stay there!'

Vissarion let go of the boy and set about unbuckling the leather belt that hitched loose cloth trousers to a swollen gut.

'A severe beating, Joseph Dzhugashvili, that is the only thing that makes you see sense.'

Joseph obeyed the order to stand still and made no attempt to protest. He had long since learned that it was hopeless to argue. Inside, he felt the indignation that always burned when his father strapped him. Perhaps he was only eight years old. But he knew how to hate.

Vissarion slumped heavily on a stool, shifting it with his rump to avoid a renewed cascade of water spilling from the roof. He tugged at either end of the belt in a mock test of its strength and motioned to the boy to lean across his knee.

Joseph bent and within seconds felt the leather rasped powerfully across his buttocks. He tried his very hardest to stifle a whimper of pain, but it was impossible. The sound encouraged Vissarion.

'What? Can't take it?' he mocked. 'Where is the man in you? What have I sired? I won't have you reach adulthood a mouse!'

He continued the thrashing, increasing the ferocity of each stroke. Joseph cast his eyes around the shack, looking for something – anything – that would take his mind from the pain. There was a noise outside. His attention focused on the door. He saw the handle turning and the door opening and felt a surge of hope as his prayers were answered. His mother Yekaterina appeared, her black shawl pressed flat against her body by the rain. She shuffled in backwards, clasping a basket of mushrooms and using her free hand to brush what water she could from her breast.

She turned with a start when she heard the crack of another lash. For an instant, she froze, too shocked to react to the dreadful sight that confronted her. Then she exploded, hurling the basket to the floor and kicking it hard against the wall.

'You!' she cried at Vissarion. 'Leave him alone. Brute! Let him go.'

She threw herself across the room, landing on top of Joseph across Vissarion's knees. She twisted on to her back and pulled the father's whiskers. He yelled 'Bitch!' and punched her in reply, sending her tumbling to the floor among the scattered mushrooms. She lay there, panting like a mad dog and shouting.

'Why are you here? Why are you not in Tiflis, earning money for your family? I can smell that once again you have spent it all on satisfying yourself. Filthy, stinking drunkard!'

Vissarion stood up. Joseph fell alongside his mother. He was alarmed by her face – mellow and content while his father had been away these past months, now distorted with anger at his return.

'The factory is closed for seven days,' Vissarion said, apparently stung by Yekaterina's onslaught. His words became more obviously slurred as his concentration wavered. 'Repairs to machinery. I wrote to tell you I would be coming.'

'So the good boot-maker returns to his home to beat my little Soso. What a husband! What a father! Go back to Tiflis, brute. There are more wine taverns there for you to spend your wages. Have you made enough money yet to start making shoes here in Gori again, as you promised?'

She jumped to her feet, clapped her hands an inch in front of his eyes and snapped: 'Ha! You are no more than a hobo!'

Vissarion lost control again. Swaying back on his heels for leverage, he pushed her roughly away. She stumbled backwards against the thick pine mantel above the vacant fireplace.

'Your little Soso,' he sneered, pointing at Joseph. 'He is *my* boy, and he is impudent. He will have to learn some respect. He would not tell me where you were.'

Yekaterina wrung her hands in hopeless frustration.

'He could not. I left before dawn to pick mushrooms. I did not tell him where I was going. He is used to it. He is a clever boy, clever enough to fend for himself.'

'So *that* is a caring mother?' Vissarion countered. 'No wonder his brothers died.'

'And you . . .' Yekaterina waved an arm at the sodden walls of the room and the dripping roof. 'This is what you have given him. A watery hovel where his floor is wet, his clothes are wet and his bed is wet.'

Vissarion took a step forward and raised his hand.

'No gratitude! No gratitude!' he shouted. 'Perhaps I ought to end my misery and kill you. So, how would you like that?' He glanced at Joseph, who had risen to his knees. 'Kill you,' he uttered again. 'Kill you both.' He

16

returned his attention to Yekaterina, made a fist and tried to punch her mouth. But the drink made him slow and clumsy. Yekaterina flicked her head to one side and launched her own attack, clawing at Vissarion's face with rough fingertips.

Joseph watched as they tripped over each other and fell grappling in front of the fireplace. He knew he had to do something and took the opportunity to crawl unnoticed into the shack's other room, which his mother used for cooking and he for sleeping.

In the corner was a chipped wooden table where Yekaterina prepared meals. It was invariably cluttered with lurching piles of pans, plates and cutlery, and today was no exception. Joseph, taking care not to dislodge anything and thus raise a racket, fumbled in the dark for the long-bladed knife with which his mother chopped vegetables.

He found it tucked into an earthenware jug and gripped its handle firmly. He pulled it out and ran a finger along the edge of the blade. The ritual was unnecessary as the boy had spent hours sharpening it with a stone the previous day. But he did it all the same.

He climbed slowly to his feet and tiptoed back to the door, peering around the corner with weasel eyes locked in concentration at the battle unfolding before him.

Vissarion, his superior strength telling, rolled on top of Yekaterina. He pinned her shoulders to the floor and butted her in the face with his forehead. Yekaterina shrieked and kicked out uselessly with her feet.

Joseph crept out into the open without being noticed. He looked at Vissarion's bull neck and wondered how far into his father's flesh the knife would penetrate. Would it pierce his throat and leave him gasping for breath? Or would the blade, once lodged in muscle and gristle, need an extra twist to ensure a rapid death?

Joseph felt confident that if the latter was necessary, he could do it before his father had a chance to pull out the knife.

The boy took hold of the blade between thumb and forefinger. He held it vertically in front of his eyes, taking aim at the rich, protruding artery piping blood between Vissarion's head and shoulders.

Joseph balanced himself on his toes and threw the knife with a delicate, restrained touch beyond his years. He watched the glinting arrow arc through the air, levelling off to home in on its victim, and performed a little skip of anticipation.

But the boy's new hope turned just as quickly to despair. The instant before knife plunged into flesh, Vissarion lost his balance and tumbled on his side. And the target, there for the taking, was gone.

The knife shot through thin air above Vissarion's flank before digging deep into the pine mantel. Its handle vibrated feverishly and suddenly the shack was full of its resonant rattle.

Vissarion let go of Yekaterina as if she was a hot coal. He glanced at the knife, then looked aghast at Joseph, wanting to demand an explanation but finding the words trapped in his gullet. Joseph saw the fury building up inside him and knew he was done for unless he could get out of the house.

He made a dash for the door. Vissarion leaped up, grabbed an iron poker from the fireplace and tried to intercept him. But the boy was too fleet. He unlatched the door with one flick and ran out into the rain.

Once, he felt the ground shudder as the poker crashed down an inch from his ankles. And briefly, he heard the

18

splashes of Vissarion's chasing footsteps. But he did not look back or hesitate. He knew his father was too drunk to keep up the pursuit for long – and so it proved.

Joseph made for the outskirts of Gori and walked in the hills. The storm cast a charcoal cloak over his favourite sight, the distant snow caps of the Caucasus mountains, at which he often gazed for hours on end. So he divided his time between climbing rocks, easier in the rain with bare feet, and throwing stones at birds.

He tried to imagine how simple life would be without his father, but it was too unlikely to consider for long. His thoughts became dominated with worry about the fate of his mother, and at dusk, brought on prematurely by the thick cloud, he crept cautiously back to Cathedral Street.

Watching out for Vissarion, he knocked on the door of his neighbours, the Vasinskis, and told them what had happened. They took him in, dried him and covered him with a blanket. Mrs Vasinski, a slothful but kind-hearted woman, gave him a bowl of steaming cabbage broth and, as a treat, a spoonful of his favourite walnut preserve.

'It will be the end of you if he catches you tonight, child,' she said, combing Joseph's bedraggled hair. 'You'll stay here until morning and then we'll see what's to do.'

Mrs Vasinski felt pity for Joseph and wished she could bring herself to hug him. But something strange, a deep misgiving rooted in her soul, always stopped her. She complained about it later to her husband as the boy slept.

'I will grant you that nature has not been kind to him,' she said, measuring her words thoughtfully. 'But through all his illnesses and through all his beatings, I have never – not once – seen that child cry.

'It's not normal.'

2

Quester's task was to blow a path up the mountain wide enough and flat enough for the job to be finished later by a road gang. He didn't know what the government were planning to build at the summit, though he had heard whispers that it would be some sort of listening post. It seemed logical, what with the close proximity of China, Pakistan, Afghanistan and, particularly, the Soviet Union. But as long as they paid him, he didn't much care.

After three weeks of controlled explosions and the subsequent clearing of rubble, he had come to the most difficult part of the project – a giant overhanging section of rock known by the locals as Mother because of its resemblance to a pregnant womb.

Quester had drilled ten funnels at appropriate stress points and filled each with cartridges containing plastic explosive. He arranged the charges in a vertical spiral. Each had its own umbilical detonating cord – plastic-coated with a core of explosive – undulating over the contours of the rock like strands of spaghetti and linked to a neat line of electronic detonators. These were spaced so that each detonator would only set off its own cord. A conical pattern of wires stretched from the detonators to a master box containing a radio receiver and ten terminals.

Quester had calculated that if he fired each charge in turn from the base upwards, rather than detonate the lot in one go, falling rock would be diverted away from the village to which he had now returned.

All that was needed was the flick of a switch and a

resolute push on the ten red buttons of the transmitter Quester held tensely in his right hand. He had waited two hours to carry out these simple manoeuvres, but suspected he would have to delay at least another two.

The villagers were in the valley below Mother, locating their livestock and shooing them away from the danger area by slapping their backsides with sticks and sheaves of dried grass. It was a laborious business. A goat here, a chicken there. They grazed and foraged across a vast area of the hillside and valley, with neither help nor control.

Quester had foreseen the problem a week ago. But nothing he could say could stir the villagers into premature action. They would clear their animals when Quester was ready to push his buttons – and not one second before.

'To you, a goat is a goat. To them, a goat is the difference between life and death.'

Vijay sensed Quester's growing impatience. He was a student from a wealthy family – Brahmins – who Quester had taken on in Delhi as his interpreter and gofer. Vijay could have slumped in a hammock amid the sumptuous greenery of South Delhi's most exclusive suburb, Vasant Vihar. He could have spent the rest of his life sipping ice-cold nimbupani sherbert while servants cleared dead leaves from the swimming pool. But he had preferred to branch out on his own and, as he put it, get his hands as dirty as a miner's.

Quester liked him. He had been the only person of interest at the British embassy party, to which Quester had been invited upon his arrival in India. Oh yes, everyone was curious about a new listening post.

Vijay rested his foot lightly on Quester's, to stop it tapping.

'Surely the world can wait another two hours for your

fireworks,' he said. 'You must learn to relax. Rome was not built in a day.'

Quester gazed the 500ft up to Mother and cast his eyes around her rugged, dusty domain. Early afternoon shadows were giving way to late afternoon shadows. Longer, blacker, more confusing. Quester was painfully aware that in Kashmir, dusk dropped like a lead curtain, swiftly and uncompromisingly. He pulled his foot from beneath Vijay's and resumed his tapping.

'What are you – a bloody guru?' he said. 'Coaching Western man in the mystical ways of the East? Stick to what you know, Vijay. I need daylight for my fireworks.'

'Why? You said everything was ready. The rock fall was planned. What difference does it make whether it is day or night?'

'It is still a dangerous business. Would you rather walk in the jungle by day, or by night? Ask the tigers which they prefer.'

'You're being facetious.'

'And you're being a pain in the arse.'

'Such a short fuse!' Vijay cried. 'You don't need daylight. You need a woman.'

Vijay wished he could suck back the words and swallow them. Quester had told him what happened to Rosanne on the way from Delhi. If Vijay had been standing beside a fire, he would have thrown himself on it.

Quester scowled at him, but saw his discomfort and said softly: 'I'm tired, that's all. It's hard to sleep in a sauna. Go and see if you can find out how much longer.'

Vijay turned to walk down the sloping track separating the two rows of huts that made up the village. He returned ten minutes later with a helpless shrug of the shoulders. Quester sighed, leaned back against the wooden wheels of a donkey cart and lit another cheroot.

The two youngest children of his host, the goatherd, looked up at him with puzzled expressions. Kiran, who was eight, and her brother Ramesh, who was five, shared the same tree-bark brown eyes that made every child in the mountains irresistible. Their ragged clothes, matted hair and barefoot poverty could not mask their supreme natural beauty. In his time at the village, Quester had grown deeply fond of Kiran and Ramesh, and they of him.

'Where's your mother?' Quester asked them. Vijay translated. They replied in Kashmiri – and looked lost.

'She's with their father and their older brothers and sisters,' Vijay said. 'Somewhere in the valley. The children don't know where.'

Quester decided to cheer them up. It would help pass the time – and he enjoyed playing with children. They had no pretensions.

He picked up a dead branch bleached white by the sun and used it to draw a face in the dust. A circle for the head, three dots for the eyes and nose and a turned-down sad-looking mouth. He sketched another beside it, identical but for a U-shaped mouth giving the face a happy smile. He pointed to the first, then jabbed Kiran and Ramesh in their stomachs as if to say: 'This is you.' He pointed to the second and jabbed himself, giving them an exaggerated grin to emphasize the point.

The children laughed.

'Aha!' Quester exclaimed. 'Now you are the happy ones.'

He pointed to the second face and jabbed them in the stomachs again. They understood, and laughed louder.

In an instant, their laughter was drowned by a thunderous explosion from above, followed at once by a second, sharper, blast.

23

Quester shot round instinctively in time to see a massive cloud of dust and debris shooting from two gaping holes ripped in Mother. There was a sickening series of cracks, groans and moans – like those made from the base of a tree trunk as it is felled – and great fissures appeared in the overhanging rock.

Quester shouted 'No!' but it made no difference. He could *feel* the great weight of granite pressing down . . . with nothing left to support it.

Huge sections of the rock gave way in a sudden rush and crashed down the mountainside towards the valley, breaking into a cascade of boulders along the way. There was no clever sequence of explosions, no ridge of stone to divert the landslide. Rocks bounced. Earth crumbled and slid. There was a roar like surf pounding over a gravel beach.

'Christ!' Quester panted in blind, helpless panic. 'There are people down there!'

It was too late for them. The rockfall cut down everything in its path. Trees, bushes, animals – and villagers with no time to flee. They watched disbelievingly as the giant, solid wave hurtled towards them and put their arms across their heads in a futile gesture of self-protection.

Even at this distance, two or three hundred yards, even above the rasp of devastation, through the billowing haze of dust, Quester could hear their screams. Men's screams. Women's screams. Children's screams. Screams of old people who had survived eight decades, only to be buried by earth and stone raining from the sky in their ninth.

The catastrophe lasted two minutes, until the floor of the valley was filled with rock and a dreadful silence that seemed impossible just an instant before.

No-one who witnessed the slide could move. Quester trembled. Vijay stood with his mouth wide open, gaping at the awful spectacle. Kiran and Ramesh looked puzzled again.

It was Quester who spoke first. His cracked voice betrayed the horror he felt inside.

'Vijay, get someone to look after the children,' he said. 'Then see if there is anything to be done. There will be wounded. There's some medical stuff in my room. Bandages, antiseptic, a small amount of morphine. You'll need that.'

Vijay was in shock, rooted to the spot.

'Vijay!' Quester shouted. 'Move, Vijay! You're needed. Get everyone *out* of the village.' He pointed to a neighbouring hillock. 'Take them higher, up there. Who the hell knows what could happen next.'

The student snapped out of his trance. He took the children by the hand and led them away, looking over his shoulder at Quester.

'What are you going to do?' he asked.

'Go up the mountain. Find out what went wrong. Only two charges have exploded. That leaves eight. Anything could go off after that magnitude of disturbance. Don't let anyone come back into the village or go into the valley until I give the all-clear. Here . . .'

Quester threw Vijay a walkie-talkie, the companion to the black box strapped to his waist.

As he made for the entrance to the new mountain road, the villagers who had not been in the valley gathered around him. They said nothing, but he could feel their eyes. They were knives, spears, scimitars. Glinting metal with poisoned tips.

Quester felt a weight of guilt on his shoulders equal to anything the mountain had pressed down on the holes blown in Mother. He tried not to let the villagers see the tears spilling over his cheeks.

* * *

Quester saw the devastation more clearly the further he walked up the mountain. It was a dreadful sight. The falling rock had cut a swathe 100 yards wide through brush, grass and scrub, spreading out into a pool of cracked granite as it reached the valley.

Survivors stumbled screaming from the lake of stone. Some pointed back to where loved ones were trapped, dead or dying. Others just ran.

Quester quickened his step. He was the technician. He was the one who had to find out what went wrong. He was the one who had to prevent a repetition.

It could happen any second and Quester knew he could be walking towards his death. But it was a duty he could not shirk. And looking at the plight of those below him, he had neither time nor inclination to be afraid.

His mind was transfixed by thoughts of what set off the two charges. A sudden earth tremor? He hadn't felt one before the explosions. An unexpected electromagnetic signal setting off the detonators? Unlikely in such a sparse area so free of electronic gadgetry. Perhaps some of the village children had climbed the peak and fiddled with the detonating cord, or even with the explosive itself. God knows, they had been warned often enough to stay away, in the strongest language. But curious little fingers had been responsible for worse.

Then Quester found himself thinking the unthinkable. That he had made a mistake. A terrible, fatal mistake.

The walkie-talkie crackled and Vijay called from the village.

'They are moving,' he reported. 'But there's a lot of blood to be cleared up first.'

'Get them out!' Quester snapped. 'Wounds can be dressed later, in a safer place.'

'I'll try. But they are in an awful state.'

'What news of casualties?'

'At least twelve dead so far.' Vijay hesitated, then spoke barely audibly. 'Kiran and Ramesh are orphans.'

Quester didn't answer. He could not. The word 'orphan' paralysed him. He knew what it was like to be an orphan. Deprived, loveless, bitter. Confused. In his mind he saw the faces of Kiran and Ramesh as they had been just minutes before, laughing with delight at his sketches in the dust. He stopped climbing and had to vomit before he could carry on.

He began to ache all over. The pain in the thigh which had troubled him the previous night returned with a vengeance and he felt an urge to take hold of the throbbing flesh in his hand and tear it out.

He was nearing Mother now, the scarred rock taking on a menacing appearance she did not have before.

Her outline was silhouetted against the pastel orange light of early evening. Quester could see the hole blown in the centre of her womb – and knew at once that it had been Charges 4 and 5 which had exploded. Charges 1, 2 and 3 – those at the base of the rock which would have taken the landslide further away from the village – were still intact. Above the gaping, windswept hole, a massive rectangular slab of stone looked ready to fall with the tickle of a feather.

Quester picked his way across the rubble. He took one step at a time, putting the weight of one leg carefully down on each foot before committing the rest of his body.

He checked the lower funnels first. The cartridges of explosive were normal, stable, lying dormant as if they had been there for centuries, untroubled by the mayhem that had erupted around them. Quester traced the detonating cord of each back to the master box. He found nothing irregular. The same was true of the cords leading around the explosion crater to Charges 6 to 10. Those linked to Charges 4 and 5, though, had vanished – replaced by twisting lines of white ash.

Something had set them off.

The master box . . .

It had to be a fault in the master box.

The black plastic box, no bigger than a hardback book, rested alone and exposed fifty yards away on a flat rock directly above the village, ready to receive its signal from below. Its base was weighted by lead to prevent movement and its cover was held on by two hand-tight butterfly screws.

Quester felt his heartbeat quicken as he slipped his fingers around the screws. It was the instinctive reaction of a man defusing a bomb. For if the fault lay within the master box – a sloppy connection, a dud terminal, a rogue wire – then a bomb was what it was. Any recklessness, any slip, and there was certain to be at least one more explosion, and possibly eight.

His hands became greasy with sweat and it took several minutes to free the cover. Quester stared at it for a moment. It was almost as if he did not want to take it off, dreading what he might find inside.

He could delay no longer. He pressed his palms against either flank of the lid and lifted it off with the gentlest touch, his body taut and prepared for the shock waves he was sure would hit it the next instant.

What he saw took his breath away.

Ten wires, in parallel lines a centimetre apart. But two had been disconnected from their end terminals.

The wires leading to Charges 4 and 5.

Someone had been there!

Not a child. Not an amateur. Someone who knew what he was doing.

Whoever it was had disconnected the two charges from the master box and reconnected them to something else to cause the explosions. What? A battery? And why? Why would anyone in his right mind want to send a rockfall plummeting on to the heads of a dozen helpless Kashmiris? And why just Charges 4 and 5? Why not send the whole lot up and destroy the village as well?

Quester reached for his walkie-talkie to tell Vijay of his discovery. He felt a strange combination of relief and fear. Relief that he had been exonerated. Fear brought on by a sinister mystery.

There was a noise behind him. A scratching, like a rat clawing at a door. Quester half-turned, but it was too late.

The rock hammered into the side of his head, forced down by an unseen hand.

He was lifted off his feet and fell to the ground with a sensation of weightless spiralling, like an astronaut in space. He landed on his back and felt the pain – searing shards of agony ripping across his skull and into every crevice in his body.

The rock was brought down on his head again and again. Viciously, remorselessly. Bone cracked and splintered. Flesh tore. There was dust in his eyes and a soupy warmth in his mouth as he tasted his own blood. He had only half a face, he was sure of that.

'Nothing more than you deserve.' *A voice, rasping and faint at the same time. Impossible . . .*

The rock rammed into him for the final time. There was a slapping noise as his jaw was broken, like a swimmer diving into water at the start of a race.

Other sounds followed. Metallic. Squeaky. Frenetic. Screws moving on threads. Someone was tampering with the master box again, rigging another wire to more plastic explosive. Quester felt his chest heaving. He wanted to shout out, to warn someone – anyone – but could not. There was another ear-splitting explosion behind him, as ferocious as the first two. Great stones thudded to the ground around him. Around them.

Breathing. Heavy, distorted breathing on my face. The stench of nicotine. A thumb opening my eyelid. I see nothing. I am dead.

He is standing over me, looking at my crumpled, bleeding body. The voice again. Louder. Clearer.

'Nothing more than you deserve, Colonel. Now I must find Lydia and attend to her.'

Sun on my face. Hot, so hot. Footsteps . . . running . . . running away. Fading. Fading into the distance. I'm getting cooler. I see a forest, a stream, cabins in a clearing. It must be Heaven.

Narym. West Siberia Plain. 1912.

The cabin was a mess, its floor littered with discarded letters, soiled clothes, dried mud and the paraphernalia of trapping and fishing.

Sverdlov coughed – and Joseph laughed.

'That tuberculosis will kill you in the end, you know it,' Joseph said. 'How many years do you think you have left?'

Sverdlov ignored him and tried to concentrate on his book. There was no kerosene, so he pressed the pages nearer the single candle that lit the cabin during the endless night.

They were unlikely room-mates, even for a couple of revolutionaries sharing a common exile in Siberia. Sverdlov, the gentle, scholarly but sickly Jew. Joseph, the crude, domineering and robust Georgian.

Joseph wouldn't let Sverdlov be. He kicked the book

so it flew from the scholar's hands and crashed against the cabin's log walls.

'Listen,' he said innocently as if he had done nothing offensive. 'I need your help.'

Sverdlov held on to his dignity. He took off his egg-shaped spectacles and rubbed his eyes, smarting again from the strain of reading in near-darkness.

'I will go blind,' he muttered to himself. 'I'm sure of it.'

He replaced the spectacles and glanced sideways at his book, now resting languidly on the floor, its cover torn. He looked contemptuously at Joseph and asked: 'What is it?'

'A name!' Joseph bellowed. 'I must have a new name!'

It was fashionable among young Bolsheviks to continually switch surnames in the hope of staying one step ahead of the Okhrana, the Tsarist police. Sverdlov, a proud man, had never seen the point of it.

'They will arrest you no matter what you call yourself,' he said.

'No faith, no drive, no guts,' Joseph countered. 'What do you think of Stalin?'

'What . . . ?' Sverdlov was barely concentrating.

'Stalin! Man of steel! It sounds fine, doesn't it? A good word, reflecting both the strength of our historic movement and the material we will need to build a new Soviet nation.' Joseph became excited. 'After all, has not Rosenfeld become Kamenev, the man of stone. And has not Skriabin transformed himself into Molotov, the hammer? The only one to have screwed it up is Bronstein. Do you know he took the name of Trotsky from one of his prison warders? He is even more of a fucking fool than I thought. But what can you expect from a Jew?'

Sverdlov was outraged. He leaped from his chair and shouted: 'Keep your poison! What do you know?'

31

Joseph realized he had insulted Sverdlov and apologized in his own way. He waved a dismissive hand and said: 'I did not mean you, Sverdlov. As Jews go, you are reasonable to live with.'

Sverdlov, who did not like to fight, backed off and went outside to calm down. He stood stroking his wispy beard, staring blankly at the pillars of smoke that rose in perfect parallel lines from the 150 cabins that made up the Narym settlement. Away to the right, the beginnings of a river slipped stealthily through the forest and the bogs. There was no wind, no sound. And despite it being July, no warmth.

Sverdlov was wearing a thick fisherman's sweater under his jacket, but even so he shivered. He felt more isolated than ever.

'I must leave this place,' he said as he walked back into the cabin.

'Escape?' Stalin, sitting on his bed untangling a fishing line, had his back turned.

'I have a plan,' said Sverdlov. 'I'm going next month.'

'It's 2,600 miles back to Petersburg.'

'I am well aware of that, Comrade *Stalin*,' Sverdlov said sarcastically. 'What I am not sure about is whether I am running to escape the gendarmes or to escape you.'

'Good! You used my name!' Stalin said gleefully. He grew impatient with the fishing line and threw it to the floor still in a hopeless tangle.

'Pick it up!' Sverdlov said indignantly.

Stalin turned and glared at the scholar with what Trotsky called his 'yellow' eyes.

This time Sverdlov stood his ground. He cast a hand around the rubbish on the floor and said: 'You are an animal. Look at it! And it is all your doing. Where you go, rats follow. We are stuck in this forsaken place together. Why do you not contribute to the chores that must be done? When was the last time you gathered wood for the stove? When was the last time you lit it, or even stoked it?'

Stalin grinned aloofly. He filled a clay pipe with makhorka tobacco kept loose in his pocket and put a match to it.

'Because such matters are more pressing for you than for me,' he said. 'So it is only correct that you should accept the lion's share.'

He blew out a cloud of atrocious smoke.

'What do you think of it?' he said, knowing it would irritate Sverdlov. 'I have a tame gendarme. I give him rabbits, he gives me tobacco. When I threaten to tell his superiors of our arrangement, which I will do soon, he will give me papers to get me through the Okhrana checkpoints when I, too, slip away to Petersburg. Simple, isn't it?'

The noxious cloud reached Sverdlov and he coughed violently, holding a hand against the pain in his chest.

Stalin's grin grew wider.

'That tuberculosis will kill you in the end,' he said.

3

'And so one life ends and another begins. Through this holy anointing, may the Lord in his love and mercy help you with the grace of the Holy Spirit. May the Lord who frees you from sin save you and raise you up.'

Quester heard the words. Some distinctly, some muffled. But he heard them. At the same time, he felt a tugging sensation, as if he was the prey caught between the unyielding jaws of two rival predators. He was stretching, being stretched, until muscle became rubber and bone became gelatine.

What was happening? He couldn't tell, but he knew he was frightened.

The stretching went on. Rubber shredded. Gelatine disintegrated. All that was left was a pool of water, evaporating into a hot, thick mist and floating upwards.

It was then that he saw them. He was looking down from above. Whether he was in the room or outside he couldn't tell. But he watched as they stood in a cluster around the bed. There were five of them . . .

On the left was a priest. Old and weary, he wore an unkempt black robe with a soiled collar. Half-moon spectacles balanced precariously on the end of his nose as he read the last rites from the limp, time-worn card he had placed on the bedside table. He made the sign of the cross with his left hand and dipped the fingers of his right hand into a silver bowl filled with anointing oil.

Beside him stood a doctor in a spotless white coat. He was middle aged, but boasted suave, thick grey hair groomed in great waves to complement the deep, curved lines of knowledge that carved across his recently sun-tanned face. He had his arms folded and was scowling impatiently as if urging the priest to make haste.

Next to the physician was a nurse, much younger and clearly less experienced with the rigours of working in intensive care. Overcome by the awfulness of it all, she discreetly turned her shoulder from the doctor so he could not see the tell-tale trickle that had escaped her eye.

The fourth person in the room was a figure of authority, despite being much younger – and shorter – than the doctor. Quester estimated his age was mid to late thirties, but he had an air about him that commanded respect. The deferential smiles and sideways glances of both doctor and priest illustrated the point. He was formally dressed in a light grey suit and white shirt, with a pastel-pink tie that did little to divert attention from his pale skin. His hair was his most striking feature, dazzling blond and spiky like the tips of a porcupine's quills.

Quester did not know him – and his attention turned to the fifth and final spectator. A woman in a long, trans-lucent robe. Satin, perhaps, or silk. But strangely unsuited to the sanitized coldness of an intensive-care room. And hardly fit for wearing in front of a priest, of all people.

Nevertheless, she was a striking – and somehow familiar – figure. She stood with her back towards Quester, tall and erect, perfectly poised on slender legs that showed through the fabric of her robe. Long, glowing red hair tumbled down to the spectacular curve at the base of her spine. She half-turned – and Quester caught a glimpse of her face.

Rosanne!

No . . . it couldn't be. Rosanne was dead. Gone. Buried in the ground. More than two years ago.

Quester stared at the woman, studied her every movement. She was walking around the edge of the bed,
towards the head poking lifelessly from a neatly pressed
fold of undisturbed sheets. The effortless grace was there,
just as it had always been. And the casual flick of the
head to remove stray strands of hair from her eyes . . .

It *was* Rosanne!

She looked mournfully at what she could see of the lost
patient's head. The top half was masked by bandage and
the rest was overshadowed by the large respirator tube
thrust down an unprotesting gullet. Electrodes probed
into both skull and chest. Colourless plastic tubes dropped
from saline and food drips suspended on a stand, and
vanished under the sheets.

Beside the bed, the needles of dials on a renal dialysis
machine flicked to left and right. The bright line on the
green monitor recording heartbeat showed a regular
hump corresponding to – and dependent on – the impulses
of the life-support machine.

'The man in the bed,' Quester cried. 'Me! You know,
Rosanne, don't you? It's me.'

The sound of his words crashed around the room,
picking up volume as they bounced off each wall. Each
word merged with the previous and the next until they
were a distorted mass of syllables with the awesome
energy of thunder.

Yet no-one heard them. There was not a flicker of
recognition from the quintet below him. They were talking between themselves, that much was clear. Yet he
could hear them no more than they could hear him.

'Rosanne! Oh God, Rosanne . . .'

She bent to kiss what flesh she could find between the
bandage and the respirator tube. Instinctively, she raised

a hand as if to stroke his hair. But it, too, was covered and her hand remained limp and awkward in mid-air.

She straightened herself and turned away. Quester saw her face again – and turned to ice.

He had expected grief, tears, a tremble of the lips and a sorrowful shake of the head. But she was *smiling*. A warm, entreating smile as if she was glowing inside with a deep, dark-velvet pleasure.

Quester knew something was wrong. He was dying – and Rosanne was glad. It couldn't be true.

He sensed that now, more than at any other time, he needed to summon every ounce of willpower he had ever possessed. He had heard of others who had been given the last rites. How they had heard the priest from inside their locked cocoons of gauze. How they first had to convince themselves they were not going to die, and then convince the rest of the world.

Quester rallied his concentration and wrapped it around the word 'survival'. He saw every letter in large three-dimensional shapes coloured red with a yellow background. He spelled out the word again and again.

S-U-R-V-I-V-A-L. He ate the word, drank it, caressed it, worshipped it. No other word existed.

Beneath him, the priest pulled the bible from his pocket and slipped the rites card inside its cover. He went to shake the doctor's hand. The doctor accepted the gesture and watched the clergyman leave, puffing out his cheeks in an exaggerated display of relief. After taking one last glance at Quester, the spiky-haired stranger also departed, looking almost flippant as if thinking, 'Oh well, another one bites the dust.' The doctor opened the door for him and dipped his head. The stranger walked past without recognition.

The doctor briefly stepped out into the corridor to

watch him go, then re-entered the room. He spotted the nurse's damp display of emotion and frowned at her reproachfully.

But he ignored Rosanne. An omission which Quester could not begin to understand, so flagrant was his wife's behaviour. She was clinging on to the rail at the foot of the bed, leaning back with her hair dangling behind her, swaying to and fro and breathing deeply to take in the air as if she was a choked city dweller reaching the sea for the first time in her life.

The nurse, still sobbing, motioned reluctantly to the umbilical respirator tube. The doctor nodded and spoke a few words to her. She walked towards the patient and raised an arm to pull out the tube and end a life.

'Survival!' Quester shouted it and sent thunder rolling around the room once more. A great wind blew up, swirling and raging, though it disturbed not a hair on the nurse's head. Within seconds, it accelerated to hurricane force and developed into a tight, roaring tube of air, wide at the top but tapering to a needle-sharp point at its base.

Quester was sucked into the eye of the maelstrom, spiralling down its length at tremendous velocity. He screamed louder than he had ever screamed before. The roaring stopped. The storm subsided. All was peace and calm.

'Are you sure? Absolutely certain?' The nurse's voice, shaking and insecure. There was something about its resonance and its pitch which gave Quester hope.

'Christ, give me strength!' The cynical doctor's simmering anger with the raw recruit boiled over.

'I'm sorry,' she offered. 'It's just . . .'

'Just that you can't believe anyone can die?' the doctor interrupted. 'We're all going to die, Teardrop. You, me, everyone. No more breathing, no more heartbeat. No more screwing with your boyfriend on a Saturday night. Just rigor mortis, decay and decomposition. That's what you've got coming, Teardrop. Today, Mr Tom Quester. Tomorrow, you.'

'But he's such a strong man. I can feel it. He's . . . I don't know . . . *special*.'

The doctor lost the remaining scrap of his patience.

'Now look! I didn't ask to have you here, moping about and generally getting in the bloody way. It's part of your training. So learn, girl, learn! This man was ninety-nine parts dead the moment he had his accident. He spent two months in a hospital in India, Pakistan or wherever the hell he was. And it has been three months since he was transferred back here. In all that time, he has made not one iota of progress. He has failed every test for life known to mankind. He may have flesh and bone, Teardrop, but he's as dead as a bloody Dodo. So pull that bloody tube out and let the bastard stiffen up in peace.'

'One more try,' the girl pleaded. 'He deserves it.'

'What do you mean, he *deserves* it?' the doctor asked incredulously.

'He has no-one to stick up for him. No relatives. No family. No-one to stop you!'

'Learn one more thing, Teardrop. That was gross insubordination. I'll let you get away with it this time because you've got good tits. But one more time and you'll be on report.'

'No-one,' the girl repeated. 'He's the loneliest man I've ever met.'

'Met him, have you?' the doctor gave his voice a cutting edge of sarcasm. 'Been getting up in the middle of the night and giving you the odd quickie on the floor, has he? Clever guy! Although I suppose you did say he was a special kind of man – '

The nurse, revolted by the doctor's remorseless crudity, did not reply. Quester could tell she was a special kind of girl.

'Anyway,' the doctor sighed. 'We dug up some bloody third cousin twice removed, or whoever that weirdo with the hair was. He said we could switch off. Signed the papers.'

'He didn't care. It was almost as if he was glad Mr Quester was dying.'

'So he's got a few quid coming in a will. He was all that was required. Read your textbooks, Teardrop.'

'One more try . . .'

'Nurse Warren! I am tiring of this conversation, which, frankly, I find rather juvenile. I have a busy day ahead and I'm already behind. Now do as you are told! Pull the fucking tube out, inform the fucking mortuary and call a fucking porter!'

A swing door clattered. There was no more talking. The doctor had left to go about his business. Quester was alone with the nurse.

He sensed movement in his throat. The nurse had wrapped a hand around the respirator tube and was tugging. Gently, as if she didn't want to hurt him. He could feel plastic sliding out from deep inside him.

Survival!

It was slipping away from him – and this time he was powerless to stop it.

He wanted to shout, to scream, to reach up and pull the tube back into his chest. But there was nothing he could do. He had no strength, no way of fighting back.

The slithering in his body stopped. He felt a thumb pushing under his right eyelid, forcing it open.

He saw a fierce, blinding light of the purest white. It stabbed into his brain, probing, hurting. He knew he had

40

to close his eye to prevent the laser boring out through the back of his skull.

'Doctor!' the nurse screamed. 'Doctor! Come back!'

He heard a pair of heels clicking rapidly across the antiseptic tiled floor. The door clattered again as the nurse ran out of the room. She returned a moment later. There were two sets of footsteps. The doctor was with her. The nurse was panting, trying to talk between gasps for air.

'His pupil shrank when I opened his eyelid,' she said. 'I saw it!'

'If you're making this up, I'll see you out of this hospital, young lady.'

Quester felt another thumb on his eyelid. Rougher, more impatient. He saw the light again, felt the pain again.

'Good God,' the doctor uttered.

'I told you,' the nurse shrieked. 'He's alive!'

Quester felt a wave of relief break over him and was swamped with a warm sensation of security. For the first time in months, the rigid cage of concentration he had needed for his renaissance could be unlocked, just for a short time.

Immediately, instinctively, he allowed his mind to wander. He drifted, luxuriously, on a magic carpet of euphoria. Across vast oceans, around great castles, over glaciers and through deep gorges. He wanted to imagine and enjoy all the scenery and spectacle he had been forced to yield in exchange for a world of shadows and a hospital bed.

He did not stop until he floated into woodland and saw a group of picnickers basking in a sun-filled clearing.

*Stalin's dacha at Zubalovo, outside Moscow. Summer
1932.*

The raucous sound of playing children could not bring a
smile to Nadya's face. She was in a dark depression, as
she had been for weeks. She glanced sideways at her
husband, sitting cross-legged on the grass telling a joke to
Molotov, Beria and Voroshilov. Something about a
whore, an ass and a perverted coalminer.

'I'm going for a walk,' Nadya announced quietly.

Stalin looked at her angrily. She had disturbed his
concentration as he was about to deliver the punchline.

'Then go,' he said, flicking his fingers at her. 'What are
you waiting for?'

Nadya rose to her feet, shielding her eyes against the
sharp afternoon sun. Everyone agreed that though she
could be melancholy, her meticulous beauty made her a
wife fit for a master of men. Round-faced and Oriental in
appearance, her short hair was parted in a perfect line
directly in the centre of her crown. Her large eyes, proud
bone structure and clear complexion gave her a mystical
allure. And her loose floral dress was custom-made for
such an airy day.

She took the arm of her closest friend Polina Molotov
and they stepped over a ragged line of picnic baskets into
the dappled shade cast by a sparse copse of silver birches.
Nadya stayed silent as they walked. Polina, sensing that
something was seriously amiss, did not press her.

It was only when they rested a moment, deep into the
woods, that Nadya suddenly burst into tears.

'What am I going to do?' she said with complete
despair. 'He is a monster. The man I married is a cruel
monster.'

Polina glanced nervously around to see if anyone had
heard. It was not uncommon for secret policemen to

follow Nadya, whether she was strolling in the Kremlin, studying at the textile college in Moscow or picnicking at the dacha. This time, as far as Polina could tell, there was no-one. She eased Nadya on to a fallen tree trunk and wiped her damp cheeks with the frilled cuffs of her blouse.

Nadya wanted to talk. Polina, who had long been Nadya's shoulder to cry on, said she was listening. Nadya, trying desperately to shrug off her misery, began surprisingly brightly.

'When I was a teenager in Petersburg, living with Father and Mama, he used to pop in to see us whenever he could. He was always running from the Okhrana, of course, but made time to visit us despite the risk. I remember one cold, cold Shrovetide. Mama and I had our noses pressed to the window watching the low Finnish sledges slip by, their pretty ribbons floating in the breeze and their bells jingle-jangling as they rattled over ruts in the ice.

'The drivers were calling out to people, "Jump in and I'll give you a ride!" The people looked at each other and giggled like schoolchildren. Some clambered aboard and clapped their hands with delight as they watched the plaited manes of the horses bounce up and down in front of them.

'Suddenly a voice like gravel called out from behind us, "Who'd like a sledge ride? Well, get dressed and hurry – we'll stop one straight away!" It was Soso! Mama and I couldn't believe our eyes. We thought he was in exile in Narym with Sverdlov.'

'*The* Sverdlov?' Polina interrupted. 'The one who became president?'

'Yes. He died of tuberculosis, just as my husband said he would.'

'Go on . . .'

43

Nadya took up her story again.

'Soso laughed and told us he had escaped. We were so excited – and impressed. It was the FOURTH time he had escaped from exile. How wonderful! He bullied us to get a move on. "Come on, get dressed why don't you? We're going on a sledge." Mama and I grabbed our fur coats and followed him downstairs. Soso waved down a sledge and called, "Driver, driver, over here! What about a ride?"

'We got on, the driver cracked his whip and we were away! Wind in our hair and such *cold* noses. Mama and I couldn't stop laughing, especially when Soso mimicked the way the driver kept praising his stumpy little horse. Soso joined in our caterwauling as we bumped over a snow-drift, certain we would fall from the sledge at any moment.

'We glided down Sampsonievskaya Prospekt and past the station where a steam train took passengers to Lesnoy. Soso ordered the driver to stop. Then he turned to Mama and said, "I'll get off here and you can ride back home." He kissed us both, jumped off, paid the driver and hurried away to the station without another word. And that was the last we saw of him for two weeks!

'Oh, I tell you, Polina, when I married him I thought he was the finest hero of the Revolution. I thought marriage to such a man was the highest form of service I could offer to Bolshevism. And, of course, there was a true and deep bond between us. But now . . .'

Nadya's words tailed off and for a moment she looked as lost as a newborn fawn abandoned in the forest. Polina was ready for another cascade of tears, but Nadya composed herself and carried on, gathering strength as she spoke.

'The students at the academy, they are the ones who

are telling me the truth. They don't know who I am, you see. I use another name. Many have relatives or friends living in the country. They tell me of the horrors of Joseph's drive to collectivize the farms. How anyone who disagrees with him, or stands in his way, is shot or stabbed by his murder squads. How his victims are numbered in millions. *Millions*, Polina, do you hear me? How the chaos has brought disease and famine in its wake. And how famine has brought cannibalism. Can you honestly believe that? Cannibalism in Russia today? That is the gift my hero of the Revolution has bestowed on his people. My heart bleeds for them.'

Polina heard a twig snap in the distance and put a cautionary finger to her lips.

'I won't shush!' Nadya shrieked indignantly. 'He has spies everywhere. Let them tell him! I don't care any more.'

'Of course you do.' Polina, still watching for shadows, took Nadya's hand and tried to reassure her.

'Do you know, he treats me with less regard than he treats his servants,' Nadya said. 'He calls me names, he spits at me and he goes into a rage when I warn the children of the perils of alcohol. The other day, he deliberately gave Vasily and Svetlana a glass of wine in front of me. Just to annoy me, you see.'

'He is a Georgian,' Polina offered without conviction. 'It is a Georgian habit to give drink to children at dinner.'

Nadya wouldn't have it.

'He does it to spite me, that is all,' she said. 'No more and no less.'

Voices approached from the right, amplified by the stillness of the woods. Stalin appeared through the birches fifty yards away, the open collar of his tunic exposing a white vest stained with splashes of red wine. Beria, drunk, fat and panting in the heat, clung on to him for support.

'Who is that man?' Polina asked, eyeing the pair primly.

'Lavrenty Beria,' Nadya replied with a shiver of disgust. 'Head of the NKVD in Transcaucasia. Another killer.'

'He's new to Zubalovo, isn't he?'

'Relatively. It is his third time here, I think. But I despise him already. The way he looks at me. The way he looks at any woman, for that matter. He is a scoundrel. I have asked Joseph many times to keep him away, but the slimy man has ingratiated himself with the great Stalin in a fashion I have not seen for some time.'

Stalin bowed melodramatically as he reached the two women. 'Ladies!' he bellowed. 'So this where you are hiding. With the pixies and the elves.'

Polina smiled out of courtesy. Nadya did not. It made her retch to even look at either man today. She took Stalin to one side, leaving Beria to size up Polina Molotov.

'I have asked you before, Joseph,' Nadya said in a hushed voice. '*Please* do not invite that man to our home. I do not like him and I do not wish to be in his company.'

Stalin glanced over his shoulder. Beria, immediately alert to Stalin's attention despite his intoxication, squinted through small, round spectacles and smiled. Stalin turned back to Nadya.

'Matters of state,' he said. 'I need him here.'

'To me, you do not appear to be discussing matters of state,' Nadya countered.

'To me, you do not appear to be a hostess attending to her guests,' Stalin said. 'Instead, you prefer to idle away the hours with your friend, the Jewess.'

Nadya was offended and prayed Polina had not heard.

46

'She is the distinguished wife of a distinguished member of your Politburo,' she protested.

'She is still a fucking Jewess,' Stalin said with a grin.

Nadya, her face flushed with fury, wheeled away and stomped off through the ferns. Stalin ran after her and growled: 'Where do you think you are going?'

Nadya kept walking. 'To the dacha,' she said.

'There is a more obvious place for you to go,' Stalin said.

'Oh?' Nadya said flippantly. 'And where might that be?'

'To hell, my dear.' Stalin tugged at her shoulder and spun her around. 'Go to hell!'

4

Quester was conscious only in short bouts. From his bed
he could see the nurse who had saved him on the day he
survived five weeks ago. It was night, and she was reading
a book under a conical shaft of saffron light from a lamp
attached to the arm of her chair. Quester tried to talk,
but the ventilator mask that covered his mouth only
allowed him to grunt. The nurse heard it. She smiled
sweetly, rose to her feet and pulled Quester's mask to one
side so that it hung loosely on his collar bone.

'Nice to see you again,' she said. 'It's 2.30 in the
morning. You can keep me company for a while.' She
nodded at the mask, a plastic semi-sphere with a rubber
sealing strip, connected by tube to a mechanical ventilator. 'You can do without this for a few minutes, if you
like. But no longer. Your lungs aren't working properly
yet. And we all know what happens when lungs don't
work.' She drew a finger across her throat and smiled
again.

Quester felt as stiff and heavy as a steel girder. He was
confused, aggravated – and tired. So very tired. He
opened his mouth to talk. It required enormous effort
and he could manage only short, stunted phrases.

'Name,' he said, turning his head a fraction to look
directly at the nurse. He could not see her features clearly.
His eyes would not focus, no matter how hard he strained
them.

'Nurse Warren,' she replied.

'No. First name.'

48

'Kelly.'

'Or Teardrop.'

'You heard!' she exclaimed. 'That's amazing.'

'I was alive.'

'I know. Thank God for that.'

'No. Thank you.'

Kelly was embarrassed. She was barely twenty and Quester was the first patient about whom she could genuinely put her hand on her heart and say: 'I helped save this man.' She did not know how to react to his gratitude.

'Doctor. Bastard.' Quester said. 'All bastards.'

Kelly laughed. She lifted Quester's head gently so she could pump air into his pillow. He felt a sharp pain sear across his skull – and remembered.

'Tried to kill me,' he said. 'Man with rock. Tried to kill me.'

Kelly tut-tutted.

'No-one is trying to kill you,' she said.

'Not now. Then. He did. On mountain.'

'The mountain where you were found – in Kashmir?'

'Kashmir. Yes.'

'You had a nasty accident. I've been told the story. Something blew up and you were caught by debris. It was an accident.'

'No!' Quester became agitated. Why wouldn't she listen?

'Ssssh. It doesn't do to get upset in your condition.'

'Listen! Someone inside master box. Then hit me with rock. Smashed skull.'

Kelly eased his head back on the pillow and scuffed a hand across his sheets to flatten them.

'I've heard all about your dreams,' she said. 'They're

on your medical file. But that's all they are. Dreams. Nothing to worry about.'

Quester's agitation turned to anger. His fingers curled into claws and he tried to shout. But he had no air, no breath.

Kelly saw what was happening and became alarmed. She acted quickly and put the ventilator mask back over Quester's mouth. As he sucked in the oxygen he became calmer. She decided against calling a doctor. She had coped and all was well.

She waited ten minutes before removing it once more. All the time Quester's eyes, wide open and wild, watched her, followed her every step. She was unnerved and had to keep telling herself he couldn't move.

'I stay calm,' he promised when he could talk again. 'But you listen.'

Reluctantly, she nodded her agreement.

'Ambushed me. Called me Colonel. Why?'

'Have you been in the Army?'

'Never. No services.'

'I don't know then . . .'

'Lydia. Said he must attend to Lydia. Who is Lydia?'

'Don't you know?'

'No. Rosanne. Where is she?'

'I thought we were talking about Lydia.'

'Rosanne.'

'So who is she?'

'Wife. She is alive.'

Kelly was confused. She had been told Quester's wife was dead. And if she was alive, why had she not been called upon five weeks ago to make the vital decision about his life-support machine? Why had it been left to a distant cousin?

'Where is your wife?' she asked.

'Here. In room. Day I survived. Priest, doctor, you, stranger and Rosanne.'

'But how could you know?'

'Saw. Heard.'

Kelly, the new professional, tried to cast her mind back to her psychology textbooks. Words like delusion and hallucination occurred to her, but she was not sure how to respond. She became angry with herself but knew she had to make a choice. She tried the truth.

'I was the only woman in the intensive-care room that day,' she said. 'I'm sorry . . .'

'Rosanne there!' Quester protested. 'Red hair. Silk robe. You remember.'

Kelly cleared her throat, as if she was about to deliver bad news.

'I hope you'll forgive me if this is the wrong time to mention this, Mr Quester. But I was told your wife died of cancer several years ago.'

'True,' said Quester, unruffled. 'But she was here.'

The nurse could not reply. What could she say? Quester asked about the stranger.

'He was a cousin. From your family in Austria.'

'No family in Austria.'

'He flew over from Vienna.'

'Mother, father, died when I was baby. Brought up in orphanage. No family anywhere. Only Rosanne.'

Kelly could not stifle a fatigued sigh of despair. Quester heard it.

'*Why?*' he demanded with a sudden severity in his voice. Its tone and strength took Kelly by surprise.

'Why what?' she said defensively.

Quester summoned every ounce of his stamina and launched into a breathless tirade.

'Why won't you believe me?'

51

He lost control and became hysterical. She *had* to believe him.

'Explosions. One! Two! Mountain giving way. Falling down side. People there. Christ! Crashing on to them. Buried. Blood. Vijay! Move, Vijay! Take them higher. Kiran and Ramesh are orphans. Oh God! Ten wires. Two disconnected. Charge 4. Charge 5. Rock in his hand. Hitting me. Breaking skull. Half a head. I know, I know. Nothing more than you deserve, Colonel. Now I must attend to Lydia. So hot. Cooler. Cabins in forest. Two men alone with the night. One threw knife at father when he was child. Has a wife. Unhappy. Not like mine. Rosanne! Oh, Rosanne . . .'

His words were stifled as Kelly clamped the mask over his mouth. She ran out to call a doctor.

'A sedative?' she said as they returned. 'Can he take one?'

The doctor did not reply. Quester felt the sting of the needle in his arm – and then nothing more.

How many hours had he been unconscious? It seemed an eternity. Not for the first time, the sheer tedium of his existence – for that was all it was – made him fit to burst with exasperation. He had seen badly injured people in hospital himself. Explosives and accidents went hand in hand. He had always thought they looked so peaceful, so content, as they laid back in their beds, eyes closed whether they were sleeping or awake. He had reckoned without their minds. Shattered limbs do not paralyse the spirit. A body rests, heals itself. But the brain keeps churning. Relentlessly. Mercilessly. Even mine, he reflected, even with half a skull.

His head flopped languidly to one side. She was there, a hazy silhouette reading her book in her private pool of light. It was still night. Which night? The same, the next or the one after that? It really didn't matter.

There was a knock on the door. It was opened an inch and the voice of a doctor came through the gap.

'Nurse Warren?'

'Yes.'

'Ah, they told me I would find you here. You are wanted in casualty. Major road accident. A coach, I think. They need all hands. Me, too, on my one night off this week.'

'But . . .'

'But you were told to stay here at all times, just in case.'

Quester knew the voice. He didn't know where, or when. But he knew it was not friendly.

'He'll be all right, nurse. He's not going anywhere. I'll meet you in casualty. Chop-chop!'

A pair of steel-capped heels clicked away down a corridor. Kelly leaped to her feet and shouted 'Coming!' after him. Quester sensed her checking him over. He still could not see her clearly.

She left – and he heard her sprinting down the corridor.

Strange, but he felt somehow abandoned. His weeks of recovery in the hospital bed had been interminable, but at least he had shared them with a partner. Kelly. Now she was gone and he was like a child. Alone in the night. Frightened.

He tried to place the doctor whose voice he had just heard. A thick, guttural voice. Perhaps the slightest hint of an accent. His concentration was disturbed as he sensed another presence in the room.

Someone was there. By the door. Hovering. Watching.

'Kel . . .' He tried to call out the nurse's name. But the

ventilator mask was rigidly in place and he did not have the energy to fight it.

Whoever it was came closer, until Quester felt breath on his face. He smelt nicotine – and immediately recognized both the stench and the mystery voice.

The man on the mountain.

Quester panicked. He tried to move, to flee, but it was futile. Not a muscle in his body responded to the pleadings from his brain. The man spoke – and Quester knew he was trapped.

'Regrettably, I cannot stay long, Colonel.'

Quester forced his eyes open. But he could not make out the intruder. The man was still a voice.

'I have come to pass on my congratulations at your survival,' he said deliberately. 'Frankly, there was a time when I thought you were bound to die. Perhaps, on this occasion, you will not be so fortunate. One-to-one, Colonel, that is how it has been between us. Only this time the odds are in my favour . . .'

Quester felt a hand grasp the ventilator mask. It was pulled off his mouth with the lightest of touches and left to dangle under his chin. On the mountain, the man had been a savage. Tonight, he was a velvet-gloved assassin.

The smell of nicotine dissipated.

'Until we meet again, Colonel, wherever that may be.' The voice faded away as the man left the room.

At first, Quester was not afraid. By taking short, controlled intakes of air, he found he could inflate his lungs sufficiently to keep the breathing process operative, if not vigorous. But his mastery lasted less than a minute. His concentration flagged and the co-ordination between mouth, nose and lung evaporated. His breathing became jerky and inhibited. He screamed at himself to relax, but his alarm only made matters worse.

He broke out in a cold sweat and lost his nerve completely. There was nothing he could do to reverse the decline. His brain sent messages, but they were not received.

He felt the lining of his throat becoming clammy. The sides were pressing in towards each other, until they touched. They stuck together. There was no gap left for air. Only tiny pockets forced their way through a hinged flap of flesh.

Quester heard the terrible sounds he was making. The sounds of a dying man.

On the mountain it had been so quick. Now he had time to feel true terror.

His lungs were flaccid, useless. His larynx was raw, burning hot. His heart pounded its last beats against his rib cage like a mallet against iron.

'Oh my God!'

Kelly saw the spasms that had gripped Quester's body and rushed across the room. She scooped the ventilator mask in her hand and pushed it over his mouth, holding it there as if her life, too, depended on it.

'Oh, Mr Quester. I'm sorry! I'm sorry!' she panted. 'How on earth did you move it? I didn't think you had the strength. It could have been terrible. Please don't tell anyone. Please . . .'

Quester lunged maniacally as if he had been given a massive electrical shock. Kelly wrapped her free arm around his chest to try to hold him down, but it was no use.

His mind was sparking, powered by an unseen but awesome charge of energy. He could see it all so clearly. An instant ago, he had been fighting for his life in a hospital bed. Now, he was in the thick of a ferocious onslaught as a remonstrating wife hurled bitter insults at her husband.

'This will end badly!' he shouted to himself.

Voroshilov's apartment in the Kremlin. 7 November 1932.

The banquet became livelier towards midnight, when the drink took its effect. Among the men, only Stalin was sober. He had kept to water rather than vodka. No-one could tell the difference and it enabled him to remain quick-witted enough to absorb the indiscretions of the piss-heads around him. Such slips of lubricated tongues, particularly those voicing a degree of criticism, were noted and filed away for future use. Perhaps, he thought whimsically, he ought to write his observations on paper. His mind was becoming too cluttered.

Molotov stood and proposed his second toast to the 15th anniversary of the October Revolution, forcing everyone else to make one more supreme effort to clamber to their feet.

All except Nada. Seated far away at the opposite end of the grand table to Stalin, she remained pinned to her chair, staring remorselessly at the plate of sturgeon and vegetables piled high in front of her. Stalin scowled reproachfully at her, but she did not notice. Neither did she hear the ripple of polite applause that greeted the end of Molotov's little speech.

Stalin got stuck into his food. In between mouthfuls, he talked with his neighbour, Beria. They spoke in Georgian, which annoyed all the other diners, who could not understand and therefore feared some dreadful plot was being cooked up against them. In the event, Stalin and Beria were discussing the merits of women.

'So Lavrenty, I am told you favour the Olympian type,' Stalin said, nudging Beria's elbow.

'As long as they are good Communists,' Beria said, his guard never slipping.

'Of course,' Stalin said, winking.

Beria thought better than to wink back and Stalin filled the void.

'But come, come, be honest,' he said. 'I am also told you like practically any arse in a skirt. Athletic or gross. Communist or imperialist. Provided, as the wartime saying goes, you can attack from the rear.' Stalin guffawed. Beria made a show of laughing, but grimaced inside.

'Do you like Moscow women?' Stalin asked.

Beria nodded. 'In general, I find them amusing.'

Stalin rapped him hard on the knuckles with his fork. 'I have not known you too well for too long, but I realize already that you can sometimes talk nonsense,' he chided. 'Amusing? Amusing? What kind of gibberish is that? What do you mean, eh? Do they make you smile, or are they a good fuck? Speak plainly, Beria, call a spade a spade. We speak plainly here in Moscow, which is where you will soon be, I have no doubt of that.'

Beria's discomfort was eased by the implication of promotion and he dipped his head in gratitude. Stalin gulped down the remainder of his meal, shoved his plate away and belched loudly. He plucked a papirosa cigarette from a crystal tumbler and wet its cardboard mouthpiece with his tongue. Beria offered a match.

'Well?' Stalin demanded.

Beria looked confused. 'Well what?' he said.

'Aren't you going to ask me?'

'Ask you what, Comrade Stalin?'

'Aren't you going to ask me what sort of women I favour?'

The penny dropped.

'But of course,' said Beria. 'I was just about to. What sort of women do you favour, Comrade Stalin?'

Stalin looked across the table to Nadya. She had not moved an inch. Her eyes were still fixed on her meal, now cold and uninviting. Stalin waved an arm at her.

'There is only one woman for me, Lavrenty, and you see her before you.'

Beria caught his breath. He was convinced he had been trapped into suggesting Stalin was promiscuous, and searched quickly for a way out.

'I positively *knew* you would say that,' he said, pretending to admire Nadya.

'And yet . . .' Stalin took another pull on his cigarette. Beria waited, unwilling to commit himself further.

'And yet,' Stalin continued. 'Sometimes I wish she would be just a little livelier, a degree or two warmer. Just a shade more, well, attentive. She spends far too much time studying French or music or I don't know what. It is not as if she has to. All that is required of Nadya is to run a good household and be charming to our friends and colleagues. But look at her tonight! She has not enjoyed herself for one moment. What am I to do, Lavrenty? Please . . . I would be grateful if you would tell me.'

Beria did not dare make a suggestion. From his close proximity, he could sense a dangerous frustration welling up inside Stalin. Lips were thinning until hidden by that bulbous moustache. Eyes were closing until they were mere slits in his face. Beria knew an explosion was imminent and tensed every muscle in readiness.

Stalin wrapped a hand around a freshly-opened bottle of wine. He gave it a powerful push, sending it sliding down the table towards Nadya. As it crashed noisily into a silver candelabra, he shouted at her: 'Hey, you! Have a drink!'

Nadya looked up from her plate and glared at Stalin with a burning resentment in her eyes that took him aback. She began to tremble and had to take a deep, deliberate breath before she could speak.

'Don't you *dare* "hey" me,' she hissed.

She leaped to her feet, sending her chair toppling backwards. Then she pointed an accusing finger at Stalin and let rip with a tirade that stunned every dinner guest into silence.

'Look at it!' She waved an arm across the table. 'Fish, vegetables, fruit, the finest vodka and wine. Candlesticks and caviar. A feast fit for a Tsar, wouldn't you say? And all this, Joseph Vissarionovich, while Russians eat each other to fend off starvation! Well then, I will add to this wanton outrage.'

She slipped a hand under her plate and tossed it into the air. Sturgeon and potatoes flew in every direction. Glasses smashed. Wine splashed over screaming women.

'Is this what Lenin set out to achieve?' Nadya yelled. 'What happened to the spirit of the Revolution? What happened to all the promises made to our great working people? What happened to their historic chance to improve themselves? What, I ask, happened to the *truth*?' She became hysterical. Tears streamed down her face and she hammered her fists on the table. 'And what happened to *you*, Joseph Vissarionovich? How did my hero Soso turn into the murderer Stalin?'

There were gasps of anguish around the table. Eyes flicked between Nadya and Stalin, waiting anxiously for his reaction. But Nadya denied him any time to think. She gathered her gown above her ankles and rushed crying from the room, leaving behind two rows of open

59

mouths and a man who felt he had been clubbed half to death.

Polina Molotov scurried after her. They walked arm-in-arm inside the towering perimeter walls of the Kremlin. The winter air was freezing, but neither felt the chill. It took Polina several minutes to calm Nadya's rage. It didn't help when she said: 'You must be careful.'

'*I* must be careful!' Nadya shrieked. 'My dear Polina, *everyone* must be careful. He sees plots against him around every corner. He finds fault with no matter who. Even you, Polina Zhemchuzhina. You are Jewish and therefore a potential Zionist conspirator.'

'Surely not!' Polina, a leading Party figure in her own right, was genuinely shocked.

'As surely as your husband survives only by "yessing" Stalin at every opportunity.'

'My husband is quite capable of standing on his own two feet at the head of the Soviet Union,' Polina protested.

Nadya could not stifle an ironic laugh. 'You are intelligent enough to realize I am speaking the truth,' she said.

Polina let it ride to allow Nadya's temper to cool. They walked in silence until they reached the foot of the Potneshy Palace, which housed Stalin's apartment. Nadya looked up at its pointed roof and sighed. The flames inside her, which had brought with them a welcome burst of adrenalin, had been quelled by a relentlessly familiar gloom.

'I'm sick of everything,' she complained. 'Even the children. I'm sick of them, too.'

It reminded her of Yakov, Stalin's son by his first marriage.

'I'm thirty-one – only seven years older than Yakov,' she told Polina. 'He turns to me for affection and understanding. The boy gets precious little of either from his father. He tells me some terrible stories. How Joseph constantly harries him with criticism of his marriage, his approach to his studies and his character . . .' Nadya lowered her voice instinctively. 'I haven't told anyone this before, but poor Yakov tried to kill himself with a gun. Mercifully, he failed. And do you know what Joseph told him? He laughed and said, "Ha! You can't even shoot straight!"'

Nadya gripped Polina's wrists and tried to force a smile. But it would not come. She whispered: 'Enough of this, you must be tired of my troubles.'

Polina kissed her on both cheeks and said: 'Will you be all right?'

Nadya nodded. 'Of course. Thank you, Polina Zhemchuzhina,' she said warmly. 'You have been a good friend, the best a woman could hope for.'

She turned away and walked briskly through the palace door and up to the apartment. She went straight to her bedroom and sat at her dressing table to write a letter. She sealed it and scribbled 'J. V. Stalin' on the envelope.

She reached for the bottle that contained her favourite perfume. Using a lace kerchief, she dabbed the fragrance on her neck, behind her ears and between her breasts. She looked at her hair in the mirror and pinned back the only loose strand she could find.

Then she opened the drawer and took out the small Walther revolver that her brother Pavel had brought her from Berlin as a gift. She checked it was loaded and put it to her head.

She murmured, 'I'll show you who can shoot straight,' and pulled the trigger.

5

It was a treat to see Kelly. Four months had passed since
the assassin pulled off the ventilator mask – and it had been
nearly twelve weeks since Quester left behind his watchful
saviour in intensive care. He was up and about now, nearly
fit enough to go home, and was filling in time by helping the
hospital staff with their chores. Making beds, cleaning
floors, lifting patients. It kept him occupied.

But he missed Kelly. During his days of darkness, she
had become his ally, his confidante. His friend.

He had arranged the rendezvous on the pretext of
formally thanking her for her endeavours on his behalf.
The real reason was that he simply wanted to see her
again, to maintain contact. He sent a message to her via a
sympathetic staff nurse and they met in the hospital
garden. He dressed for the first time since Kashmir,
pulling a pair of shorts and an unpressed white T-shirt
from the suitcase that had been flown to England with his
battered and bloodied body. Fortunately, they were suitable for one of the rare hot days of the British summer.

Kelly, off-duty, arrived in matching lemon blouse and
light cotton trousers. Quester realized that even though
his recovery was properly under way the last time he had
seen her, he had still been unable to fully appreciate her
beauty.

She looked a picture. Her shining, wispy blonde hair
was shoulder length, with a fringe cut so it flopped to one
side, always threatening to fall over her right eye, but
never quite doing so. She had a habit of jerking her head

to one side when she was making a point, which briefly sent her locks flying, enhancing their vivacity.

She had distant pale blue eyes and a bright, willing smile which displayed the most perfect rows of pearl-drop teeth Quester had ever seen.

But it was her skin he admired the most. Smooth and unblemished, peppered with the softest, finest down, it made him want to stroke her.

'How are things in intensive care?' he asked as they exchanged an awkward handshake. He cursed himself inwardly. His conversation could be so clumsy when he addressed attractive women.

She sat opposite him on an ornate iron chair matching the round table between them. She laughed and said: 'Not so hectic since you've been gone.'

He poured her a glass of orange barley from the jug he had prised from the dragon who ran the hospital canteen.

'What we need now is a bottle of vodka,' he said.

Kelly pretended to search for one in her handbag, and shrugged her shoulders in mock surprise when there was none to be found.

'I wanted to . . .' Quester hesitated, unsure of how to express his thanks sincerely. She put up a hand to halt him.

'None of that nonsense, Mr Quester.'

'Tom,' he insisted.

'What do you think I was there for?'

'Whatever it was, I am extremely grateful. You will always be much more than a nurse to me.'

Kelly was embarrassed and shifted uneasily in her seat.

'That's what they all say,' she said unconvincingly.

For the first time, Quester realized she had an accent. It was Transatlantic, but not nearly as sharp as most he had heard.

63

'American?' he asked.

'I was born there, in New York,' she replied. 'But my parents moved to Canada when I was three. Toronto's my home town. Actually, I made a lot of English friends there. I get on with European people, for some reason.' She shifted her eyes to the lawn at her feet and lowered her voice. 'When my parents died, I don't know, I just didn't want to stick around. I felt I wanted to go somewhere new, away from the memories of my mother and father. Make a fresh start. So . . .'

'So you packed your bags and came here.'

'Uh-huh.'

'I'm sorry about your parents. They must have been young.'

She looked up at Quester. She felt she could talk to him – and she was braver now.

'Car crash,' she said. 'On the freeway. A guy in a Porsche coming the other way. He lost control and vaulted the barrier. Straight into mum and dad. They both survived for quite a while, but in the end their injuries were so bad they couldn't quite make it.'

'God . . .'

'So I became a nurse. Dedicated to sticking people back together again. Maybe if I had been in their hospital, I told myself, maybe I could have tipped the balance their way.'

'You did for me. Twice.'

'You are a strong man. It was your willpower that pulled you through.'

Quester relaxed. Kelly's company was like a strong drink at the end of a hard day's work. She made his heart light and his head free of concern. And although he was more than twenty years her senior, it made no difference. It troubled neither him nor her.

'How's your head?' she asked him.

'Welded, patched and riveted.'

'I didn't mean your skull.'

'The grey matter?'

'Between your ears.'

'Fine.'

He was lying. He had been plagued by visions, dreams and nightmares. A few pleasant, green and verdant. But mostly violent. Battlefields, bombs and the spilled guts of soldiers. He viewed the worst through a scarlet filter. It neutralized the blood.

He was well enough now to keep the secret of his visions to himself. The tin god doctors had told him that if all was well, he could finally go home at the weekend, and he did not intend to give them any excuse to change their minds. He loathed the hospital. Loathed the way their rules controlled his life. Loathed the unreality of it all. It was time to go – nightmares or no nightmares.

'Only I was worried,' Kelly said.

'About what?'

'You know . . . about whether the accident had caused any, well, permanent damage. You were in a terrible state at times. Saying someone tried to kill you. Seeing your poor wife standing beside your bed.'

Accident . . . assassin . . . Rosanne.

Quester was not a man to leave things unsaid to those he cared for or respected. He had to tell Kelly the truth. To remain silent would be a deceit towards someone who had given more than enough of herself to him.

'Kelly, look at me,' he said.

She frowned quizzically at the strange request, but rested her chin on her hands and gazed at him with a smile.

'Do I look in any way unbalanced?' Quester asked.

She shook her head, trying not to laugh.

65

'Then I must explain,' he continued. 'Those things I told you about before. The killer on the mountain. How he called me Colonel. And Lydia, remember her? And me seeing Rosanne. They're all true. Every one.'

'Oh, no,' Kelly's smile vanished and she let out a long, painful groan. Disappointment radiated from her. Quester could feel it settling on his shoulders.

'I thought that was all over and done with,' she said.

Quester wanted to stop. He wanted to absorb Kelly's friendship without erecting barriers that did not have to be erected. But he could not stop himself.

'He came to London, the man from Kashmir. He tried to kill me again. He was the one who took my mask off. I didn't touch it, Kelly. I swear . . .'

She became angry. Her lips thinned and her cheeks reddened.

'Don't say it,' she pleaded.

'I have to! It's the truth! Now you tell me. When you ran down to casualty that night, there was no emergency. There had been no coach crash, had there? The "doctor" who told you to go there. He just wanted you out of the way, that's all. It was him who tried to kill me. Don't you see?'

'Stop it! Stop it!' She clenched her fists and put them over her ears.

'Why would anyone tell you there had been a coach crash?'

'Young doctors. Trainees. Juniors. They're always giving fake messages to nurses. It's their idea of a joke.'

'He tried to kill me again, Kelly.'

'There wasn't time.'

'He didn't need much.'

'No-one was there! You brushed the mask off with your arm. A reflex action. Your body was convulsing, your limbs were flapping all over the place. I'm sorry. I should have been in the room.'

'He called me Colonel again.'

'No, please, no. I'm very fond of you, Mr Quester. Tom. I don't know why, but I am and that's it. But if you go on like this, I will *have* to tell someone, don't you see that? It would be my duty. It would be criminal for the hospital to let you go before you are ready.'

'Ah, the hospital.' Quester was relentless. 'Throughout my time here – nigh on seven months – I have been having private treatment. The best possible attention in intensive care, with my own little minder, you, to constantly hold my hand. As soon as I am able, I am transferred to my own private room, away from the rabble. Television. Telephone. Tape deck with a sophisticated selection of cassettes spanning all tastes in music. But I am not a member of any private health scheme. I am comfortable, but not wealthy enough to afford this kind of care. I am not an employee of a company with a conscience. I have no secret benefactor. So where is the money coming from? Who is paying for my stay at the spa?'

'Your cousin, of course. The one from Austria. I thought you knew.'

'I told you, I have no family in Austria. I have no family anywhere.'

'You *have*! He paid a year in advance, in cash. I know. The whole hospital was buzzing with the story. You think things like that don't get around? Now the authorities are trying to trace him to give him a refund because you are being released.'

'He is the one! The man who called out to you to go to casualty. A foreigner. I heard his voice.'

'You have a rich cousin, that's all.'

'An imposter who tried to kill me.'

'You're not trying to convince me. You want to convince yourself.'

'No. It's important to me that you believe me.'

'God, I can't stand it!' Kelly burst into tears. She leaped from her chair, catching her knees on the table and upturning her drink. 'I must go before I hear any more. I'm sorry . . .' She turned and half-walked, half-ran towards the wrought-iron gates that led to the road at the rear of the hospital.

Quester rose to his feet and watched her go. He did not know how to stop her.

'Why do you always apologize?' he shouted after her.

She surprised him by turning to wave as she reached the gates. She was dabbing her eyes with a handkerchief, but managed to call: 'Take care.'

He looked down at the glass of orange barley, rocking gently on its side, spilling the last of its contents into a growing pool on the table.

'It was the truth, Kelly,' he muttered under his breath. 'The truth, the whole truth and nothing but the damn truth.'

Home for Quester was a houseboat on Taggs Island, a sliver of land in the middle of the River Thames near Hampton Court Palace. A genuine oasis in the thick of London's suburbia, it featured a spruce collection of houseboats – some grand, some modest, but all well-maintained – moored around a central reservation of lush grass, gravel paths and a concrete perimeter road sectioned off by speed bumps. In the centre was a lagoon of still river water on which more houseboats floated. There were flowers and shrubs everywhere, thriving in the succulent ground. Between them wound little flagstone

68

paths, leading to decks decorated with figurines and pot plants and protected by brightly painted chain-link fences. Names like Skipper and Thames Queen reminded outsiders they were now on marine territory. The island's only link with the more sure-footed outside world was a long, arching bridge to the riverbank, wide enough for a single car, narrow enough to keep out unwanted trucks.

It was a perfect compromise for Quester. He needed the energy of the city to keep himself stimulated. Needed to walk the crowded streets of central London sucking in vigour from interesting faces and places.

But he needed a refuge, too. A haven to which he could retreat quickly and easily. Away from the ear-shattering noise, the dust, the drilling and the debris which went with his work. A place where life went by at the same pace as the lolling river which surrounded it.

His houseboat was of the smaller variety – dwarfed by its two-storey neighbour – and needed little upkeep. Geese, ducks, swans and moorhens came and went. Casual pets, accepting food if it was offered, untroubled if it was not. People lived there because they were different from the herd. And because they did not want the herd to intrude on their privacy, which suited Quester fine.

He set about restoring the tiny patch of greenery beside the houseboat which he considered his garden. It was marked out by clay pots that last summer had been filled with geraniums – flowers that could look after themselves – but were now cracked and barren.

The neighbours who owned the floating mansion, a Cypriot couple called Amaniou, had kept the grass down as best they could with a scythe, but it was still ragged and out of control. Quester attacked it with a pair of shears.

'I'm sorry about what happened.' Mrs Amaniou, fattened by a lifetime behind the counter of a fish and chip shop, passed with a bag of groceries.

Quester glanced up. She was looking down on him with an expression of deep pity.

'What do you mean?' he said, without greeting her first.

'The accident, of course. In Asia somewhere, wasn't it? Terrible.'

'How do you know about that?'

'It was in all the papers. How those poor peasants were killed. How you were so badly injured. Are you better now? It has been so long. You look so pale. And so much thinner than you were when your picture was in the papers.'

As he squatted on the grass, Quester suddenly felt like an old racehorse put out to pasture.

'I'm fine,' he responded, leaping to his feet to emphasize the point.

Mrs Amaniou was unconvinced. 'You are weak,' she said. 'You need food. Tonight, I will bring you a good meal.'

Quester watched the fat woman leave, waddling from side to side like the Canada geese that fell in behind her in readiness for their daily ration of sliced bread.

It had been Kelly who had sowed the first seeds of doubt.

'You're not trying to convince me. You want to convince yourself.'

Now Mrs Amaniou, too, was concrete-sure the whole episode had been a simple accident. Awful, dreadful, but one of those things.

Perhaps it had been. Perhaps the certainties of the mountain savage and the velvet-gloved assassin were

70

uncertainties. The strangest things happened when you were hit on the head.

He tried to believe it until his fifth day on the houseboat. He was sitting on the sun deck with a magazine when he glanced across to the riverbank.

He was there!

At the end of the bridge, leaning back against its metal railings with one foot crossed in front of the other. The sun reflected harshly from his white skin and picked out the sharp peaks of his spiky fair hair. Plumes of blue smoke rose from the pipe hanging lazily from his lips.

The fake cousin. The killer who wanted him dead.

Quester felt a tremor rattle through his body. He was transfixed by the sight of the assassin. The man was motionless, unconcerned, casual. And so arrogant, absorbing the warmth of the day in shirt-sleeves as if the sun owed him.

He returned Quester's stare with poise and control, yet made no attempt to approach. Watching was enough. Action was inappropriate.

A pair of pleasure cruisers burbled by on the river. Children and grandmothers shouted and waved at Quester, but he took no notice. The cruisers were mere interruptions in his view of the assassin.

Their eyes met again. Neither blinked.

Why was he there? What did he want?

The man smiled, a slow crease of his bulbous lips that sent a shard of ice down Quester's spine. The predator was mellow and content – a big cat who had just enjoyed a meal and was not anxious for another.

Quester realized he would have to take the initiative. He wondered briefly if he possessed the courage, but he could not find an alternative. He would confront the man, question him, demand his identity. Find out why he was

71

there, watching. Discover the truth about Kashmir. The man held all the keys.

He slipped inside the houseboat to put on a pair of trainers. When he returned on deck, the assassin had vanished.

Quester knew there was no time to lose. He leaped on to the island and ran for the bridge. A car chugged towards him. Its driver was dazzled by the sun and did not see the oncoming athlete. Just as Quester swerved to avoid it, so the driver yanked his steering wheel to send the car in the same direction. Quester thudded into its wing and fell. The guilt-ridden driver was astonished to see him scrabble to his feet and race off without waiting for an apology.

Quester bolted over the bridge as if it was about to collapse. Even the sprint tired him and as he reached the far side, he threw his arms around a post box and clung on to it for support. He looked around. The assassin was eighty yards away, half-lost in the shadows of a mature horse chestnut tree that soared from a raised pavement on the other side of the busy riverbank road.

Quester sucked in a chestful of air and headed towards him. As soon as he moved, the man ducked behind the tree and disappeared again.

Quester approached cautiously and quietly. What if the man was still on the other side of the trunk, ready to reach out and grab his wrist? What if he had a knife or a gun? Quester had not stopped to consider the possibility, but now it put fear in his heart.

He stayed four yards away from the tree, giving himself room to manoeuvre. He walked around it, taking sideways steps and staying light on his feet in case he was forced to flee. At the point where he was sure he would see the man, he leaped into the air and landed with muscles tensed for the showdown.

Nothing! There was no-one there.

He heard a shrill whistle behind him, like that of a shepherd marshalling his sheepdog. He spun around. The assassin was there, the same distance away from him that he had been before, only this time in front of a petrol station on the other side of the road.

For a moment, the two sized each other up above the blurred roofs of passing cars. Then Quester crossed the road. The man ambled behind a parked truck – and was gone again.

The truck pulled away as Quester reached it. There was no-one left standing where it had just been.

Quester felt his heart pumping. He turned his head in swift jerks, looking desperately for the answer. A passing jogger stopped to ask if he was all right. Quester did not reply. He was too preoccupied. The jogger ran on, glancing anxiously over his shoulder.

Another whistle!

Quester saw him. Seventy yards further on, again on the opposite side of the road. He was leaning backwards against an iron fence that bordered the park beyond. He had wrapped his arms around the spikes that topped off the fence and did not appear to be breathing hard.

Quester could think of no alternative to pursuit, but the pattern remained the same. Stop. Go. Vanishing. Reappearing. They traversed a chestnut-bordered green in fits and starts, leader always four or five trees ahead of follower.

The assassin headed across a traffic-clogged roundabout and past the heraldic unicorn and lion that looked down on the gates of Hampton Court Palace, sweeping into the palace grounds without a backward glance. Quester, confused and agitated, followed at the prescribed distance. They crossed the Tilt Yard, a spectacular garden where in centuries past rival knights jousted on horseback. Quester knew his modern foe was more devious. He glimpsed a heel here, a shoulder there. The man was twisting, turning corners behind brick walls or beds of shrubs, yet never failing to leave a clue to his chosen path.

The game continued in the main garden at the back of the palace, where fir trees had been trimmed to form perfect pyramids, their lower branches resting on finely clipped lawns and their upper stems rising sharply to a point.

The assassin would show himself briefly then vanish behind the nearest fir. When Quester investigated, he would appear beside another, grinning with the confidence of a man in the habit of winning.

Quester broke into a dripping sweat and began to wonder if it was real. He was going around in circles . . . chasing ghosts.

He slumped on the steps of a fountain and wrung his hands in frustration. He looked up at a crowd of Japanese tourists – and realized they were already looking at him.

'Staring at the loony?' he snapped.

They did not understand, but his manner made them move on.

'Hey, Colonel! Over here!'

The spiky-haired man was fifty yards away, beckoning at a gate leading to the palace's famous maze.

Quester was exhausted and could barely pull himself to his feet. But he managed. He *had* to manage. He reached the gate and walked along a path towards the maze. The man stood outside it, pointing to the entrance.

'The ultimate location for a chase, wouldn't you say?' he called.

Quester saw the trailing hand of his quarry disappear into the hedgerows – and followed.

It was a hot Saturday and the maze was crowded with tourists. Quester found it oppressive, but there was a determination welling up inside him bordering on obsession. He had to find the man. And he had to find him now!

He searched for half an hour. Along narrow passages to the inevitable dead end. Around the clearings in the centre of the maze, where the elderly and the tired rested on benches. He studied every face that passed him, listened to their accents. He saw French, German, American, Italian, Japanese, Spanish. But there was no-one who even resembled the man he was following, and no-one with the same accent.

Gradually, he began to walk faster. He felt the onset of panic, though he could not explain it. Before long, he was running through the crowd. Those who stood in his way, he pushed aside. Their shouts of protest joined the excited screams of children and the laughter of the lost in a cacophony that bore down on his shoulders like a lead weight. He was losing control. He knew it, but he could not prevent it.

His head ached and the cramp in his thigh which had troubled him in Kashmir had returned. But his only answer was to keep going, keep searching for the man who could tell him *why*.

'Where are you, you bastard?' he shouted.

He ran faster, shoved harder. Nothing, he was convinced, would stop him now.

He was wrong. As he rounded one more corner, he was gripped by the firm arms of an official with a peaked cap.

Quester struggled like a demon, but the keeper was resolute and would not yield.

'Come along now, sir,' the keeper said. 'You're spoiling it for everyone else. You can't go round here like a bull in a china shop. It's not safe.'

The rebuke penetrated Quester's fevered mind. For a moment, he looked open-mouthed at the official as if the man had appeared out of thin air. Then he shook his head and felt the warm return of calm. He glanced around and saw the hostile eyes of those he had pushed, pulled or knocked over. A teenage girl waved a broken camera strap at him and yelled in Spanish.

'Yes . . . yes,' he uttered, holding up his hands in apology. 'I'm sorry. I don't know what came over me.'

The keeper led him to the exit gate.

'Too much at the pub,' he said accusingly. 'Don't come back.'

Quester walked back to the houseboat on the verge of collapse. His whole body hurt and most of his clothes had been ripped in one place or another during his rampage through the maze.

He had failed. Yet no-one understood. He was totally alone.

He changed into a pair of swimming trunks, poured himself a large vodka and went on deck to lie in the sun.

There was a shout from the end of the bridge and the spiky-haired assassin waved his greeting.

Quester rushed into the bathroom and cowered in a corner, squatting and pushing his back into the angle where the bath met the wall. A fierce trembling erupted in his fingers and toes, spreading quickly into his limbs and through the rest of his flesh.

He fixed his eyes on his knees, not daring to look up in case he saw the face of the assassin. A blast of Arctic coldness swept through his bones. Yet at the same time he was clammy and flushed.

'Oh Christ,' he uttered under his breath. 'Madness . . .'

The visions exploded with greater intensity than ever before. He saw billowing vermilion fireballs, severed limbs flying across a backdrop of steel-grey sky and a bucketful of blood spilling onto an endless plateau of packed snow. He heard the cries of men torn apart by jagged lumps of metal – and added his voice to the chorus of terror.

He screamed until his throat was raw.

A field outside Stalingrad. 1942.

The shell exploded – and the soldier died without blinking. The two others manning the forward machine-gun post were hurled backwards through the air, their great-coats shredded by the force of the explosion. They landed heavily in the cold claws of broken snowdrifts and blood the colour of the ruby stars on their tunics spread rapidly across white crystal, its vivid hue fading to soft pink as it was absorbed.

In the trench behind, snatches of the captain's hysterical screams of encouragement could be heard between the pounding of the shells.

'Remember the city you are fighting for, comrades. Stalingrad! It is no ordinary city.'

He paused, to give the message a greater sense of history. Fifty yards to his right, an unseen swarm of rifle bullets, homing in a few inches from the ground, rattled remorselessly into a tangled barricade of crossed logs and barbed wire.

'Fight! Fight! Until the last drop of blood is spilled. Do not disgrace our Supreme Commander, comrades. Do not allow the Panzers to defile his name. We will fight for every field, for every street, for every house.'

The Nazis could have heard him. The shells stopped raining, the bullets stopped shrieking. There were no frightened men looming through the evening mist behind bayonets.

An uneasy calm descended over the Soviet trenches. Cigarettes were lit by shaking hands in tattered gloves. The stench of cheap tobacco smoke settled like smog over a twisting line of men laughing nervously at bad jokes.

When they were sure they would not be killed, the medical corps scurried from their bolt-holes like mice after cheese. They lifted bodies blown from one crater to the next and pressed rags against the torn muscle and sliced skin of those who had survived for another day.

The captain, Turkish in appearance, rubbed the stinging from watery crimson eyes. He paced up and down behind a row of sandbags, on the brink of both exhaustion and delusion.

'My men, my men,' he muttered to himself. Then, louder so others could hear, he said: 'In this cold place, I feel a glow of pride like an iron poker left in burning logs.'

'Spoken like a Bolshevik, captain!'

The gruff voice cut through the thin air so that everyone looked around. They recognized him instantly, though none could believe he was there, standing above them on the edge of the trench.

He was much smaller, squatter and greyer than he looked on the posters. And they had never known about the ugly pockmarks on his face. But his intense, stabbing eyes, his stately stance and, above all, his name, gave him a commanding presence that made them shudder in both awe and fear.

As dusk approached, the temperature had dropped to

minus twelve. But Stalin did not wear a greatcoat. He tucked a hand Napoleon-like between the buttons of his ash-grey tunic and rested a gnarled cane on a scarlet epaulet, tapping the glinting gold star sewn tightly on its cloth.

A broad smile spread almost unnoticed beneath his forest of a moustache. He looked up at the boyish features of Rokossovsky, marshal of one of the three armies fighting to save Stalingrad. He transferred his gaze to the small group of officers who had accompanied him to the front carrying leather bags full of vodka and cigarettes. Then, without uttering a word, he turned his eyes back to the captain in the trench, his ceremonial manner conveying to the others that they, too, should focus their attention on the good captain.

'Name!' Stalin said abruptly.

The captain stood to attention and saluted.

'Ronsky,' he said in a faltering voice. 'Captain Andrei Ivanovich Ronsky, Supreme Commander.'

Stalin took his hand from the warmth of his tunic and rested it on the captain's shoulder.

'Where are you from?'

'I am a Georgian,' Ronsky said proudly, knowing it would find favour.

'I, too, have my roots in Georgia, in the town of Gori. Cathedral Street, actually. Number Ten. Yes, yes, a very happy childhood.'

'I am glad of that, Supreme Commander.'

'I have news for you, Captain Ronsky,' Stalin said. 'Good news . . .'

The captain waited. He hoped he would be posted elsewhere, away from the front, but suspected he would not.

'Relief is at hand,' Stalin continued. 'A counter-offensive has been launched to the north, to the north-west and to the south.' He motioned to Rokossovsky. 'The marshal here is commanding one of the great armies that are attacking the Germans from the rear. Soon the scum laying siege to Stalingrad will themselves be besieged. We will thrust a bayonet up the arse of Hitler and twist it until his intestines fall out.'

Stalin bellowed with laughter. Ronsky was shocked by the Supreme Commander's unexpected crudeness, but joined in. Troops who had heard looked at each other and grinned.

Stalin ordered the distribution of the vodka and ciga-rettes. The officers slid into the trench and trudged in different directions, giving each man a pack of cigarettes. Vodka was in shorter supply. Only eight bottles were handed to those soldiers standing immediately adjacent to Ronsky. They were given strict instructions to take one mouthful only, as a toast to Stalin's health, before passing the bottle to their neighbour.

Stalin took out his pipe as he watched and fumbled in his pocket for a nugget of tobacco. Rokossovsky offered a match. Stalin beamed expansively as he overheard the whispered message being passed down the ranks.

'Stalin is with us!'

'Yes, Stalin is with you,' he said. 'And Stalin will be too strong for even twenty German and Rumanian divi-sions. If only Hitler knew what a target he had in his sights.'

He turned back to Ronsky, breathing out a cloud of smoke and swivelling his pipe to dig the wet mouthpiece into the captain's shoulder.

'Your task,' he said, 'is to hold the Germans at bay until my counter-offensive becomes fully effective.'

The captain nodded with neither expression nor understanding of what the job entailed.

Stalin prepared to leave, but turned back with a last razor-edged glance, accentuated by its hood of thick eyebrow, that stiffened Ronsky to the bone. Stalin mouthed his words clearly and deliberately, to ensure they were engraved on the captain's soul.

'Tell your men they must not allow themselves to be captured. If they choose to save their skins by giving in to the enemy, they will be traitors to Russia. One day, Andrei Ivanovich, they will answer to me. And their situation will be far, far more serious than anything they can expect from the Nazis.'

His voice rose in anger at the very thought of a single soldier laying down his arms to surrender.

'Tell them that, Captain Ronsky. Make sure they understand. They will answer to *me*.'

6

Quester saw his agent – a purple-faced Old Etonian named Heywood-Taylor – as soon as he felt fit enough to work again. Blessed with the wisdom of experience coupled with a shrewd far-sightedness, Heywood-Taylor was nearing retirement age, yet showed no signs of relinquishing the reins of either the Pall Mall Special Projects Agency or his plethora of other directorships. Quester had never met a man with so many high-level contacts in both industry and government. If there was a project in hand, Heywood-Taylor knew about it – and knew how to find the right specialist personnel to carry it out.

Quester admired his tenacious style. Heywood-Taylor had responded by warming to Quester and finding him a constant supply of explosives work which paid dividends for both men.

Over the years, their business arrangement spilled over into friendship. They talked out future plans over lunch rather than in an office and both had been guests in the other's home. Quester expected Heywood-Taylor to grab his cigars and whisk him off to the Italian restaurant around the corner from the agency.

But he did not.

And there were other surprises. Heywood-Taylor, normally gushing with enthusiasm, was quiet and evasive. The lines on his face were carved by worry rather than age. And he found it difficult to look his friend in the eye. When he dropped a cigar he was trying to light, Quester asked if he was ill.

Heywood-Taylor picked up the cigar with a grunt of effort.

'That is an irony, to be sure,' he said in the gilt-edged voice that had charmed and influenced the world's diplomats and – more importantly in Heywood-Taylor's view – their wives.

'Why?' Quester could not disguise his bewilderment.

'Because that is the question I was about to ask you,' Heywood-Taylor explained.

Quester smiled. 'Then ask it,' he said. 'You know what the answer will be.'

'As agile as a mountain lion and ready to roar.'

'Something like that.'

'And where will you roar?'

'Anywhere you send me. What's happening to the dam in Brazil?'

'Nothing,' Heywood-Taylor said seriously. 'Nothing is happening.'

'Have they run out of cash?'

Heywood-Taylor shrugged his shoulders.

'Come on,' Quester challenged. 'You *always* know the answers.'

'Not this time,' Heywood-Taylor replied. 'There are no answers.'

'So forget Brazil. There's a suspension bridge in Sri Lanka, a Metro system in Poland, an airport in Papua New Guinea . . .'

Heywood-Taylor lit his cigar – and shook his head.

'What do you mean?' Quester protested. 'I've been reading the trade mags, talking to other boom merchants on the phone. They're all packing their bags.'

Heywood-Taylor glared darkly at his friend. Quester recognized the expression. It was the same look of pity he had received from his neighbour, Mrs Amaniou.

83

'Have a Scotch,' the agent suggested.

'No!' Quester said sharply. 'Tell me.'

'All right.' Heywood-Taylor's tone was full of regret, but he came sharply to the point. 'I'm afraid, Tom, that you have been blackballed.'

The word hit Quester like a kick in the gut.

'There's nothing I can do about it,' Heywood-Taylor continued. 'You have been placed on a list of banned personnel, those no longer trusted to carry out work that involves . . . well, that involves such risk.'

'List?' Quester cried. 'What list?'

'A confidential list. It circulates internationally. It is surprising how many business establishments and governments see it, both in the West and in the Eastern bloc. Once one's name is on it, it takes a miracle, or some form of underhand dealing, to get it erased. Unfortunately, I am neither saint nor crook. Nor, I suggest, are you, Tom.'

'Why?'

'You know why.'

Quester saw neither rhyme nor reason. He did not want to become angry with Heywood-Taylor, but could not help it.

'Let's have this out,' he said coldly.

Heywood-Taylor matched his aggression.

'So be it,' he responded quickly.

'I have an exemplary record, both of skill and safety,' said Quester. 'Before Kashmir happened, there was not a single accident.'

'But Kashmir *did* happen. It was a disaster of major proportions. What was the final death toll? Thirty? Thirty-one? It is a tragedy that no-one – no-one, Tom – wants repeated.'

'You think I don't know that?' Quester snapped. 'God,

I can never forget. But is there to be no forgiveness, either?'

'It's not as simple as that, and you know it.'

'I don't know it.'

'The circumstances. The aftermath.'

'What in Christ's name are you talking about?'

'Your claims that someone else was responsible. That someone tampered with the master box.'

'They are not claims. They are facts.'

'You see what I mean? How can you talk about facts when you have no proof?'

'So, is my word no longer good enough for you? For anyone?'

'Not against the evidence produced by the Kashmiris.'

'What evidence?'

'They found what was left of the master box. It was all but destroyed by the second explosion. They say it was old, neglected and faulty. They say the corrosion was such that anything could have happened – and did.'

Quester was outraged.

'They are liars looking for a scapegoat! Do you seriously believe that an operator of my experience, of my *calibre*, dammit, would even consider using second-rate equipment?'

Heywood-Taylor sighed heavily.

'No . . .' he said. 'But faced with your version of events . . .'

'Go on,' Quester challenged.

'That some lunatic appears out of nowhere to tamper with the master box, blows a lump of rock sky-high and then tries to kill you. With what motive, Tom? Why on Earth would anyone want to murder thirty innocent and helpless Kashmiri villagers? Why would anyone want to murder you, for that matter? As far as I am aware, you have not an enemy in the world. So who is this mystery assailant? Where did he come from? Where is he now?'

'Say it,' Quester interrupted. 'You're going to say it, so say it.'

'If that is what you wish,' Heywood-Taylor said. He looked at Quester firmly, almost harshly, before continuing as forthrightly as he could manage. 'A sceptic might think that this maniac is an illusion, invented by a person to cover his guilt.'

'A person? You mean me!'

Heywood-Taylor held up his hands as if to prevent a barrage of abuse.

'Hold on,' he said. 'I did not say the mystery murderer was deliberately invented in an act of callous deceit. I know you would never do that, Tom. It is not in your nature. But there remains the question of your subconscious. The exploding rock hit you pretty hard and . . .'

'Strange things happen when you are hit on the head.' Quester finished off the sentence with an air of inevitability. Heywood-Taylor, full of resignation himself, carried on.

'Strange things go on happening,' he said. 'Your medical file is awash with them.'

'You know about the Colonel and Lydia?'

Heywood-Taylor nodded sorrowfully.

'How? I thought medical files were confidential.'

'There are methods. I am an agent for governments. An international broker. There are methods.'

'You make me sound like a spy.'

'You have worked on many confidential assignments.'

'With no knowledge of them.'

'That is how it should be. And, if I am not mistaken, how you prefer it. Yet you must still be positively vetted by the powers that be. In your case, it has been simple.

86

You have no political axe to grind and have therefore been able to get on with your task in peace in both East and West.'

'Until now.'

'No-one wants an explosives technologist who may be mentally unstable.'

'I am not! That is a slander! I was injured, but now I am perfectly well.'

Heywood-Taylor hesitated, but he had to say it . . .

'Then why did your neighbours find you dressed in your swimming costume in your bathroom, obviously distressed and screaming about a man nobody knows and nobody saw? A man who allegedly lured you into the maze at Hampton Court, for Heaven's sake. Think about it.'

'He was . . .' Quester was about to tell Heywood-Taylor that the man in the maze was the spiky-haired assassin from Kashmir, but stopped himself.

What would it achieve? How could it sound like anything but one more confirmation of his insanity? He bowed his head in defeat.

Heywood-Taylor, relieved but saddened, put an arm around his shoulder.

'All is not lost,' he said quietly. 'Rest. Take a long, long holiday. Then change your name. Find a new agent. And don't tell me about any work you are offered.'

Quester did not reply. In his mind's eye he saw the fat smile of the blond killer, and wondered why he was doing this to him.

'I know it will hurt your pride,' Heywood-Taylor continued. 'But the pain will fade with time. Do you have money?'

'Some savings,' Quester said absently. 'A few thousand, I think.'

Heywood-Taylor walked over to the computer that rested incongruously on a mahogany bureau crafted at least two centuries before. He tried to lighten the atmosphere, leadened by Quester's sagging hopelessness.

'The office girls laughed when I bought this thing,' he said. 'Of course, they thought an old goat like me would never be able to master it. But I did. Inside two days, wouldn't you know. That showed 'em.' He tapped the computer's keys and read the resulting message. 'You are still owed four thousand, two hundred and thirty-six US dollars for the job before Kashmir. The demolition of the power station in Caracas, wasn't it? I'll have it changed into sterling and paid into your account in the morning. It will make up for the hole in your pocket left by Kashmir. They wanted to keep you out there. Charge you with criminal negligence. Did you know that?'

Quester was a million miles away.

'Only good work by the chaps in the Delhi embassy got you out in one piece. Give them a buzz if you get the chance.'

Quester made for the door. Heywood-Taylor brushed past his shoulder to open it. He reminded Quester to keep in touch and insisted that the end of their business association should not affect the sanctity of their friendship.

'Look after yourself,' he said as Quester left.

Quester turned and half-smiled to assure Heywood-Taylor he bore no grudge.

'I'll survive,' he said. 'I'm getting good at it just lately.'

Quester finally got through to Kelly.

'You'll have to be quick,' she said. 'They don't like nurses taking calls at work.'

'Come across,' he pleaded. 'Tonight. Please. I need to talk to someone.'

'A shoulder to cry on?'

'Maybe . . . I don't know.'

'I'll be there.'

Quester felt a strange combination of surprise and relief. Surprise that Kelly had agreed so readily. Relief that she had agreed.

'Thank God,' he whispered to himself.

She asked for directions. He gave her his address and told her he would pay for a cab.

'It must be urgent,' she said.

'It is,' he replied. 'I've never wanted to see someone so badly.'

He cooked her a Chinese meal in a wok he had been given in Hong Kong. As they ate, he told her what happened at the agency.

He could see the doubt that remained in her eyes. But he was growing accustomed to it and no longer felt bitter.

'Blackballed,' she said. 'It sounds terrible.'

'I still don't understand it,' Quester sighed. 'It makes no sense.'

'Nothing makes any sense.'

She saw the hurt etched on his face by her remark.

'I'm sorry . . .' she said.

He shook off his disappointment. 'I've told you before you must stop saying sorry,' he said.

'May I be allowed one more apology?'

'Can I stop you?'

'No.'

'So then . . .'

89

She stretched across the table and put her hand on his. It was warm and comfortable.

'I'm sorry for what I said in the hospital gardens – and for my hysterics. I know now that I didn't even try to understand you . . . and that hurts me as it must have hurt you. I have thought a lot about it. About you. And now I am ready to admit that what you told me was the truth as you see it.'

Her final four words took the edge off Quester's gratitude, but it was a start.

'You must tell me more,' she continued. 'Perhaps there is something locked inside you – and I can help you open the door to set it free.'

'Not now,' Quester said quietly. 'Not tonight.'

The night was still and sultry, and they climbed on deck to breathe it in. The river sparkled with reflections of the coloured bulbs decorating the Amanious' houseboat next door. And there was a tranquillity in the air that nothing could disturb. Not the voices from the opposite bank, where men and women talked on the balconies of a tall wooden chalet, brought in pieces from Switzerland a century before and reassembled above a boatyard. Not the raucous cries of ducks swooshing in to land on the water in their ridiculous, feet-first fashion. Not even the muffled bass drumbeat of a passing discotheque barge.

Kelly pulled a bottle of vodka from her substantial handbag.

'Ah, what do you know, this time I *have* found one,' she said with a smile. 'Me have firewater. You have mixer?'

They both laughed. Quester fetched some orange juice and ice to make screwdrivers and they sat side by side on the deck with their feet dangling in the water.

As the night wore on, they moved closer, until their

90

legs were touching. Kelly's feet drifted in the current until she found her toes playing with Quester's beneath the surface. She looked at him with a sincerity he knew he would never forget.

'I must tell you something,' she said softly. 'I've tried, but I can't hold it inside me any more.'

Quester waited. It was as if he knew what she was going to say.

'I'm very attracted to you, Tom. I know it's ridiculous. After all, we hardly know each other. You are more than twenty years older than me. And most times I have seen you, you have been swathed in bandages, not looking at all handsome and barely able to even notice me. I realize this will sound utterly stupid, but I have been attracted to you since you were first wheeled in to the hospital, long before the incident with the life-support machine. Do you think that's possible?'

Quester smiled. He reached out and tucked her hair behind her ears.

'If that is how you felt, it must be possible,' he said.

'It was as if you were giving off some sort of . . . I don't know . . . some sort of energy. Your arms were by your side, limp and helpless. But they were reaching out to me, begging me to touch you, to help you. I didn't understand. I still don't understand.'

'Do you have to understand?'

There was a sudden urgency in Kelly's voice.

'I want to know why, Tom, *why*?'

Quester rose slowly to his feet and held out his arms. As Kelly looked up at him he said: 'I am reaching out to you. I want you to touch me.'

She flung her arms around his legs and held them as if she was clinging on to life. Time and again she whispered: 'Why?'

Quester put his hands under her shoulders and eased her up. He kissed her lightly on the cheek and said: 'Because I feel the same way.'

Their lovemaking had an intensity that neither had experienced before. There was no fumbling, no awkward discovery of taste and preference. Their bodies were in concert as soon as they met in the bed, moving together, exploring together with an unquestioned familiarity that heightened their passion.

They were lovers forced apart by war, reunited by peace. They were lovers riding on a trade wind. They were lovers ready to die rather than spend their nights alone.

Every time the one caressed, the other responded. They stroked each other's skin in times of tenderness, tore at each other's flesh in moments of wildness.

The last time he entered her, he moved slowly and rolled over so they were both on their sides. She pushed his hand down so he could touch her most sensitive place at the same time as he rocked inside her. The day's first light was seeping through the windows and both wanted to make the most of their final chance.

Kelly squirmed and groaned and pushed her breasts against Quester's chest. He felt her getting hotter and stickier, though he would not have believed it possible.

She licked beads of sweat from his neck and whispered: 'Come with me. You'll know when. I want you to come with me.'

He slowed down even more. He never wanted it to stop. She was too delicious, too succulent. His whole body absorbed her.

But she took over. She cried, 'I love you,' and twisted and turned her pelvis on his axis. He responded, thrusting and stroking until she yelled 'Oh God! Come with me! Please!'

She shuddered violently and dug her teeth into the meat of his shoulder. He allowed his resistance to explode into atoms and joined her in ecstasy. They wanted to melt into each other, become a single person for one fantastic moment.

When they were ready, when the fever in their muscles gave way to serenity, they looked at each other and kissed deeply.

A solitary tear escaped Kelly's eye and tumbled over her cheekbone on to the pillow.

'Together,' she said.

She was on duty at six. Quester watched her climb into a taxi and went back inside the houseboat. He decided not to sleep. He wanted to stay awake to relish the memories of the night.

Sweet, deep purple memories.

He went to the bathroom to shave and studied his face in a mirror. It was fatigued, but passable. The strain of the day had been mellowed by the wonder of the night. He knew the removal of his stubble would be a further freshener.

He shaved with a razor blade. As he drew it across his skin, he thought of Kelly.

Kelly's warmth, Kelly's smile, Kelly's willing body. For a moment, he closed his eyes and saw her mop of blonde hair floating in the breeze as she flicked her head from side to side.

He lost concentration on what he was doing and cut himself just below the chin. Soap seeped into the wound and made him wince. When he opened his eyes, a trail of blood, filled out with water, was trickling down his neck.

He stared at it, became transfixed until he saw nothing else. The effect was as dramatic as it was dreadful. His mind went blank and in an instant he lost his grip on reality. He was powerless to prevent it. The memory of Kelly was gone. He could no longer remember the magic of what they had just shared. There was only a river of blood, flowing between two mud banks that caved in as the scarlet stream clawed at their foundations.

He blinked, but it was no use. His face had disappeared from the mirror. In its place was a macabre, flickering spectacle, like an old silent movie, all in black and white except for the natural hue of the blood.

There was a forest. Internment camps amid the trees. Three of them. Rickety wooden buildings. Dirt compounds enclosed by wire fences. Floodlights. Watchtowers.

Men in uniforms were taken out and loaded into lorries like cattle. Hundreds, thousands were driven away on tracks winding between the pines. Their destinations were vast pits dug in clearings. Heavy-coated men with rifles and revolvers forced them to stand in a great line around the quarries. Despite being threatened, they held themselves erect. They had such dignity, such poise.

Then, one by one, they were shot in the back of the head. Their bodies crumpled and slid into the pits, each falling on top of the one shot before. When there was no space left in the pits, the men who had done the shooting filled them in with soil and covered them with bracken and pine needles.

Twelve thousand five hundred men had been wiped from the face of the Earth.

The vision danced before Quester's eyes. He shook from head to toe and found it difficult to breathe. He reached up to the shelves where he kept a ball of cotton wool. His trembling hand knocked everything else out of the way. Toothbrushes, glasses, aerosols and bottles crashed to the floor. He did not tear off a piece of cotton wool, just pressed the entire ball against his neck.

It was only when he covered his blood that the men with the guns climbed back into their lorries and drove off.

But the horror was not over. Other men in other lorries drove back to the graves, armed not with guns but with spades. They dug up a sample of a few hundred bodies, filling the air with a terrible stench. A professor wearing a green frontier guard's cap busied himself dissecting corpses. He waved a bit of stinking green liver on the tip of his scalpel and shouted: 'See how lovely and fresh it looks.'

Quester shouted, 'Go away! Leave me alone!' His stomach churned and he was sick. He fainted and collapsed to the floor amid his own vomit.

The Kremlin. April 1943.

Stalin hit the desk so hard that Beria flinched.

'Bastard Goebbels!' he shouted. 'Now look what you have done, Beria. The whole world is talking about Katyn Forest.'

Beria held his hands in front of his chest in a gesture of innocence, like a clergyman about to pray. Stalin punched a crumpled piece of paper into them.

'It is a communiqué to be published through *Pravda*,' he said. 'Here, give it back.'

Beria did as he was ordered. Stalin unravelled the paper and read aloud the words he had scribbled on it earlier.

'Goebbels's gang of liars have, in the last two or three

95

days, been spreading revolting and slanderous fabrications about the alleged mass shooting by Soviet organs of authority in the Smolensk area, in the spring of 1940. The German statement leaves no doubt about the tragic fate of the former Polish war prisoners who, in 1941, were in areas west of Smolensk engaged on building, and who, together with many Soviet people, inhabitants of the Smolensk Province, fell into the hands of German hangmen after the withdrawal of Soviet troops.

'With this faking of facts, and these stories of Soviet atrocities in the spring of 1940, the Germans are trying to shift on to the Russians the blame for their own monstrous crime. These professional German murderers, who have butchered hundreds of thousands of Polish citizens in Poland, will deceive no-one with such lies and slander.'

Stalin crumpled the paper again and threw it at Beria's feet.

'Pick it up,' he said. Once again Beria did as he was told, though he felt a stab of humiliation in his chest.

'At least that is one order you have obeyed,' Stalin observed sarcastically.

Beria straightened himself.

'I don't understand,' he said.

'You fucked up at Katyn, that is for sure,' Stalin continued.

Beria braced himself. It was time for self-defence. There was no way out.

'But I was following instructions to liquidate the camps. Your instructions, Supreme Commander.'

Stalin flew into a rage.

'I issued no such order! I told you to *take care* of the Poles, meaning they were too much of a drain on the Russian war effort while they stayed in the camps. My obvious and clear intention was that they should be freed to fight alongside our glorious troops.'

Beria gasped audibly. He could not believe what he was hearing. He wanted desperately to call Stalin a liar, but did not possess the courage. As head of the NKVD, he of all people knew the fate of dissenters. Stalin glared at him, daring him to protest. He did not.

'You are in luck,' Stalin said suddenly. 'The Red Army are certain to recapture the Smolensk area by the end of the year. We must be ready. The NKVD must be ready. I have made plans. I will do your job for you. You are just like the rest, Beria. Without Stalin to lead you, you are a blind kitten who would fall off a precipice and be squashed flat at the foot of it. So, do you want to hear it . . .'

'I would be grateful, Supreme Commander,' Beria said.

'The key question that will be asked,' Stalin began, 'is whether the Poles were buried by Russians in the spring of 1940, or by the Germans in the late summer of 1941. You will send agents behind enemy lines to prepare the ground for when we retake Smolensk.

'They will find a man of repute, an academician or somesuch, who will testify to a committee of inquiry that he was compelled to become the assistant burgomaster of Smolensk under the command of a Nazi burgomaster. He will declare that his chief, who is bound to flee from the advance of the Red Army, had told him the Polish officers were to be liquidated. And he will produce a notebook or a diary which belonged to the chief with certain incriminating entries related to the Poles.'

Stalin barely paused for breath, so complete was his plan.

'Your agents will find a servant girl from the former NKVD villa in Smolensk taken over by the Gestapo. She

97

will tell how trucks drove into the forest and how, soon afterwards, with her employers absent from the villa, she heard shots being fired some distance away.

'Your agents will find a railwayman who will explain how it was impossible for the Russians to evacuate the Poles from the camps in 1941 during the German advance, because the railways were in a state of chaos due to the Russian retreat.

'Your agents will find another witness who will testify that on the roads leading to Katyn Forest, he met large trucks covered with tarpaulins and giving off a rotting stench of corpses. This will infer that not all the killings were carried out at Katyn. That many bodies had been brought by the Germans from elsewhere. Old bodies, earlier victims of the war. Goebbels insists the corpses in the Katyn graves perished in 1940. You follow my drift . . .'

'And why not?' said Beria, feeling a degree of relief. 'If the Germans killed them in 1940 and then transported them to Katyn, why not? When we exhume the bodies, we will find a mixture of those killed in 1940 and those killed in 1941. Pathologists will confirm it. There will be other evidence dug up from the graves. Newspapers, letters, dated both years.'

'So your turnip head is working at last,' Stalin chided. 'A pity it was boiled and pulped at Katyn.'

'The operation was correctly carried out,' Beria protested. 'German ammunition was used. Geco bullets picked up by the Red Army during its advance into the Baltic states.'

'But, you foolish fat-arse, you buried the Poles in sandy soil. The bodies were preserved, mummified. If you had dug your pits in damp soil, the Germans would have found nothing but unidentifiable skeletons.'

Beria dipped his head guiltily. It had been a bad error of judgment. There was no denying it.

'Either way,' Stalin went on, 'you will emerge as the main culprit, whether the world decides that the Poles were killed in 1940 or whether they were left behind in 1941 for the Germans to murder.'

'It is my responsibility to make sure I am not incriminated.'

Stalin stamped a heel on the floor in a strident display of anger.

'It is your responsibility to make sure *Stalin* is not incriminated!' he yelled.

'Of course, Supreme Commander,' Beria conceded swiftly.

'We must beat bastard Goebbels at his own game. After all, our allies in Britain and America can hardly say they agree with him, at such a time in history.'

'But the Polish government in London . . .'

'What of them?'

'They have already started vicious attacks upon us over Katyn.'

'Let the fascists crow. They are German agents. No-one listens to them. We will strengthen our support for the Union of Polish Patriots here, in the Soviet Union. By the winter, we will have a 15,000-strong force of Poles fighting alongside their comrades in the Red Army. And when this war is over, we will not tolerate such hostility from so-called Polish leaders. We will make absolutely sure there is a friendly government in Warsaw.'

Beria beamed.

'Why are you so smug?' Stalin cried. 'You have nothing to be smug about, I can assure you. Now get out of here and wipe the shit from your pants. And make sure the communiqué gets to *Pravda*. I want it published as soon as possible. Do you think you can manage that?'

'Of course.' Beria winced inside, but disguised his indignation.

'Yes, of course you can manage the duties of an errand boy.'

Beria turned and made for the door, grateful for the opportunity to escape. Stalin sat at his desk, studying a map of the latest front lines and muttering: 'All this trouble over a bunch of fucking Poles.'

He called out as Beria reached the door.

'Hey, idiot. Watch yourself. You know too much . . .'

7

Quester was like a mouse beneath a sky full of hawks. He sensed a powerful danger, glanced to left, right and above, dreading the shadow that at any moment would plummet from above to cover him, grasp him and carry him off to who-knows-where.

His shredded nerves made him bad-tempered, even with Kelly. She told him of her love of art and he took her to the National Gallery. But he could not shake his surliness. And their difference in taste irritated him to the point of distraction.

She marvelled at vast, rolling landscapes, particularly those featuring cornfields.

'The bigger, the wider, the better,' she said, holding her arms at full stretch in what she knew was a futile attempt to embrace the scenery. 'It's almost as if you can breathe the air.'

'No imagination.' Quester, who could only immerse himself in surrealism, did not waste words. 'The artist simply paints what he sees.'

Kelly turned sharply, shocked by Quester's attitude.

'Oh yes . . .' she said in a shrill voice. 'You try it!'

'I don't know what you're getting upset for. I am merely pointing out the truth . . .'

'As *you* see it, Mr Bloody Wonderful.'

'. . . the truth that our tastes are totally incompatible.'

'Jesus!'

Kelly's strident cry made everyone in the gallery look

at her. She blushed, and strode quickly into the next hall. Quester followed, grabbing her shoulder from behind.

'Why don't you say sorry to them all?' he said. 'That's what you always do, isn't it? Say sorry.'

Kelly pulled her shoulder from his grip.

'I don't understand,' she said. 'Why are you being so aggressive? You've been a wild man all week. I haven't been able to put a foot right as far as you are concerned. What have I done to you? First, you say you love me. Then you treat me like some piece of fluff you've picked up off the street. Is that it, then? A fortnight or so of passion and sweet nothings, then throw the bitch in the dustbin? Is that the sort of man you are?'

'Maybe.' Quester was abrupt. 'I don't know. And you sure as hell don't, either.'

Kelly felt her chest pumping and dampness in her eyes. She turned on a sixpence and rushed to the exit, reaching it just before she burst into tears. Quester was conscious of the disapproving scowls of spectators. They wanted him to run after Kelly, to whisk her off her feet and tell her he was sorry. He shuffled slowly out of the gallery to spite them.

'Go on, catch her up,' one old man urged.

'Mind your own business!' Quester snapped.

Kelly waited outside, her sobs moderating as she told herself to be tolerant, to be patient with a man who has fought back from the brink of death only to be confronted with a brick wall.

Quester kept his hands in his pockets as he reached her, though he was beginning to feel guilty.

'Bastard,' she muttered.

'Bastard today, lover tomorrow,' he said.

'That's the real truth of it. Only I don't know how to cope with your moods. You're like the pendulum of a clock that has been wound up too hard. Maybe one day it will snap off.'

'Don't let it.'

'You've got to try, too.'

'Then let me talk to you.'

They walked to a café in Soho. Quester ordered pancakes and coffee and tried to explain.

'My dreams are becoming more real. They used to happen at night, inside my head. Now they happen at any hour of the day or night – and they are everywhere. Projected on to walls, shining through windows, coming out at me from mirrors. They are three-dimensional. Sometimes I cannot tell the difference between imagination and reality. It's getting to me, Kelly. Scraping my nerve-ends with sandpaper. I don't know how much more I can take without losing control altogether.'

Quester reached across the table and stroked Kelly's cheek with the back of his hand. It was the first time he had touched her that day. He looked at her with an expression of utter helplessness.

'Something is happening to me, Kelly. I am changing inside, I can feel it. And there is nothing I can do to prevent it.' He paused as if he was ashamed of what was coming next. Then he said: 'I'm frightened.'

'Go to Kashmir,' Kelly said out of the blue.

'Why?' Quester could not follow her thinking.

'That's where it all began. And that's where you'll root out the answers. See if you can trace the Colonel and Lydia. Find out who they are, what they mean. Demand to see your master box. Convince yourself the accident was not your fault.'

'There!' The switch inside Quester clicked again and he raised his voice angrily. 'You can't leave it, can you? *Convince* myself? Why should I have to *convince* myself of anything. I *know* it was not my fault. Now I can see what you're driving at. You put it all down to guilt, don't you? That's what is causing the changes in me that are gnawing at my bloody stomach lining. Guilt. Well, let me tell you, Fraulein Freud or whoever you are, you keep reading your ivory tower textbooks. Me, I'm for the real world.'

Quester got up to go.

'You're being childish again,' Kelly said.

A waitress arrived at the table with their pancakes and coffee. Quester took a pancake from her tray and threw it into Kelly's lap.

'Now *that's* being childish,' he said, and left.

He phoned her before she went on duty.

'God, I'm so sorry.' He said it over and over again.

'Now it's you who can't stop apologizing,' Kelly said.

'But you never have anything to apologize for. I do. It must have been so humiliating.'

'It was.'

'God, I'm so sorry . . .'

'Don't be.'

'Look, if you want to tell me to jump in the river I'll understand.'

'No, don't do that. I'll see you tomorrow. I'll come over. I've got the whole day off.'

'Thank you. Thank you so much, Kelly. You're a jewel and I love you. I really do, you know.'

'What will you do tonight?'

'Walk. Think. It's the Saturday before Bank Holiday. There's always a fair on the green near here. I'll probably take a look. People always laugh at fairs. It'll cheer me up. Help me forget my shame.'

'See you tomorrow.'

* * *

104

The fair *was* good therapy. Quester wandered across the green and looked at faces. Blurred faces creased in a mixture of joy and terror as they sped round in circles at ever-increasing speeds. Faces pushed, pulled and contorted by the G-forces of the more robust rides. Cunning faces of old fairground women enticing passers-by to take their chances at this or that. Drooping faces of small children, desperately trying to conceal fatigue so their parents would let them stay just a little longer.

The later and darker it became, the more the carnival atmosphere grew. Quester's heart grew lighter with it. He was one of the oldest there, but it didn't matter. In fact, it was pleasant to see an occasion dominated so intensely by youthful exuberance.

'*You're being childish again.*'

Kelly's scolding at the café came into his mind. Maybe he was. Maybe this whole experience, from Kashmir on, was some sort of return to childhood.

Quester chuckled at the thought. If that was the case, it wasn't such a bad thing, judging by the whoops of delight piercing the night air around him.

A father with a broken arm asked Quester if he would take his boy on the dodgems. Quester obliged, and enjoyed himself. He felt exhilarated, a mood amplified by the cars' fizzing sparks, the remorseless backdrop of loud, thumping music and the frantic pace of it all.

He saw the boy back to his father, received the man's thanks and backed away with a wave.

His heel caught a stone protruding through the grass. He spun off balance and fell. A shard of pain tore through his right thigh and he cried out. A swarm of people hurried to his aid. The father offered his good hand. Quester accepted it and pulled himself to his knees.

It was then that he saw it.

105

There!

On the far side of the fair, above the green tarpaulins of the sideshows and a frenzied horizon of spinning chariots, was the Big Wheel. A pool of light had been sprayed on it to pick out lurching seats as they sped across the peak of their circular journey.

Now and then, for an instant, the heads of the riders in the seats could be picked out.

There! Quester saw it again.

A globe of shining fair hair, flashing in the night sky like the beam of a lighthouse.

Even at this distance, eighty yards or more, Quester was sure it was him. The assassin, returning to torment him once again.

Quester pulled himself to his feet, ignoring inquiries about his condition by those who had helped him. He shook his arms to rid himself of them as if they were lepers.

'Let go! I'm all right!' he insisted. They withdrew, bewildered and angry.

Quester tried to run towards the wheel, but the pain in his thigh was too great. He was conscious that he was limping, though it had no relevance. He had to reach the wheel before the ride finished. He had to trap the assassin and confront him.

In the distance he could see the wheel slowing to a halt. Then, jerkily, one chair at a time, it disposed of its cargo and took on a new load.

Quester dodged through a labyrinth of coconut shies and candy floss caravans. *Come on leg, damn you, you've got to carry me there before it's too late.*

The leg could not meet the challenge. Quester reached the wheel just as it whirred into action again. He watched, unable to see the new passengers in detail and hoping against hope that the assassin had stayed on for a second ride.

He had not.

Instead, he was standing thirty yards away, beside a ghost train. Brazen. Running his fingers through the spiky hair that Quester had come to detest.

The pantomime began again. Quester headed towards him. The assassin disappeared. Quester ran past the pay kiosk into the ghost train, stumbling through the darkness and tripping clumsily over metal rails. A train rattled past. A young girl holding tight to its sides saw him – and screamed. Quester ran past fake skeletons and fake vampires. He brushed aside fake cobwebs. He would willingly have encountered a real villain, but the man was nowhere. He pushed out of the clattering doors at the end of the line, startling the attendant who had no idea he was inside. The assassin waved at him from behind a toddler's roundabout.

The chase went on for half an hour. Vanishing. Appearing. Vanishing. Appearing.

Quester knew he was rushing headlong into a tunnel without an end, but could do nothing to stop himself. The fair, just moments ago a place of laughter and delight, had turned into a murderous quagmire of bogland, where children were grotesque dwarfs and their parents fire-spitting dragons.

Soon, the monstrous illusion was bearing down on Quester until he was sure he could stand it no longer. The burbling organ of the carousel became the raw larynx of a wounded beast, emitting screeches that split his head. Diesel fumes from generators seeped into his nostrils and made him retch. The fairground's manic rides flashed before his eyes, boring through his retinas and on into his brain.

Up. Down. In. Out. Forwards. Backwards. Sideways. Faster! Faster! You must go faster!

People are screaming. Everyone is screaming. There is a great terror here, waiting to devour them.

Quester saw the assassin again. Unmistakable. The snowy hair. The light raincoat, strange clothing on such a balmy night.

Only this time he had slipped up. He had his back turned. He did not know Quester was there, a mere stone's throw behind him.

Quester focused his bitterness on the man. It was not difficult. He had never in his life before felt such pure hatred. He would make the callous bastard pay for what he had done, that was for sure. Now. Now was the time when the assassin would pay his dues.

There was an empty cola bottle to Quester's right. He picked it up, grasping it by the neck and holding it above his shoulder. He crept towards the man slowly, carefully, one pace at a time so as not to alert him.

The man did not turn. Quester had him at his mercy.

He shouted 'Now!' and brought the bottle down on the man's head. The glass shattered into fragments under the impact. Quester was left holding the jagged remains. As the man fell to the ground, Quester rammed the stem into his neck. Blood spurted from the wound and splashed across Quester's face.

Quester laughed. He poked out his tongue and curled it around the sliver of spittle that was escaping his mouth. He tasted blood as well, and laughed louder.

'This time I've got you!' he yelled, digging the glass dagger into naked flesh one more time. 'This time there's no escape. As assassin assassinated. What do you think of that?'

Quester heard someone shout, 'Get him!' From the

corner of his eye, he saw a fist flashing towards him. He felt a sharp blow on the cheekbone and was knocked sideways off his feet, landing beside the prone figure he had just attacked.

The last thing he saw was his victim's face. To his horror, it was not the assassin from Kashmir . . . nor anyone else he knew.

Molotov's dacha. December 1943.

Polina Molotov gave a stylish touch to the dacha. It had a warm, womb-like quality, particularly in winter. Great log fires crackled in every hearth, sending dappled orange patterns over their marble surrounds. Bronze vases stood atop wooden monoliths, filled with fresh flowers sent from nurseries in Moscow. Framed pictures of Russian peasantry doing heroic deeds in fields hung on panelled walls. There were candlesticks, clocks, chaise longues and pot plants.

Stalin berated it as 'a country landowner's house before the Revolution'.

He declined Polina's offer of a hot brandy and walked out in the snow. Molotov, Beria, Voroshilov and Kamenev pulled on their boots and greatcoats to follow. Polina felt duty-bound as hostess to join the walking party, but took along a maid for company.

Stalin told the story of how he, along with Churchill and Roosevelt, had escaped a Nazi murderer's bullet at the Teheran summit between the Big Three two weeks before. Apart from Voroshilov, the others knew every detail – after all, it had been a famous victory for Soviet espionage. But no-one allowed their concentration to falter.

'I cannot think why old Adolf should wish me dead,' Stalin said. 'We may be on different sides, but we are not

109

so different. I do not share Roosevelt's view that Hitler is mad. He is a very able man. He is just too greedy and too swayed by thoughts of prestige. And, of course, he cannot equate his military aims to the capabilities of his forces.'

'But his potential would have been greatly increased had he succeeded in killing you, Supreme Commander,' Molotov offered.

'Fat chance!' Stalin broke into raucous laughter. 'When the trusted Nazi officer sent to Teheran to control the operation, Major Walter Shultz, is in fact Comrade Ilya Svetloff of the GPU, and has been for many years!'

The others echoed his laughter.

'I am told that a German vixen posed as his wife,' said Voroshilov. 'What happened to her?'

'Svetloff bust her radio,' Stalin explained. 'She could not guide down the plane carrying the agents who were coming to get me. When she realized what was happening, she chased Svetloff in her car. But we chased her and forced her into the parapet of a bridge. She was mincemeat, of course, but that's only to be expected if you try to murder Stalin.'

'How did Roosevelt react?' Voroshilov asked.

'I told him of Hitler's plan. They're coming to get us, I said. Operation Long Jump, it's called, I said. Roosevelt nearly long-jumped out of his wheelchair. He crapped himself. Even stayed at the Soviet embassy so he could be protected by Beria's people.'

'And Churchill?'

'Winnie just lit another cigar and mumbled some garbled nonsense to himself. He was not ruffled. He was more upset by my suggestion that once the war is over, we should shoot at least 100,000 German officers just to make sure there is no more trouble from that quarter.'

Voroshilov laughed. Stalin did not.

'You don't think it's a good idea?' he said. He turned to study the Marshal, bemused by the large gap between Voroshilov's nose and lips. Did he have a closely trimmed moustache or was this vast area covered by mere stubble? Stalin could never tell.

'Your forehead slopes back like a gorilla's and you do not give an impression of intelligence,' he said. 'You are the Marshal at the head of the Soviet war effort, yet you are unpopular with our soldiers. So what do I care about your opinions?'

Voroshilov was shaken, as was everyone else. The party lapsed into silence as they walked on.

They reached a frozen pond, dusted by the morning's light fall of powdery snow. Polina and the maid had drifted away from the men and were strolling and chatting amiably on the opposite bank of the pond. They linked arms to ward off the cold. Stalin saw them and turned to Molotov.

'Look at them,' he said. 'A pair of fucking lesbians.'

Molotov did not react.

'My wife has taken a special interest in the maid,' he said. 'She is an interesting girl. A gifted dancer. She hopes one day to be a ballerina with the Bolshoi. My wife . . .'

'My wife this! My wife that!' Stalin interrupted. 'Don't you realize that every time I see your wife, I see my Nadya. They were together on the night Nadya lost her senses. Who knows what ideas Polina Molotov put into her head?'

'None, I am sure of it,' Molotov said in his wife's defence.

'Well, *someone* made my closest and most faithful friend betray me. Who are you suggesting it was?'

'I . . . I don't know.' Molotov's voice was shaking.

'Zionist conspirators,' Stalin hissed. 'Do you think your wife was a part of a Zionist conspiracy?'

'No. It is unthinkable.'

'Or perhaps a plot by agents of the British. I have my doubts about *you* on that score, Molotov.'

'My wife has no more purpose this day than to be the perfect hostess, to look after us all.'

Stalin shoved Molotov hard on the shoulder so that he shot out on to the frozen pond. There was a groan and a crack and a pocket of ice beneath his feet gave way. His legs and torso plunged into the water and he only saved himself from going under by thrusting out his arms to form a T on what remained of the ice.

Stalin looked at the spectacle and laughed fit to burst. Molotov was powerless to move unaided and was turning blue with cold.

'Fish him out, Beria,' Stalin said. 'Before his balls turn to iced raisins.'

Beria waddled out uncertainly on the ice, testing its strength with every step. Stalin looked across the pond to where Polina Molotov was standing transfixed, her hands pushed into her cheeks with anxiety.

'Here, perfect hostess,' Stalin called. 'We've found someone for you to warm up.'

After supper, the maid was commanded to perform. The chairs of the dacha's largest room were pushed to the walls and its rugs rolled up to leave a polished wood floor. The audience took their seats, Stalin fulfilling his promise to sit next to Molotov to make up for any hurt feelings.

A small group of musicians pressed into a corner around a grand piano. They played Tchaikovsky and the maid, ushered in by a proud-looking Polina Molotov, performed the dance of the dying swan.

She was a sleek girl, wearing a white leotard that enhanced her natural grace. And she was of an age, about eighteen, where her finely honed ligaments had yet to develop into ugly bulges of over-stressed muscle.

Beria became aroused as he watched. Polina saw his expression of lust and scowled. She felt a wave of disgust sweep over her. The girl was practically like a daughter. Yet here was this sweating jackal, looking at her as if she was a piece of raw meat.

Late at night, when all the others were asleep, Beria went to the maid's room. He told her she was too old to train for the Bolshoi, but if she did as he asked he would see what he could do. If she did not, she would be sent packing from Moscow to take her chances in the Siberian snow.

'Before you say it,' he warned crisply, 'the Molotovs will not be in a position to help you. There is nothing they can do if I decide that you are a common criminal.'

He took off her nightdress, but ordered her to slip on her ballet shoes.

'Stand on tiptoe, like you do when you're dancing,' he said.

The girl, weeping, did as he commanded.

He turned her round and bent her over a dressing table, stretching her arms so her fingers reached out over the edges.

'Keep standing on tiptoe, now, like a good ballerina,' he said.

Then he unbuttoned his fly and entered her roughly from behind.

After a moment, the girl lost her balance and came

down on her heels. Beria smacked her hard on the buttocks and she raised herself again.

Beria took his satisfaction and rearranged his dress, telling the maid to stay where she was.

'My good fortune that you are not a virgin,' he said. 'Who was your first man?'

The maid shivered. It reminded her of three years ago, back in the Ukraine. A brutal farmhand who forced himself on her in the corn shed. Her father had clubbed him half to death and then moved Heaven and Earth to make sure his daughter reached Moscow, where, he was certain, this kind of thing would not happen.

'Speak up!' Beria barked. 'Cat got your tongue?'

The maid sniffed back her tears. She was thinking: He was the first; you are the second. But she said quietly: 'I don't remember.'

'So many lovers, eh? I would not have thought you were the type, judging by your appearance. All eyelash-fluttering innocence.'

Beria went to leave. As he opened the door, he took one more look at the maid's nakedness and said: 'Molotov was right. You *are* a gifted girl.'

8

Quester was surrounded by madness. In the bed to one side of him, a grey-faced man of about forty was scolding himself aloud, oblivious of Quester's staring eyes. The other neighbouring bed contained an older man with wispy hair who counted his fingers over and over again as if he was determined to reach infinity.

Quester wondered what sort of sight he presented to the world. He did not know if he was mad. What he did know, as soon as he regained consciousness, was that he was no longer in control of his destiny. It was as if there was a voice inside his head, determining his actions and telling him what to do. It was a forceful, persuasive voice and grated on his nerves.

'Shut up, damn you!' he shouted.

A doctor heard him and walked over. Quester looked up and remembered the lines of an old song.

Dashing young men in their clean white coats and they're coming to take me away, ha-ha . . .

'Mr MacDonald disturbing you?' the doctor said, nodding at the man who was scolding himself.

Quester thought for a moment, his tensed eyebrows making deep furrows in his temple.

'Er . . . yes,' he said eventually.

'Don't worry,' the doctor said. 'He never goes on for long. A man can only take so much nagging from his wife.'

'Is that who he is? His wife?'

The doctor nodded and smiled. 'She literally drove him round the bend.'

Round the bend. The words put the fear of God into Quester.

'Where am I?' he said suddenly.

'Does it matter?'

Quester became angry.

'Put yourself in my place!' he snapped. 'Of course it fucking matters.'

The doctor held up a hand of apology.

'You're at a hospital for psychiatric disorders,' he said calmly.

'A loony bin?'

'We do not like to refer to it as that.'

'Is it time for my injection?' Quester said aggressively.

'I'm sorry. I don't understand.'

'Well, that's what you bastards do, isn't it? Pump people full of sedatives so they can no longer think for themselves.'

The doctor laughed.

'You're too suspicious by half,' he said. 'And you've been watching too many movies. We're here to help.'

The voice inside Quester's head told him not to get agitated. You need rest, it said. There is a long journey ahead. Relax. Sleep.

'Journey. What journey?' he muttered.

'I beg your pardon?' the doctor said.

Quester's words faded as he drifted away.

'Nothing,' he said. 'Nothing at all . . .'

The man in the uniform introduced himself as Chief Inspector Filmore. He was young for such a rank and had an unusually sorrowful air, as if he did not really wish to pursue a career in the police but could not think how else to organize his life. At the bedside, he spoke with the courteous formality that he felt was expected of him and seldom strayed from his task of gathering information.

'Mr Quester?'

'Yes.'

'Strange name.'

'Strange person in a strange place.'

'One Christian name. Tom.'

'Yes.'

'Not so strange.'

Filmore smiled, pleased that he had topped Quester in their first exchange. He kept the initial contact to a minimum and switched tack immediately. 'Naturally, there will be charges,' he said. 'Assault. Malicious wounding.'

Quester was surprised.

'Not murder?' he said.

Filmore apologized. 'Of course, you had no way of knowing. The gentleman suffered concussion and needed eight stitches in a neck wound. It looked a lot worse than it was. Blood always does, I find.'

The policeman saw the relief on Quester's face and immediately redressed the balance.

'The glass only just missed his jugular vein, though. You're lucky.'

'Not if I meant to kill him.'

'Did you?'

Quester acquiesced.

'No, not him.'

'Who then?'

'Someone.'

'Name?'

'I don't know his name.'

'Then you'll find it difficult to find him, let alone harm him.'

'You're not taking me seriously.'

'Has anyone else?'

The remark silenced Quester and he retreated into thought. Filmore put on another hat, that of sympathetic copper, to tell the patient what he could expect.

'There will be a court appearance, of course. But, having regard to your accident in Kashmir and your subsequent behaviour, I doubt you will be harshly punished. Provided, of course, that you agree to have further treatment here. Your troubles have been explained to your victim. He is an intelligent man, a college lecturer or somesuch, and bears no undue malice.'

'Pass on my thanks,' Quester said. Filmore studied him to see if he was being facetious. Quester added: 'I mean it. Tell him he is a thoughtful person.'

'Is that the message from both of you?' Filmore asked.

Quester frowned in bewilderment.

'What on Earth are you talking about?'

'Just that the doctors are talking in terms of split personality, schizophrenia, that sort of thing. How else can your antics be explained?'

How else . . . how else?

It was as if Quester had been hit by lightning. For the first time, he could sense what had happened, what was happening and what was going to happen. He couldn't be sure. That would be too much to expect. But it was a start.

There is a long journey ahead.

Quester felt like a bloodhound on the trail of a burglar who had bolted into a forest. He sniffed in the undergrowth, glanced up to see the way ahead. He had the scent. There was no doubting it.

But he would keep it a secret for now. No-one would believe him anyway.

He looked at Filmore, smiled and said: 'The question is, where will it lead to?'

The stark, unfeeling walls closed in on him within days – and the voice told him to escape.

'But how?' he asked. 'What do I know about escaping from anywhere?'

'You'll find a way,' the voice replied. 'And you know everything there is to know about escape.'

He considered the alternatives.

Make a bolt for it? That would be absurd. He would attract immediate attention and would be caught before he could reach the street.

Climb through a window at the dead of night and flee across the roof? The windows were locked and he had no clothes apart from the pyjamas they had forced on him. It was not a recipe for success.

'Walk out,' the voice told him. 'Remember the snow and the men in white? How no-one could see them because they blended in with the background?'

'I do!' Quester said aloud. 'The white-suited men in the snow. Dashing young men in their clean white coats.'

'That's the connection,' said the voice. 'If it worked once, it will work again.'

Quester felt an awesome pressure building around him. There was not much time. The journey had to be made. He would escape tomorrow, during the day.

He phoned Kelly just after dawn and asked her to collect his passport, credit cards, driving licence and some clothes from his houseboat. When she asked why, he told her they were thinking in terms of releasing him on condition

119

that he visit a specialist in Paris. An expert in diagnosing injuries and mental conditions of those exposed to loud and stunning detonations. It hurt him deeply to lie to Kelly, but it had to be done.

'I talked them into it,' he said. 'I know the guy through the trade. He looked after French troops attacked by the Viet Cong, before the Americans moved in.'

'So are you going to see him?' Kelly asked.

'Yes. Of course. I don't know why I didn't think of it before.'

'Good . . . I'm so glad.'

'I won't have much time. I'm determined to make it to Paris by tonight. But I'd dearly love to see you first.'

'I could meet you at the houseboat.'

'No!' Quester rifled his mind for a reason. 'I have some other arrangements to make. I'll see Heywood-Taylor. Tell him what I'm doing. Persuade him to take me back on his books once I'm cured. His office is nearer your place. I can do everything in one fell swoop. I'll see you there. Just collect my stuff, OK?'

'OK. See you later.'

Quester started his search at 8 A.M. He had shaved and combed his hair for the first time in seventy-two hours, and looked presentable. Now, his immediate ambition was to find a small room, containing one doctor and nobody else. Preferably a large physician of similar build to himself.

The voice had been right. As he padded the corridors of the hospital, glancing to left and to right, he felt a surge of excitement. The deviousness of escape was coming naturally and he knew what was required.

Surprise. That was the main element. If you have surprise on your side, you will win. It had always been so.

No-one asked where he was going. No-one would, as

long as he remained in pyjamas and slippers. Just as no-one would question him once he had his white uniform.

He found what he was looking for an hour later. As things turned out, it was not a doctor, but a black porter called Henry, cleaning bedpans in the sluice room.

Quester walked in, sizing up Henry as he approached his back. Young. Six feet two. Broad shoulders stretching the cloth of his starched white jacket. Muscular legs pushing out the creases of his pressed white trousers. He was perfect.

'All alone, Henry?'

The porter turned and squinted at Quester through small, circular gold-framed spectacles.

'Welcome to paradise, Mr Quester,' he said, making a show of holding his nose. 'Ain't you got nowhere to go?'

'What could be better than paradise?'

'Ah, but it ain't finished yet.' Henry motioned to all four corners of the dingy room. 'There's gonna be a swimming pool there, a jacuzzi there, a cocktail bar there and a sofa full of sexy little sweethearts there.'

Quester's eyes followed him for a while, but stopped at the door. It had a mortice lock with a key. Good, he thought.

Henry, pleased to find company, especially someone who would listen to him, became more profound. He moaned about the bedpans and the soiled sheets and his general lot at the hospital.

'Bad day?' Quester asked.

'They're all bad days, ain't they?'

'How's the running?'

'Better. I did an eleven-two for the 100 yesterday. And I'm running for the club in the county championships next week.'

'So, there you are then. You'll soon be able to sprint away.'

Henry opened his arms wide.

'What – and leave all this?' he said.

The porter turned to rinse the next bedpan. Quester, summoning a controlled aggression which he did not know he possessed, made a fist and punched it hard into the base of Henry's skull. The porter's knees crumpled and he fell to the ground with hardly a sound. Quester rushed to close the door. Then he stripped Henry of his white uniform, his shirt and his tie and dressed himself in the plundered clothes.

'Sorry for the deception, Henry,' he muttered. 'You see, I have to sprint away, too.'

He looked at the prone porter at his feet, half-expecting him to speak. Quester filled the void himself.

'You'll have a nasty headache when you wake up, nothing more.'

How could he be so sure? Where did he obtain such knowledge about the effect of a particular type of blow?

He could answer neither question, but somehow it did not matter. He was sure, that was the beginning and end of it.

Quester slipped out of the sluice room, locking it behind him and sliding the key into a pocket of his newly acquired jacket. He headed around a corner and turned deliberately into the nearest ward. He strolled from one end to the other, pausing to rearrange a bunch of flowers leaning lifelessly over the lip of a vase, and on through a pair of swing doors.

He walked on, smiling with satisfaction. No-one had challenged him. No-one had even spoken to him. He was dressed in white and he had faded into the background.

For a moment, he was elated at the prospect of freedom

122

and sniffed the air as if he was in a lush, remote meadow peppered with buttercups. As he did so, it suddenly dawned on him that he had made a terrible mistake. He had not pre-checked the location of the hospital exit.

He did not know his way out.

He felt a burst of panic in his chest and his confidence was torn out of him as if by some huge hand. He had planned to walk calmly to the exit, allowing people to see him, even greeting them if necessary. Now, he was pacing from one side of the hospital to the other like an animal in a cage. Every corridor was an alley in a maze, every person who passed him a threat.

His pace quickened, despite his attempts to control it. He could feel beads of sweat on his forehead.

One half of him said Slow Down or you'll give the game away. The other half could see a nurse banging on the door of the sluice room.

She will call for help. They will break down the door and find Henry unconscious. Someone is trying to escape, they will cry. The alarm will be raised – and he will be trapped. Time, time. There's no time.

He turned another corner into another corridor. He passed another ward. The voice of a sister rang out behind him.

'Henry! Is that you, Henry?'

Quester looked round without thinking. The nurse saw his white face and said: 'Oh, sorry. Have you seen Henry?'

Quester shook his head and prayed the sister would not ask him to run an errand. She considered it for a moment, but eventually, to Quester's relief, flicked her fingers in dismissal.

Quester continued on his way. Though he kept himself moving in a straight line, he felt he was staggering, bouncing from wall to wall, falling and crawling along the ground. His heart was pumping and he was sure the veins on his head and neck were standing out. It occurred to him that he was ill. That was the reason they had brought him here, after all. The thought made him feel feeble. He knew he could not go on much longer.

Then he saw it. A harsh bomb-burst of light at the end of the corridor, becoming more dazzling the closer he got to it. Other hopeful signs gradually came into view. A reception desk. A commissionaire. Arrowed notices pointing to various sections of the hospital. People milling.

Quester shook himself and gathered his thoughts.

'You're there!' he told himself. 'Don't look at them. Just walk, walk and keep on walking.'

He threaded his way through the crowd and on into the embrace of a revolving door. It disgorged him on to a pavement, behind a metal fence protecting pedestrians from a street jammed with traffic. Quester saw a thread of black taxis and a wall of red buses – and knew that, mercifully, he was in central London. He shook his head in self-criticism. He had never thought to ask where the hospital was situated. Two mistakes. He could not afford a third.

He rifled the pockets of Henry's jacket. There was only small change, but enough for a short journey on the Tube. Soon, he knew, he would be setting off on a much longer voyage.

Kelly was exhausted. She had just returned from night duty when Quester called, and since then had fought her way across town and back again to collect what he had asked for. She dropped on her bed without undressing and was on the verge of sleep when an impatient fist rattled her door.

'Tom,' she called listlessly. 'Is that you?'

The sharpness of his reply startled her even before she opened the door. And when she saw him, she found herself taking a step backwards. He was panting and hysterical, the more fearsome because of his cool white uniform. He told her the truth about what he had done, then said abruptly: 'The Ardennes.'

'What?'

'It's where I have to go. Now.'

'You said you were going to Paris.'

'No. I was lying. I had no alternative. You wouldn't have believed the truth. You don't believe it now.'

'But . . .'

'It's where I have to go.'

'Tom, you can't. You can't go anywhere.'

'I must! I have no choice, don't you see?'

Kelly, who had never felt more alarmed, tried to calm him.

'You attacked a man. It wasn't pleasant, but it wasn't too serious either, thank goodness. Everyone is on your side, even the police. Now you're acting like a hunted criminal.'

'I *am* being hunted!' Quester cried. 'By an assassin. I have to go to the Ardennes. The answer is there. I know it is. The Colonel. Lydia. The voice told me.'

'Voice?'

'It's inside me. Telling me what to do. Helping me to see for myself.'

'My God . . .'

For a long, silent moment, Kelly gazed open-mouthed at Quester. Then suddenly, she gritted her teeth, took hold of his shoulders and shook him violently until he was on the brink of losing his balance.

'There is no assassin!' she screamed. 'There is no

Colonel, no Lydia. There is only you, Tom. You and your damned, mixed-up head. Come on, Tom, come on. You've got to try. Try, try, try!'

He saw she was petrified and realized it was impossible for her to understand. To her, and to everyone else, he had become an utter madman. Unable to make him see sense, she was trying to shake it into him.

He made her stop by staring at her and forcing her to realize that what she was doing was futile. He sat her on the edge of the bed. She shivered as if she no longer wanted to be touched by him.

'I don't have long,' he said. 'So I'll ask you just one question.'

Kelly could not help stuttering.

'W . . . what is it?'

'Do you love me?'

The question took her by surprise. But it eased her fears and she replied, 'Yes, of course,' with genuine conviction.

'Then *trust* me,' Quester said forcefully. 'I don't know all the answers. When I have them I will pass them on to you.'

'You used me,' Kelly said, her pain evident. 'You lied to me and then you used me.'

'I love you, Kelly. There is no-one else I can turn to.'

He leaned over to embrace her. She forced herself not to draw back and accepted a kiss.

'I know,' she said. 'I just wish I knew what was happening.'

Quester was on the verge of tears, but kept them at bay by inhaling deeply.

'So do I, Kelly,' he said. 'So do I.'

* * *

He flew from Heathrow to Brussels on a scheduled Sabena flight, hired a BMW car at the airport and drove through the outskirts of Liège to the Ardennes plateau.

He did not need a map. He had the name of a village imprinted on his brain and directions to reach it were superfluous.

At Malmédy, near the Spa-Francorchamps motor racing circuit, he turned left on to a narrow road which wound up through pine copses and rolling fields towards the highest parts of the range.

It was a gruelling journey. The road was pot-holed and bumpy, jarring the spine of even the most cushioned driver. Quester, already exhausted by the trauma of the day, was further fatigued by the pain in his thigh, which was gnawing at his bones once again. Several times, his head dropped as he approached one more blind, sweeping bend, its crumbling edges ready to trap the unwary and send them sliding to oblivion. On each occasion, he snapped out of his trance at the last instant as if by divine intervention, having a split second to be terrified by oncoming stone walls before negotiating the bend in a flurry of elbows and scarred nerves.

Just before sunset, he drove over the Elsenborn Ridge and down the five-mile slope to the village of Rocherath.

It was a remote place, lost in the hills near the German border. But it was where he was meant to be.

He stayed in his car and toured for twenty minutes. The village had a strange anachronistic atmosphere, unsettling to those who experienced it. Common sense decreed that it should have been as ancient as the ground on which it stood – a fossilized, mildewed collection of cottages and barns inhabited by bustling, ruddy-faced country folk. Instead, nearly all its houses had been freshly built in shining white stone. The streets were open-plan, modern . . . and as quiet as the grave. It was as if there had been some cataclysmic event in history – out with the old, in with the new – from which the population had never truly recovered.

Quester's eyes flicked frantically from building to building. But he could not find the one he was looking for.

Eventually, he saw a boy in his late teens, leaning against a wooden bus shelter astride an expensive competition bicycle. He had a pointed face like a weasel and was eating a bag of mayonnaise-coated frites, with long, curling fingers. Quester parked and walked up to him.

'Le Café Magritte?' he asked without introducing himself. 'Madame Troyes?'

The boy was shy – and further troubled by Quester's dishevelled appearance and haunted look. He avoided the stranger's eyes and shrugged his shoulders.

'What's the matter? Do you speak Flemish? All I want to know is the whereabouts of the Café Magritte. Madame Troyes is the owner.'

'I speak a little bit of English, monsieur,' the boy offered quietly.

'Then can you tell me?'

'There is no Café Magritte in Rocherath.'

'What do you mean?' Quester became agitated. 'I *know* it is here.'

The boy was winded by the stranger's reaction and clammed up. Quester struggled to control his temper, but managed to soften his voice before urging the boy to elaborate.

'I am eighteen years old, monsieur,' the boy responded. 'I have lived here all my life.' He shrugged his shoulders again, almost apologetically. 'No Café Magritte. No family Troyes.'

Quester cast his eyes to the ground and shook his head.

He did not understand. He had been so certain. Yet just as surely, the boy had told him he was wrong. He looked up with an expression of bewilderment. The boy took it as a sign that the stranger was lost. He gave Quester a consolation smile and offered his bag of frites. Quester, though he had not eaten all day, declined.

He shuffled away in a daze, leaving his car where he parked it. He wandered the lanes around the village, muttering darkly to the voice that had guided him there. 'Why betray me? What is the point? Why tell me about the one village when you mean another?'

There was no reply.

'So you have deserted me, too,' Quester mumbled disconsolately. 'I have no-one left.'

Sunset came and went. Darkness fell. Quester trudged on. Only an hour later did he trouble to look at his surroundings.

He saw nothing but shadows – and realized he was lost.

How far was he from the village? One mile? Two? And which way had he come? If he could find his car, he would drive it to the nearest hotel. Tomorrow, he would go back to London. Begin again.

He started to retrace his steps, hoping to see a spray of light in the night sky that would help him home in on Rocherath.

He walked five hundred yards before he was stopped in his tracks. On his right, lurking behind a shallow ditch, was a wide, wooden farmyard gate sandwiched between hedgerows and leading to a cow pasture.

Quester could not explain it, but suddenly he knew where he was. He put a finger to his lips and studied the gate as if it was a portrait hung in a gallery. It was no different to a thousand and one other gates, but there was no doubt. Quester knew what was on the other side.

129

He was gripped by a sensation of dread, the like of which he had never felt before. His brain told him to climb the gate, but his limbs seized. It was as if a tremendous battle was going on inside him. Mind against muscle. To the victor the spoils.

His mind won. He climbed the gate and barged through a herd of protesting cows.

'The well,' he muttered to himself. 'The well is here.'

It came out of the darkness inside five minutes. A circle of bricks, haphazardly thrown together so that sharp corners of masonry jutted out from the perimeter in several places. A small tiled roof supported on two posts. A rusty steel handle bent in the shape of a bow, entwined with cord attached to a braced wooden bucket.

Quester reached out to touch the soft green algae that he knew would be growing on the tiles. Its texture revolted him. Dry, yet somehow slimy. And totally familiar.

He held up his hand to the light of the moon. The stain of the algae criss-crossed his palm. He was gripped by a fearful terror and cried out.

He began to tremble and could do nothing to stop it. He ran away from the well, hauled himself over a fence and stumbled into a cornfield.

It was vast and the late summer wheat was high and unyielding. Yet he pushed on towards a precise point in the centre of the field. Corn grains whipped his face and rodents scurried for cover underfoot. Quester noticed nothing other than his path ahead.

The warmth of the day had been swiftly replaced by the stark chill of the plateau's night. A heavy mist rose from the field, resting on the tips of the corn and covering Quester from head to toe with tiny globules of water.

'The fog!' he shouted. 'God help me, I can't see a damn thing!'

Quester reached his target. It was still part of the cornfield, no different from any other part. But it was the place.

The trembling in his body erupted into a violent convulsion. His knees gave and he collapsed to the ground, his face digging into a mound of earth left by a mole. It smelt fresh, fertile – and horrendous.

Quester yelled for help, but his cries were drowned by a searing noise that threatened to burst his eardrums.

It was no use. His body was a punchbag. Blows rained on it from above, below, left and right. They were coming to get him and there was nothing he could do to defend himself.

In front of his eyes there was nothing but an ever-changing kaleidoscope of colour. Flashing, flickering, defying his senses to keep pace.

Noise, fear, flashing light, pain. Noise, fear, flashing light, pain. It went on and on, clawing at him, tearing him apart. He had to get away. He had to flee before it was too late. Such torture could never have been invented by man.

'Get this blood off me!' he screamed. 'Tardelli! Tardelli, get back here!'

The kaleidoscope cleared. The last thing Quester saw before he lost consciousness was a man standing above him, pointing a gun at his head.

9

Bren crouched lower in the foxhole and told Tardelli to do the same. In the distance, across the freshly laid blanket of snow and through the dense freezing fog of early morning, they heard the menacing roar of at least a dozen tanks.

'Lieutenant Tardelli! I told you to get your ass in here.'

Tardelli kept gazing over the sandbags, transfixed with fear and the sight of nothing but a swirling, iron-grey mist.

'The fog!' he shouted. 'God help me, I can't see a damn thing!'

'Get down, you obstinate bastard. They'll be here soon.'

Bren pulled at Tardelli's jacket and the lieutenant plummeted into the foxhole. Tardelli glared at his superior officer with ill-concealed venom.

'Where you go, *sir*, trouble follows,' he said sarcastically. 'Look around you. What do you see? A fucking hole in the ground, *sir*. A grave. At long last, after months of trying, you have found me my grave.'

'Shut it, lieutenant. There's a time and a place for everything. This is neither.'

'You know we're dead meat if we stay here.'

'We have orders . . .'

'Screw the orders.'

'We have orders to defend Rocherath and Krinkelt

until they're ready up on the ridge. The lives of thousands of men depend on us, don't you see that?'

'Yeah. They live and we die.'

Tardelli sprang forward, grabbing Bren's lapel. Silver breath cascaded from his panting mouth.

'You stay and carry out your fucking orders,' he hissed. 'Me, I'm going.'

Bren took hold of Tardelli's wrist with the grip of an angry man. Slowly, firmly, he prised the lieutenant's hand from his lapel. From the east, the churning of the tank engines was intensifying. They were coming closer.

'They'll open up any second,' Bren said. 'If you go out in the open, you'll be killed.'

'How many foxholes we got round here?' Tardelli asked.

'Plenty.'

Tardelli flashed a shining grin and said: 'Plenty shelter.'

He pulled himself free of Bren's grip and leaped to his feet. In an instant, he was scurrying out of the foxhole and heading into the fog. Bren tried to grab his ankles, but the lieutenant was too fleet, too determined.

'Tardelli!' Bren cried. 'Tardelli, get back here!'

There was a dull thud in the distance, coming as if from another world. It was followed by a shrill whine, growing louder and louder. The shell exploded twenty yards in front of the foxhole and inches in front of the rushing Tardelli.

Bren saw the lieutenant blown to pieces. A great rush of air swept over the surface of the field, bringing with it a cascade of Tardelli's blood. Bren's face was splashed with warm scarlet liquid. He screamed and frantically flicked at the stains with his fingers.

'Get this blood off me!' he cried. 'Damn you! Damn you, Tardelli.'

The Panzers opened up with a volley of fire. The ground burst open around Bren and he dived for cover in the foxhole. He was sprayed with pulverized earth and snow. The smell of the fresh soil seeped into his nostrils. It should have been so good, so pure. It should have reminded him of digging potatoes from the ground under a golden fall sunset in upstate New York. But Tardelli had been right. Here, it was the smell of fresh soil known by gravediggers.

There was another blast to his left. And another to his right. He heard the single, short cry of a man hit by shrapnel. He swung round on his knees and got on the radio.

'Forward post. How many?'

The reply of a panic-stricken lookout man crackled from a dented loudspeaker.

'Can't tell. Fog too thick.'

'Estimate on sound of the engines.'

'Fifteen. Maybe twenty.'

'How far away?'

'Again, can't tell exactly.'

'Estimate.'

'Two hundred yards and closing.'

'OK, keep your nerve, Hanson. Out.'

Bren calculated his chances in his mind. If he was lucky, if the Nazi gunners were unlucky, if his men responded to what he was about to ask of them, then there was a chance of survival.

There was no time for delay. He scurried out of his shelter and slipped and slid across the snow to where pairs and trios of GIs huddled in a chessboard of foxholes. Fortune ran with him. The Germans had lost their bearings in the fog and their shells were now exploding harmlessly sixty yards behind the American lines. At each foxhole, Bren issued the same orders.

134

'We can't see them. We have no targets for our mortars. But by the same token, they can't see us. So we let the tanks come right on in. Let them roll over the foxholes. Get a close-up of their bellies, then jump up and hit them from behind. Bazookas, machine-guns. Everything you got.'

'You mean, we're just gonna let them drive over us?' one GI asked incredulously.

'What's the matter? You never worked on the underside of an automobile from a pit?'

Bren saw the disbelief and the terror on their faces. Blue, cold faces. Frozen by endless days in the mountain snow. Skinned by the creeping tentacles of fog that greeted each dawn. Their teeth chattered. Their eyes were glazed by lost hope. Just when it seemed there could be an end to it all, Hitler had fought back with a vengeance. Now instead of them coming at him in a flurry of Stars and Stripes and Union Jacks, the Swastika was coming back at them. Hard.

A baby-faced captain called Cruz curled crystalline fingers around the trigger of his rifle and looked listlessly at Bren. He spoke with respect rather than anger.

'It won't work, major. We'll be wiped out.'

Bren, squatting above the foxhole on his haunches, tapped Cruz lightly on the shoulder and smiled.

'Got any better ideas?' he said.

The young captain thought for a moment, then slowly shook his head.

Bren said: 'Remember, guys, stick it up Jerry's ass,' then made for his foxhole.

He was nearly there when the Germans found their range again. He heard the whine of the shell on his tail and knew he was going to be hit. It exploded with ferocious force fifteen yards behind him. He was blown

135

off his feet and pushed into a series of manic somersaults. A burning pain shot up his flank as if someone had poured hot fat on him. He thudded into the small mound of sandbags that protected his foxhole.

Another shell was on its way. He could hear it slicing through the fog. He clawed at the sandbags, breaking what fingernails he had left, praying for grip. It came. He felt a sudden surge of strength in his arms and hauled himself over the barrier, diving head first into the foxhole just as the second shell slammed into the earth behind.

Tree roots, clods of turf and other debris fell around him. He examined himself, afraid of what he might find. His overcoat and combat pants had been shredded to rags by the blast. Every hair on his left leg had been burned off. His skin was like a baby's.

He reached for the radio with mounting trepidation.

'Forward post. Hanson. Report.'

Hanson was hysterical.

'Shadows. Looming through the mist. Light shadows, not dark. Like phantoms. Can't see them clearly. Eight . . . nine . . . ten . . . eleven. Jesus! They're . . .'

Hanson broke off. Bren shouted at him.

'They're *what*, man? What?'

'They're white. The fucking tanks are painted white. They're on me. Jesus! They came from nowhere. White tanks, white suits . . .'

The radio went dead.

'White suits?' Bren yelled. 'What do you mean, white suits?'

There was no reply.

The battle began in earnest. The merciless rattle of machine-gun fire broke out across the field. Bren heard the engine notes of the tanks rising and falling as drivers changed direction, pounded over hillocks or spun round to face the new challenge from behind. One was hit by a bazooka shell and burst into flames. Another churned through the fog straight into a ditch. It lurched to one side and stayed there, crippled and at the mercy of the GIs. They raked it with rifle fire and finished it off with a volley of grenades.

But there was something wrong. The crackle of gunfire and scream of bullets was too loud, too intense. Bren knew he didn't have enough men to produce such a cacophony.

His thoughts were interrupted by the approach of a tank. It was coming through the murk towards his foxhole, preceded by a noxious stench of diesel fumes. Closer and closer it came. Bren peered over the rim of his foxhole, holding firm to a bazooka.

He couldn't see it, but he knew it was there. Hiding behind an opaque screen of mist and smoke.

'Come on, you bastard,' Bren muttered under his breath. 'You're mine.'

It was on him before he knew it, tracks flashing before his eyes, a thin black slit in armour-plating painted white to blend with the warriors' snow-packed arena.

Bren ducked and the tank thundered overhead.

'White or not, I can see you now, Kraut-belly,' he yelled.

He leaped up and scrambled to the edge of the foxhole. The rear of the tank was already disappearing into the mist. A phantom returning home. Bren took aim and fired. The bazooka shell hammered into the tank just beneath its turret. Armour-plating was breached and the fuel tank ruptured. The tank went up with a dull boom and a billowing cloud of vermilion and black.

Bren reached down for his machine-gun, ready for the crew to make a run for it. But as he half-turned, his eyes caught a glimpse of fresh movement in the fog behind him. Lighter, more lithe.

'Infantry!' he gasped aloud. 'Jesus, they've got infantry.'

The grenadiers were like ghosts appearing through a wall. They wore white snow suits made of bed-linen plundered from villages conquered earlier, crudely stitched but devastatingly effective.

Two of them saw Bren and opened fire immediately. He felt a bullet dig in to his shoulder but was able to drop into the foxhole. The grenadiers sprinted over to finish him off. Bren pressed his back hard against the front wall of the shelter. As soon as he saw the nozzles of the German rifles, he reached up, grabbed them and gave them a sharp tug.

The grenadiers tumbled head-first into the foxhole. Bren pulled a knife from a sheath on his waistbelt and cut the throat of one soldier as soon as he landed. The other was a tougher proposition. Big and courageous, he launched himself at Bren and pinned him to the ground. Reaching to one side, he pulled a pistol from its holster and aimed at Bren's temple.

He pulled the trigger. The gun jammed.

The grenadier looked at it in horror. Bren took advantage of the distraction and pushed at his adversary with all his might. The German slipped off him, cracking his head against a metal ammunition box. Bren twisted over and plunged his blade into the soldier's back, through a kidney. The German cried out in agony and for one, fatal instant, he hesitated. Bren pushed the knife through his windpipe before he moved another inch.

Pressing a hand against the wound in his shoulder, Bren scrambled out of the foxhole. The story was the same all around him. After five years of warring with the most sophisticated arms available, it had come down to hand-to-hand fighting on a snow-covered plateau in South East Belgium. Desperate men slashed at each other with knives and bayonets. Some combatants had lost every weapon they possessed, and were reduced to clawing at each other's faces with their fingernails. A quartet of terrified GIs appeared through the mist, running to the rear, getting the hell out. Bren met them with a drawn pistol. He told them to stop, or be shot by their own major. They turned at a right angle and leaped into the nearest foxhole.

The fighting went on for two hours. The American lines were like an old stocking. Tattered, torn and peppered with holes, but holding.

Then the fog lifted as if it was a theatre curtain. The American positions were exposed for the world to see and the Germans were quick to take advantage. Three Tiger tanks whirled round and headed along the lines of fox-holes, blasting them one by one as groups of GIs cowered helplessly inside.

Bren, horrified at the carnage, radioed the artillery battalion stationed on the ridge above them.

'I'm overrun!' he cried. 'You can see the Krauts now. You'll have to hit them and we'll have to take our chances. Lay a barrage right on top of us.'

The artillery responded without delay. They bombarded the battleground for more than half an hour, churning the field into slurry.

Bren poked his head above the ragged lip of his foxhole, praying there would be no direct hit. As he turned to the north, a wave of relief rolled inside his chest. He saw the lean silhouettes of five Sherman tanks jutting over a rise. They charged to take on the Panthers and the Tigers, orange flame spitting from their barrels.

139

Two of the Tigers ravaging the foxholes were hit immediately. Their crews, uniforms ablaze, leaped for life from the burning wrecks.

Bren took advantage of the confusion.

'Fall back to Rocherath,' he called over the radio.

A swarm of GIs scrambled from their hideaways like rabbits deserting a flooded warren, falling over each other in their haste to escape the mayhem.

Bren ran with a soldier called Christie. As they reached a well at the edge of the field, the GI was cut down by a pursuing squadron of machine-gun bullets. Bren dragged him to shelter behind the well, but it was a futile gesture. Christie, bleeding from the mouth and ears, his eyes wide open in uncomprehending shock, died within seconds.

Bren's hands were covered with the dead man's blood. He tried to dry them by rubbing them on the tiled roof of the well, but the tiles were covered in muddied algae offering no absorption, its soft texture revolting to the touch. Bren looked at his palms in horror. They were coated with a stomach-churning mixture of fresh red blood and semi-solid green slime. It was a sight that he knew there and then he would never forget. Blood and slime and death. The three main ingredients of the hell in which he was trapped.

He turned and ran the two miles to Rocherath, but there was no respite there. Panthers were already engaging US tanks in cat-and-mouse street duels and infantry fought for each house.

Five times, Bren escaped screaming bullets or flashing blades by the merest fractions of an inch. Others did not. By the time fighting ceased, well into the night, the village was littered with piles of bodies, strewn between fallen telephone lines and pulverized masonry.

He found a square yard of space between exhausted,

dirt-caked troops packed into the cellar of the Café Magritte – and collapsed.

Madame Troyes, the café's owner, gave him a sip of cognac from the upturned cap of a bottle.

'It is all we have left,' she said in heavily accented English. 'There is no more food.'

Bren smiled at her and muttered: 'As long as we have cognac . . .'

'And as long as we don't have schnapps,' she replied. 'I would die rather than serve one more glass of schnapps to a fat German officer.'

Bren had known Madame Troyes for less than forty-eight hours, but had already warmed to her. Pink-cheeked and never without a flash of bright red lipstick – even now on this abominable night – she was a benevolent woman whose energy belied her fifty-four years. And, unlike many others in this border country, which had changed hands four times in the past century, she was a Belgian firmly on the side of the American liberators. Not for her the sullen reception offered to bewildered GIs by those of her neighbours who considered themselves German. She had welcomed the US 99th and 2nd Divisions with open arms and immediately offered the café cellar as a suitable field command post. Bren had cause to be grateful to her.

She unbuttoned his tunic and examined the wound in his shoulder.

'Your luck is holding,' she said, dabbing at the dried blood with a cloth lubricated by her spittle. 'In one side, out the other, like a hot knife through butter.'

'That's what it felt like, a hot knife.' Bren winced at the memory.

'Pah!' Madame Troyes scolded his display of pain. 'You are the least of my worries.'

She left him where he sat and transferred her attention

141

to a group of semi-conscious soldiers pressed into a corner. They had trench feet and there was little she could do to save them. But she could offer comfort.

A GI slumped opposite Bren stirred from his half-sleep. He looked at the officer with an expression of complete despair and asked: 'What in hell's going on, sir? It wasn't long ago they told us we'd be in Berlin for Christmas.'

Bren felt a flush of guilt. He had no answers. Clichés were all he could produce.

'No-one, not American, British or Kraut, not private or general or civilian, knows what is happening. The Ardennes plateau is a mess, that's all, soldier. A mess of blood and slime.'

Bren moved quickly to avoid an atmosphere of morosity. He had to keep their thoughts active. He had to provide a string of events, something which would focus their attention. He selected ten of his strongest men. Two were despatched to give him a head-count of the day's survivors. Two teams of four were told to shoot deer in the woods behind the village. Captain Cruz was put in charge.

'We need food,' Bren said.

Cruz looked him straight in the eye and replied: 'We need a miracle, sir.'

In the early hours of the morning, a messenger slithered down from Elsenborn Ridge.

'We've got to have one more day,' he said. 'The ground's frozen up there. It's taking time to carve out enough foxholes and gun emplacements. Your orders are to hold for another twenty-four hours.'

Bren showed him the drooping, withered faces lining the walls of the cellar.

'They've had it,' he said. 'We have no food and precious little ammunition. We were massacred today, you know

142

that. There isn't a guy here who didn't knock at St Peter's door. They have more men, more armour.'

'One more day,' the messenger repeated. 'You'll get more tanks, more guns. If the Krauts break through, the lines on the ridge won't be ready to knock them back. They'll flatten us – and there won't be anything to stop them rolling on to the Meuse river. But if we get dug in and prepare the artillery properly, they will never shift us.'

'Who are they?'

'You mean the Krauts?'

'Who else?'

'The 12th SS Panzer Division and the 277th Volksgrenadiers, under the command of Dietrich. He's jammed up here. Other Kraut armies have launched a spectacularly more successful offensive to the south. They've pushed a massive bulge in the front line. If Dietrich succeeds in taking Elsenborn Ridge – the shoulder of the bulge, if you like – then the flood gates will open. That's how vital your task is. One more day.'

The messenger left and the head-counters returned. Of the entire battalion under Bren's command, only 240 men were still alive. Of the two companies who caught the brunt of the Germans' white phantom assault, twenty-three remained.

Bren looked around him at the dread and decay that filled the icy cellar. The café's water supply had long since been ruptured. His men could not bathe, shave or clean their teeth. They used their helmets and old cardboard boxes for toilets, with neither privacy nor shame.

'Animals,' Bren murmured to himself. 'We're all animals, locked in a cage.'

He was desperate for sleep and dropped heavily on a sack of coal. It was not comfortable, but neither was it as frozen as the cellar's brick floor. He pressed himself hard against a GI for warmth. Another soldier joined them, then a fourth, a fifth and a sixth, until they formed a small pile. They were like a litter of kittens abandoned by their mother. Each giving heat and succour to the other. None sure if they would survive the night.

Dietrich, stung by a lambasting from Hitler over his slow progress, threw more men and more tanks into the next day's fighting. But the defenders of Rocherath kept them at bay with a frenzied series of guerilla ambushes.

The order to withdraw came just after dark.

'The ridge is ready,' Bren was told on the radio. 'Save your necks.'

Bren ushered the GIs from their gutted shelters and into the pine woods leading up to Elsenborn Ridge. Soon long, silent columns of men and machines were weaving between trees, across firebreaks and along meandering paths cut through the snow by troops with shovels.

Dietrich took his time to realize what was happening. But when he did, he sent a horde of grenadiers and Panthers in pursuit, and ordered his artillery to open up without mercy.

For Bren and the rest, the climb to the ridge became a race with death. As he sent word to the leading troops to quicken their pace, a volley of shells exploded around him and meemies screamed overhead. Two trees to his left were smashed into matchsticks, showering the frightened men underneath with bark, pine needles, severed branches and heavy slabs of snow.

Shrapnel cut through the air. Scores of men were hit and fell to the ground yelling in agony. As he ran, Bren stumbled on the body of Madame Troyes, face down in a snowdrift, her back split in two. Bren heard her voice as he stretched to cross her.

'*I would die rather than serve one more glass of schnapps . . .*'

It crossed his mind that he had never discovered her Christian name. Neither had he thought to ask her what had happened to her husband. Now it was too late. In a few days, she would be just another faceless, nameless skeleton in the snow. His heart bled for her.

He was half-way up the ridge. But he was near the end of his endurance and the Germans were gaining. His overboots, greatcoat and machine-gun felt heavier with each yard, until they were like lead. He threw down his weapon and took off the coat and boots. Others followed his example and the hillside became littered with discarded paraphernalia. It was cold, so very cold. But that was nothing compared to the claws of death snapping at their heels.

A manic flurry of shells exploded to Bren's right and a jagged lump of metal smashed into his ribcage. He knew at once that at least one of his ribs had been broken, the pain was so intense. He glanced down to see a burgundy stain spreading across his midriff and pressed a fist on the wound in a vain attempt to stem the flow of blood. But he stayed on his feet and kept struggling, struggling, to reach the ridge.

As he neared the summit, relief troops ran past to protect the column's rear. And artillery on the hill opened up on the Nazi pursuit force.

Bren saw the camouflage awnings flapping above flaming barrels. He staggered past slit trenches protected by sandbags framed with wood plundered from farm fences. A sandpaper voice called out urgently: 'Those needing help, this way.'

His vision was blurred and he relied on instinct to guide him to the medical tent. He collapsed on the ground and a medic homed in on him with a loaded syringe. Bren cried out as he saw the figure approaching.

'Light shadow. Not dark. Another man in white. How many? Jesus, how many more of you bastards?'

He tossed from side to side to avoid the medic's needle.

'Hold still, major!' the struggling medic pleaded.

Bren looked at him with wild eyes.

'You're wearing white – you're all wearing white,' he shrieked. 'Let me be, I'll kill you, you bastard. I'll kill you!'

'Hold still. You're delirious.'

'I'll kill you, man in white. I hate all men in white. You ought to know that by now. You come for me, but I'll have you, motherfucker.'

The needle slipped into a vein and the medic pushed.

Bren made a silent vow to get the bastard before he lost consciousness.

10

Two days after the retreat, a sergeant from Allied head-quarters arrived at the ridge in a sludge-covered Jeep. He found Bren propped in the back of a truck, his ribs tightly bandaged under a warm shield of blankets.

'They said you were in the medical tent,' the sergeant said without introducing himself. 'I looked, but you weren't there.'

'That's because I'm here,' Bren said impatiently. 'They kicked me out. There's far worse than me needing attention. Anyway, sergeant, you've found me. What the hell do you want?'

'Can you move?'

'It hurts, but I'm mobile.'

'Good – because I've come to take you out.'

'Oh,' Bren said dubiously. 'Why?'

'You're wanted by the brass.'

'What for?'

'You think they told me?'

The sergeant gave Bren a new uniform and took him to an airstrip twenty miles away. A small military transport plane was waiting, its undercarriage fitted with skis for take-off. Bren was ushered into a hold normally reserved for a cargo of nine paratroopers. He was greeted by a decorated British general who he did not recognize.

The general immediately produced a blindfold and dangled it from a finger in front of Bren.

'My orders are to put this on you,' he said stiffly. 'Your orders are to accept it without question.'

The crude black mask was pulled over Bren's eyes and tied firmly at the back of his head.

The flight was short and Bren knew the plane did not have sufficient range to fly him out of Europe. But that was all he knew. Save for offering him a hot drink from a flask, the general and the plane's two-man crew ignored him. Isolated and not trusted with the knowledge of his destination, Bren could not help feeling like a criminal. He wondered what it was all about.

The blindfold stayed on for the ninety-minute car journey that followed. There were no landmarks to absorb, no conversation to stimulate. He was left to deal with the pain from his ribs himself. But the silence away from the battlefield and the rattle of the aircraft was bliss. Bren, relaxing for the first time in months, fell asleep until his shoulder was tapped as the car came to a halt.

'Is that you, general?' he asked.

A cultured, more bureaucratic voice replied: 'The general flew away with the plane. In any event, he was a fake. No more a general than my Aunt Lucy. But I'm real. And you're my baby now.'

Bren was led up a flight of concrete steps into what he sensed was the cavernous interior of a large building.

When his mask was removed, he found himself standing in a narrow corridor in front of a towering mahogany door. He glanced to right and left, looking for a sign, a clue. He was in a mansion, of that he could now be sure. Gothic in style, it was in good repair and had apparently escaped the ravages of the great conflict. Perhaps he was in France.

He felt an urgent desire, almost child-like, to be reassured. But there was no-one to whom he could turn. Even the grey-suited man who had taken off the blindfold had disappeared in an instant without any further exchange of words.

He reasoned that as he had been placed in front of a door, there was someone on the other side. Probably someone of superior rank who had been waiting patiently for this bizarre rendezvous. He knocked on the wood with a firm fist.

Two voices in unison told Bren to enter.

He walked into a room bathed in dim saffron light, struggling to penetrate a thick, curling cloud of cigar smoke which obscured the entire ceiling. Two men sat behind a leather-covered table placed in the centre of the uncarpeted parquet floor. They were not difficult to recognize. A short, bulbous man puffing plumes of charcoal grey from a giant Havana and a gaunt, more wiry individual, his hands resting on the arms of a wheelchair.

Winston Churchill, the British Prime Minister, and Franklin D. Roosevelt, the President of the United States.

Bren was dumbfounded and froze on the spot. Churchill chuckled at his discomfort and told him: 'Come forward, Major Bren.'

Bren approached in short steps. He was told to sit and took the only other chair in the room on the opposite side of the table to the two leaders. For a long, silent moment, they stared at him, looked him up and down, sized him up. He felt he was in a shop window and found it difficult to meet their eyes.

He was shocked by the sight of Roosevelt. When he last saw him, on home territory before the 2nd Division was sent to war, the president had been full of vigour, colour and geniality. He was everyone's favourite uncle. Now he seemed so *old*. His cheeks were hollow and full of shadow. His skin was pale and had the unnatural quality of polished marble. He was clearly chronically ill.

149

Churchill did most of the talking, though he, too, was less rumbustious than usual.

'We will not detain you long, major,' he began. 'Frankly, Mr Roosevelt and myself do not have the time to dally. We are both supposed to be somewhere else. Mr Roosevelt, in particular, is expected at a meeting many thousands of miles away. He must be sure to keep that date, do you follow . . .'

Bren did not. Churchill elaborated.

'Many events of war have by their nature to remain classified – secret from others.' He stopped smoking and glared at Bren to emphasize his point. 'The truth is, major, that I cannot remember a more secret event than the one in which we three are participating at this moment. The president and I arrived here separately. Because of the distances and time scales involved, Mr Roosevelt, especially, has gone to enormous lengths to disguise his journey. There has been the minimum of security, no hoo-ha whatsoever. No-one knows that we are *both* here, in this place, at this time. No-one, that is, major, except you.'

Bren, instantly burdened by such responsibility, lost his breath and could not speak. He gazed blankly around the room, but it offered little comfort. It was stark and cold, its only decoration a hung oil portrait of an Alpine maiden whose sombre expression perfectly reflected the mood of the meeting.

'You will want to know why, major,' Roosevelt said quietly.

Bren found his voice and replied: 'Yes, sir. Of course.'

'Lamentably,' said Churchill, 'you have become accustomed to death in this abominable affair into which the human race has plunged itself. You have also become accustomed to killing . . .'

Churchill raised his eyebrows to prompt a reply. Bren said: 'I've done my share.'

'Then what you must do for us, for your country, for the Allies and for the future of mankind, is to kill someone.'

'Who?'

Churchill cleared his throat and exchanged a final glance with Roosevelt before delivering the name of the target in a voice laden with a sense of history.

'The leader of the Soviet Union,' he said. 'Joseph Vissarionovich Stalin.'

11

Quester was floating on a smooth sea of flattened vegetation. He did not know whether or not he was conscious, but he knew what was happening.

A strong man was dragging him through the cornfield by his ankles. He could not see anyone, but he could hear the man's grunts of effort. His legs were in the air; his head, torso and arms on the ground, bumping and rolling over the field's contours. His hands, hanging limply behind his head, were being cut and bruised by stones and the stunted, razor-sharp stems of trampled wheat.

He did not care where he was going. All that troubled him was the relentless pain in his right thigh, more intense now than ever before, and the pressing need for escape.

'You don't understand,' he murmured, without knowing if he could be heard. 'I have to go. I have been given an important task and it is vital that I should be free to fulfil it.'

No-one listened. Quester floated on. Only the smell of the air changed. The harsh, solid scent of the grain had been replaced by a vile, moist stench of dung.

Someone took hold of his arms. He was being swung to and fro like a skipping rope.

I'm in the air, by myself. I'm flying.

A soft landing. Comfort. Warmth.

He heard the protesting whinny of a disturbed horse. Did it have a rider? Quester knew he could not find out now. The answer would have to wait.

* * *

'What do you know of politics, of conflicting ideologies?' Roosevelt asked when Bren was ready.

'I'm a soldier, sir,' the major replied. 'It doesn't do to dwell too long on such matters. Screws you up.'

'So, you follow orders. That's one of the reasons you have been chosen for this mission. But don't pretend that you do not have a mind of your own. You have an excellent educational background and achieved the rank of major on merit rather than inheriting it from the deceased.'

'I guess so.'

'So we feel honour-bound to explain to you at least part of the reason for our desire to eliminate Stalin. After all, he's Uncle Joe, our ally in the great struggle against Hitler.'

'The fact is,' Churchill intervened, 'that we are looking beyond the end of the war. We can allow ourselves that luxury now. We are certain of victory, with or without Stalin. To his credit, the man has mobilized and motivated his forces into scoring a major success on the Eastern front, and is now sweeping all before him. In the West, despite Hitler's push into our lines in the Battle of the Bulge, of which you are only too painfully aware, we are totally confident that we will soon have the situation under control before beginning our final thrust across Germany. We are on the eve of Christmas, major. The sound of carols, the sight of holly and the scent of plum pudding. Victory in Europe will be ours long before the next festive season.'

'But that will *not* be the end of it,' Roosevelt said in a sharp tone that belied his weariness. 'This planet faces a potential disaster more cataclysmic than anything Hitler has dreamed of. It could divide the Earth in two. And it will be Stalin's doing. Yes, we sleep with Uncle Joe to

153

further our objectives now, but we are not natural bedfellows. Whatever we say about him in public is not what we think in private. Stalin has designs for Russia which will be the next major threat to world peace. He already has his eyes on several Eastern European nations which he is determined to subjugate. He will try to annexe Poland and other buffer states to throw up an impenetrable Communist-ruled barrier around the borders of Russia.'

'An iron curtain,' Churchill interjected.

'It will eradicate all hopes for peaceful and productive co-operation between nations,' Roosevelt continued. 'Stalin may well create a core of power that the US and Britain will be forced to challenge. More fighting, more death and destruction. Lord knows, we've had enough of that . . .'

Roosevelt shook his head sadly at the thought. His stamina was ebbing and Churchill took over. He looked at Bren with a considerate air, as if he sincerely wanted the major to understand.

'What you must see is that Stalin is a savage. He is as anti-semitic as Hitler, but his prejudices and vile contempt for his fellow man do not stop there. Those who he perceives as a threat – and that encompasses many millions – run the risk of his wrath. He has been more agile in mind than the Führer. Hitler tried to export his cruelty. Stalin keeps it under wraps in Mother Russia. He massacred eleven million Ukrainians because of their tendency to independent thought. He simply starved them to death by plundering their harvests and setting up border controls to prevent food from outside getting in. Eleven *million*. Can you imagine that?'

'Even his own kind are not safe,' Roosevelt interjected. 'He has already murdered most of those who stood beside him during the Revolution. We have clear indications that he will begin another bloody purge after the war. Today's comrade is tomorrow's corpse. Frankly, if we kill Stalin, we will be doing Russia a favour as well as ourselves.'

'We need to move quickly if we are to have a Soviet leader with whom we can communicate,' Churchill said. 'If Stalin dies, one of three men will take control: Molotov, the People's Commissar for Foreign Affairs; Malenkov, the Kremlin's shooting star; or Beria, the head of the secret police, the NKVD. The former two, granite-faced and robotic though they may be, we can do business with. Beria is in the same class as Stalin. Therefore, major, your task will be to kill two birds with one stone. Eliminate Stalin . . . and implicate Beria in the murder so the Kremlin will be obliged to deal with him.'

'But where? How?' Bren asked.

'The "where" is simple,' Churchill responded. 'Mr Roosevelt and I will be meeting Stalin in February at Yalta on the Black Sea. It will be a major summit to plan the last moppings-up of the war and the future of Europe. Each leader will be supported by a large delegation of advisers and experts. You will be part of the US delegation.'

'The "how" is by blowing Stalin sky-high with a bomb, leaving evidence that the device was manufactured in Russia,' Roosevelt said.

Bren held up a hand of protest.

'I have very limited knowledge of explosives,' he said. 'And none at all of Russian bombs.'

'Training will be provided.' Churchill handed Bren a plain brown envelope. 'There are two names and addresses inside, together with the dates on which you must report to them. At one address, you will learn all there is to learn about Joseph Stalin, so that you will be fully prepared to meet what is an undeniably formidable

155

foe. It will be good therapy for you while your rib heals. At the other address, you will be given comprehensive tuition in the latest explosives technology. Those named inside the envelope will both be briefed to expect you, though approaches will be made so that neither will be given any idea of your mission and neither will be aware of any government involvement.'

'And after that, I am on my own,' Bren surmised.

'Not quite.' Churchill allowed himself a brief smile. 'It is only natural that Stalin has made many enemies inside his own country. We have made initial contact with a Soviet citizen who is interested in becoming involved. We will need inside help, and we are grateful for her assistance.'

'*Her*?'

'You will see. All in good time. She will contact you in Yalta – and not before.'

Bren's inevitable question took longer to arise than the two leaders had anticipated.

'I am flattered to be here, in your presence, gentlemen. But why me? Surely you could have had your pick of a thousand known operatives.'

'Exactly,' Roosevelt replied. 'They are known to us – and to intelligence agencies. When the balloon goes up in Yalta, the Soviets will start digging. Especially if it appears that one of their own is responsible. They will put every member of every delegation under the microscope. They will be desperate to find a scapegoat from our side. Someone who is merely suspicious will suffice. You, however, will emerge as a soldier who until recently was fighting on the Western front. A straightforward, honest major who showed great courage, initiative and fortitude. A man who, when he was wounded, was plucked out of the battlefield, promoted to colonel and entrusted with strategic tactical planning behind the front line. Nothing shady. No dirt clinging to your shirt-tails. Merely a logical chain of events. You could not possibly be an agent in disguise.'

'But I'm inexperienced. I could be caught.'

'That's a chance we all have to take in any event,' said Roosevelt. 'You have not been simply picked with a pin. Your progress had been monitored even before your heroic defence of Rocherath. You are an exceptional man, a colonel now. You'd better get used to it. There is, however, one instruction we will give you if you feel you might be caught.'

'Which is . . . ?'

'Don't be.'

Churchill reached across the table and rested his hand on Bren's.

'Well, Colonel,' he said gravely. 'You have been entrusted with a mammoth task, one which must succeed. But you have not yet given us your decision.'

'I'm sorry, sir,' Bren said in bewilderment.

'Will you do it?'

Bren was conscious that his hands were clammy with sweat and wondered if Churchill had noticed. He looked first at Roosevelt, then at the Prime Minister, and slowly, deliberately, nodded his agreement.

'I'll do it. I'll kill Stalin.'

Churchill let out a loud sigh of relief.

'I'm so glad,' he said. 'You see, outside the door of this room stands a man with a gun. The chap who saw you in, actually, the one who looks like a civil servant. His instructions are that if you are the first to leave, he is to shoot you dead. Now that you are a willing party to our operation, however, I shall show my portly features to him and alleviate the need for such violence.'

Bren was shocked more than he had ever been on the battlefield.

'You mean, sir, that if I had turned you down, you would have allowed me to walk out of that door to my death?'

'Well,' Churchill grinned. 'We plainly could not have you wandering around with such knowledge, now, could we?'

Churchill rose from his chair, ready to leave. Before saying his farewells to Roosevelt, he put his hand on Bren's shoulder and chortled: 'Merry Christmas, Colonel.'

Kelly stepped from the supermarket into the eerie quiet of a shopping precinct. It had always troubled her. Bustling crowds of people, yet no noise apart from the clip-clopping of shoes on chequer-patterned flagstones. No-one seemed to talk in precincts. It was as if the concrete alleyways harboured some unseen, unspeakable menace that demanded obedient silence.

'Nurse Warren!' The cry was strident, cutting through a vaporous barrier of languid faces on hunched shoulders. Kelly stopped, looking around to find its source. Seconds later Quester's cousin from Austria, the one who paid for his hospital treatment, emerged from the mêlée. Kelly remembered what Quester had said about him and felt her muscles tense. But he greeted her with a broad smile, and she relaxed.

'Nurse Warren?' he said with a heavy mid-European accent. 'It is Nurse Warren, isn't it?'

Kelly nodded and studied the man. He was wearing a strange combination of urban raincoat and farmer's cap. Kelly wondered which part of Austria he came from. He took her shopping bags from her hands and rested them on a bench.

'So glad to have found you,' he said. 'They told me at the hospital that you and he have become close. So you can tell me where he is.'

He waited for her to speak. She realized that she did not know what to say.

'Only I don't have much time,' he continued. 'I am not in England very long. I have to go home. So . . .'

'I – I don't know . . .' Kelly stuttered. She saw a flash of impatience sweep across his face and asked: 'Why do you want to see him?'

The man reddened and said: 'I should have thought that was obvious, young lady. To see how he is, of course. To tell him there are many more members of our family who wish him well and hope to see him soon.'

No family anywhere.

Quester's sick-bed disclaimer came back to Kelly as if he had told her yesterday.

'Now look, Mr – er . . .'

'Mezera, nurse. My name is Mezera.'

'There are two things I should tell you, Mr Mezera.'

'Oh? Yes . . .'

'The first is that Tom – Mr Quester – insists that he has no family in Austria, or anywhere else for that matter.'

Mezera looked sad and shook his head.

'And do you believe him?' he said quietly.

'I don't know what to believe,' Kelly replied candidly.

'Do you believe that a man would pay an expensive hospital bill for a complete stranger? Do you believe that a man would insist on the very best treatment available without the kind of attachment to someone that can only be brought about by family? Do you believe that a man

159

would stand beside a dying man's bed and pray for his recovery without the bond of blood?'

Kelly felt guilty for entertaining any other thoughts.

A gust of wind blew her fringe over her eyes. She pulled it back and muttered: 'I'm sorry.'

Mezera dipped his head to accept the apology and said: 'No matter, my dear. I am sure there are explanations. A loss of memory brought on by his accident, perhaps. Or some sort of strange suppression of his innermost feelings. Who can say? But what was the second thing you had to tell me?'

Kelly cleared her throat. She was nervous and did not know if she possessed the strength to inform Mezera of the assassin. But she felt it was her duty. She avoided Mezera's eyes as she told him.

'Tom is convinced that you are not a cousin. He believes that you are an imposter who has tried to kill him and is still trying to kill him. An assassin, in fact.'

Mezera moaned loudly.

'Oh my God,' he gasped. 'This is dreadful. The poor, poor man.'

Mezera slumped on the bench beside Kelly's shopping bags as if he had been winded. He looked up at the nurse and asked her if it was true that Quester had been admitted to a psychiatric hospital. When she told him that it was, he moaned again and mumbled: 'Paranoia. The poor man thinks I am trying to kill him. Me, of all people . . .'

'I'm sorry,' Kelly said.

Mezera glanced at her and smiled.

'It's true what he says. The last time he phoned me – when was it, about a week ago – he told me that your beauty was matched only by your compulsion to apologize, whether or not you were at fault.'

160

Kelly blushed deeply. Mezera chuckled. They were each warming to the other.

'So!' Mezera exclaimed suddenly. 'I will visit him in the psychiatric hospital. Where is it, please?'

Kelly told him Quester had 'walked out'.

'Have you seen him?'

'Yes, briefly.'

'Then he is not staying with you.'

'No. He left.'

'Did he tell you where he was going?'

'Not in detail. He just said the Ardennes.'

Mezera fell silent, lost in thought.

Eventually, he said: 'The Ardennes. Yes, of course. It's logical.'

Suddenly, he sprang from the bench and walked away. Kelly was staggered. They had been talking, almost as friends, about a man they both cared for. Yet for no apparent reason, Mezera had cut the conversation dead, turned his back and hurried off, without so much as a goodbye.

Kelly couldn't take it. She ran after him, took him by the shoulder and spun him around. His cap fell off, revealing the shock of snowy hair that she remembered so well.

'Please!' Her voice reflected her state of utter confusion. 'You can't go like this. Will you see him? Can I come with you? Why is he behaving like this? You seem to know something. Why is it logical for him to go to the Ardennes? I have to know, don't you see? I love him . . .'

Mezera looked at her with eyes that had lost their inquisitive innocence of a moment ago. Kelly took a deep breath to compose herself and repeated: 'Why is it logical?'

Mezera's reply was measured and lacked concern.

'Because, my dear, that is where it all began for him.'

Kelly was beside herself. 'What do you mean?' she said.

She took hold of Mezera's hand. Begging, pleading for more.

As he felt her touch, something happened inside him. His jaw dropped so that his mouth fell open. He could not believe the sensations that were pulsing through his flesh. He looked at her wildly until she felt his gaze was penetrating her every cell. She pulled her hand away instinctively and hid it self-consciously in a pocket.

His stare did not falter.

'What?' she asked nervously.

His words came from deep inside him, forcing through a gullet that was tight with shock.

'You . . .' he said slowly. 'It's you. I can feel it. I am so sure.'

Kelly twined her fingers through her hair and tugged. She wanted to make sure that it hurt, to prove she was not dreaming.

'What?' she shouted, her voice cracking as she became more hysterical. 'What? What? What?'

Mezera's voice took on an unreal, distant quality, as if he was speaking to her across a vast hall.

'I knew I would find you. It was only a matter of time. I should have known you would be at his side. Incredible.'

'Talk sense, damn you! Who are you? How do you know me? What do you want with Tom?'

'The Ardennes,' he said. 'I must go there first. Find the Colonel. Then I will return for you, sweet, treacherous girl. Then I will return for you.'

He took one last look at Kelly, turned and vanished into the crowd.

She fell to her knees, knocking them on a flagstone but feeling no pain.

So it was all true. Everything that Quester had told her about, had warned her about. She wrapped her arms around her shoulders for comfort and warmth. For a moment, she wondered why she was so cold. Then she realized.

She was shivering with fear.

12

Bren was transferred to the US Third Army and assigned to General Patton's command headquarters in Luxembourg. He spent a week there, long enough to alert any spies in the camp to his new-found role as strategist. He pored over maps of Europe, sliced into portions by front lines until they looked like butcher's diagrams of pigs, and consulted with other tacticians, including the general himself. On the Friday after New Year, he left with Patton's blessing on the pretext of conducting a fact-finding tour of hot-spots.

He had memorized the information in the envelope handed to him by Churchill. His first appointment was at an Elizabethan manor house set deep in the backwaters of England fifteen miles from Truro. He raised his eyebrows in surprise as he arrived.

Its garden was coarse and overgrown, its brickwork neglected and crumbling. Several panes of its leaded windows were missing or cracked. And the Tudor beams that criss-crossed the first storey were plagued by rot, administered either by insects or by damp. It was a sad sight of decay – and gave no hint of what was inside.

Bren was greeted by a short man in his fifties whose heavy, unexercised thighs gave him an awkward rolling gait. He had thin streaks of hair slicked back with cream that spread over his scalp and made it shine.

He introduced himself as Professor Gordon Lambert and ushered Bren inside with the enthusiasm of a schoolboy.

'An American. Good, good. Americans tend to speak their minds, call a spade a spade. We British are so reserved, you know. Don't say a dickey-bird in case we offend. I'm sure I'll get a far higher quality of feedback from you.'

Within minutes, it became apparent that Lambert was the only inhabitant of the manor and that he knew nothing of Bren's mission. As far as he was concerned, he was simply conducting an experiment. And Bren, apparently, had volunteered his services as a guinea-pig.

Lambert served up an abominable lunch of lukewarm soup and bread. He spoke in academic riddles, showed little interest in the war effort and none at all in Bren's part in the conflict.

'Coming here for a few days is so much more pleasant than being shot at, n'est-ce pas?' was his sole, simplistic recognition of what had been going on around him for the past five years. Lost in his own world. Bren envied him.

For all his babbling, Lambert was not to be underestimated, as Bren discovered when he was taken down to the cellar. Here was the real truth of the decaying manor house. Hollowed out and lined with smooth, magnolia-painted plaster, the cellar was the nearest thing to luxury that 1945 could offer. Carpets, sofas, spotlights. A heavily cushioned easy chair in the centre of the floor sandwiched between a reel projector and a large screen. In one corner, sublime comfort gave way to the practical catering of a small open-plan kitchen. A gas stove, sink, food cupboards and utensil cabinets rested on diamond-shaped black and white tiles. A huge poster hung on the wall, designed like an ancient manuscript and displaying the recipe for some sort of goulash in Olde English lettering.

'I'd rather like a bed to finish things off,' Lambert said. 'Then I could stay down here forever.'

'What do you use it for?' Bren asked.

'You're about to find out,' Lambert replied with a wink. 'Actually, though you would not believe it, this is a laboratory.'

'For experiments?'

'For research into my theories on Deep Repetitive Energy Absorption into the Mind. Or taking the initials, DREAM.'

Lambert sat Bren in the easy chair and told him to relax.

'DREAM,' he explained, 'is a method by which the subject, in this case you, assimilates information on a particular topic by means of hypnosis, drugs and repetition. Now, of course, none of these techniques is new. But the combination and inter-relation of the three is completely revolutionary. My research is in its infancy, but I believe DREAM will lead to an explosive increase in man's ability to expand and use his memory.'

'So?' Bren found it difficult to fathom the benefits. Lambert felt a burning frustration born out of other people's inability to match his own extraordinary intelligence. But he had become accustomed to it and had learned to adapt. He extended his explanation, trying hard not to sound patronizing.

'The brain's resources are enormous, Colonel Bren. But we are far from being able to mine its most glittering treasures. For example, do you dream?'

'Yes, of course.'

'Can you explain why or how these crazy, ridiculous scenarios appear from nowhere as you sleep?'

'No.'

'Neither can I, Colonel. Do you remember past events in your life?'

'Some, I guess.'

166

'And not others . . .'

'That's right.'

'Do you know why you should remember only a selection, and forget the rest.'

'Not really, no.'

'Neither do I. And I could go on and on. So you see, there are countless functions of the brain that are, if truth be told, totally baffling. And yet we know they are there, so perhaps we can find a way of utilizing them to the full.'

'With what in mind, if you'll excuse the pun?'

'When you are faced with a decision which you must make quickly, on what do you base your response?'

'On what you know, and what you think will happen.'

'Exactly. And this in turn is based on information supplied to you by your memory, defined as the sum of everything retained by your mind and including its most intriguing constituent, the subconscious.'

'Explain . . .'

'Without our ability to remember past experiences, we would be wanderers lost in a world perpetually new to us –'

'No, not memory.'

'What then?'

'The subconscious.'

'Oh, I see. Well, let's just say it consists of memories which influence our behaviour without us being aware of them.'

'Such as?'

'A man comes into a room. You immediately like him. You feel drawn to him, though there is no logical reason for such an emotional response. What you don't realize is that the man had exhibited a similar mannerism to your long-lost, dearly beloved father. It may be the way he brushes a hair from his jacket. It may be the way he lights his cigarette. Whatever, the man reminds you of your father – though this actual thought never crosses your mind – and you feel a warmth for him.'

'Amazing.'

'Not at all. It's a common fact of life.'

'So why bother with DREAM?'

'The key word is control. The memory has an annoying habit of leaking, wouldn't you say? In one ear and out the other, and all that. It's tragic how much information we lose in a lifetime. DREAM, therefore, has two functions. To expand our ability to store information and to keep it *safe*. If you like, to keep a locked cupboard of secrets in our subconscious which, when necessary, can be unlocked.'

'And to what use will this be put?'

Lambert chuckled.

'You may think me over-enthusiastic. You may even come to think of me as just a dotty professor. But I'll tell you this, Colonel, I am not naïve. What are the first uses for DREAM that come into your head?'

'Military and espionage.'

Lambert sighed heavily. The speed with which Bren had seen the possibilities was as deflating as it was predictable. Even though the scientist had admitted defeat months ago, and had thrown more romantic notions for his brainchild out of the window, he still felt a stab of resentment in his stomach.

'The principal beneficiary will be the professional assassin,' he said reluctantly. 'The more he knows of his target, the more information he retains, the more his whole psyche is geared up to combat the target. And the greater his chance of success. Particularly when the difference between triumph and disaster comes down to a split-second decision that can only be based on a subconscious hunch.'

Lambert told Bren he could expect four days of intense work, broken only by meals and sleep. Each day would be a carbon copy of the first. There would be no respite, no deviation.

'The hypnosis is straightforward,' he said. 'My research will be concentrated on the repetition of information – and the drugs. These are early days. I feel duty-bound to tell you that I cannot be certain there will be no side effects.'

'What drugs are you using?'

'Classified. But I can tell you they are mild hallucinogens.'

Bren balked at the thought.

'They are necessary,' Lambert said uncompromisingly. 'They will help you to create pictures in your mind. Pictures that will be retained and stored. I call them eidetic images. Your word would be photographic memory. It is a question of efficiency, of using the available space in the memory at its optimum capacity. After all, every picture says a thousand words.'

'I thought people either had a photographic memory, or they didn't.'

'I am trying to create the ability in those who do not possess it. And I will go one step further.'

'Which is?'

'The implantation of living, moving pictures. Dreams, Colonel, dreams.'

Bren was impressed and doubtful at the same time. Lambert said confusion was the normal reaction to scientific breakthroughs.

'But how will you know if DREAM is a success?' Bren asked.

Lambert waggled a finger as if he was warning his guinea pig not to expect too much, too soon.

'It is a long-term project,' he said. 'You will return here six months, one year and two years from now to be tested on your powers of retention. I hope everything will come naturally. If not, I may have to drill through to your subconscious using other drugs.'

'Another aspect of your research?'

'Captured spies rarely volunteer secrets, Colonel Bren.'

Lambert announced the end of the briefing.

'There is work to be done,' he said as he rolled across to the kitchen section. He took a shoe box full of syringes and unmarked brown bottles from a cabinet. Then he pulled aside the goulash poster to reveal a large safe set in the wall. He unlocked it and brought out three tattered brown folders and a pair of round metal tins that Bren assumed contained film.

Lambert glanced at the folders and puffed with exasperation.

'I thought Adolf Hitler would be the natural subject for our studies,' he said. 'I asked the intelligence people for everything they had on him, but for some reason they sent me the file on someone else.'

'Who?'

'Stalin. Joseph Stalin.'

The crucifix dangled lazily in front of Bren's eyes. Beyond, past the tip of his nose, the screen was alive with a flickering newsreel film of Stalin reviewing the Red Army from Lenin's Tomb. Bren watched him, studied every twitch of his moustache, absorbed the dictator's arrogant confidence until he felt he could reach out and touch him.

There was a sting in his arm as a hypodermic slid in. He heard Lambert's voice drifting towards him from nowhere.

'Memory is based on experience. You are about to experience the entire life of Joseph Stalin without moving from this chair. You will fall deeply asleep. Deeply. Deeply. But you will cling on to the ledge that juts out above the precipice of coma. You will hear every word I speak. With the help of the hallucinogens, you will transform each word into a vision of your own. Pictures. Living, moving pictures. Dreams. Deep, vivid, unforgettable dreams. Sleep now, Colonel Bren. Let yourself walk into another world.'

The effect was stunning. Bren heard Lambert's nasal monotone for hour after hour. And for each of Lambert's sentences, he created a picture in his mind.

'Joseph Vissarionovich Stalin was born in a hovel, the son of a brutal, perpetually drunk Georgian cobbler . . .'

I see it! There is a struggle in front of the fireplace. The boy Joseph throws a knife at his father, but misses. He runs for his life.

'. . . By the time he reached his early twenties, he was a known revolutionary who had been arrested several times and sent into exile in Siberia . . .'

I see a forest and a river. Smoke rising in perfect parallel lines from a cluster of cabins. Stalin is laughing at the other man in his cabin. The man has a bad cough. Stalin does not sympathize and even makes fun of the other's predicament.

'. . . The great leader hosted summer picnics at his dacha. Henchmen like Molotov, Voroshilov and Beria were invited. But the occasions were often marred by clashes with his wife, Nadya . . .'

I know. Nadya complained to her friend Polina Molotov. She told her a story of Stalin's wondrous visits to Petersburg, when he took Nadya and her mother on magical sleigh rides. Now Nadya is so disillusioned, so sad.

171

'. . . They argued at a banquet to celebrate the anniversary of the Revolution. He treated her bullishly, with contempt . . .'

She dabs herself with perfume. Then she takes a revolver from a drawer. 'I'll show you who can shoot straight,' she says, and pulls the trigger.

'. . . He has been seen only once on the field of battle, when he paid a visit to the troops defending Stalingrad in 1942 . . .'

He distributes vodka and cigarettes along the trenches. At the same time, he warns his men that if they surrender to the Germans, they will answer to him when the war is over. And their fate will be worse than they could have imagined. Snow. I can see so much snow. It reminds me of the Ardennes. Snow and blood and slime.

'. . . He claimed Russia was not responsible when the bodies of 12,500 Polish officers were unearthed from mass graves in the Katyn Forest . . .'

He tried to blame the Nazis and organized a cover-up with Beria. He brought in a puppet professor to perform autopsies. The professor is waving a bit of green liver on the tip of his scalpel and shouting, 'See how lovely and fresh it looks!' God, I can smell it. I think I'm going to be sick.

'. . . He treats even his most senior statesmen abominably. At least they have survived his murderous purges, but they are subject to constant humiliation . . .'

He is shoving Molotov on to the ice. It breaks – and Molotov plunges into the freezing pond. 'Fish him out, Beria, before his balls turn to iced raisins.' Polina Molotov cannot believe what has happened to her husband. She pushes her hands into her cheeks in anxiety.

'. . . He is due to meet Churchill and Roosevelt at Yalta, on the Black Sea . . .'

And that is where I will kill him.

13

Quester saw two blurred black circles as his eyelids parted slowly. He squinted, straining to focus. Gradually, the circles took on a definite form . . . the twin barrels of a pump-action shotgun, pointing directly at his temple.

He followed the line of the gun to the rough hands that held it and beyond. A swarthy, unshaven peasant farmer with a curling moustache and shambolic greasy hair returned his stare. Quester could see in his eyes that he, too, was frightened. He wore a thick red shirt patterned like a lumberjack's, braces to support trousers that were a size too big and rubber boots coated with dust and chaff. He shook the shotgun to remind Quester who was in control, but his awkwardness suggested he was not a man of habitual violence.

Quester looked around to take stock of his situation. He was lying amid broken bales of straw in a stable shared with a staunch but restless workhorse.

Warmth, comfort . . . the whinny of a disturbed horse, the smell of dung. It was beginning to come back to him.

The stable was illuminated by two paraffin lights hung on hooks. The door was open and Quester could see a pair of pigs milling in the mist outside. It was still night. Quester sensed that little time had elapsed since he collapsed in the cornfield. The farmer had dragged him here and someone else had helped to throw him on the straw bales, that much was evident. He felt a burning sensation on the backs of his hands. He held them up and studied the cuts and scratches that criss-crossed his knuckles. He noticed that his watch was missing.

Had the farmer taken it? No, he looked too honest, too sincere. It must have been torn off by some root or stone. Quester did not care. There were more important considerations. He had to get away from this place.

'Alain!' The farmer called out in a high-pitched voice that came as a surprise, considering his size. 'Viens vite! Il se réveille.'

Moments later, the weasel-faced boy who Quester had met in Rocherath stumbled through the door in pyjamas and dressing gown, rubbing sleep from his eyes.

The farmer scolded him about something or other, then returned his attention to Quester.

'Alors l'Anglais! Qu'est-ce que vous foutez ici?'

'My father wants to know what an Englishman like you is doing here,' the boy explained.

Quester looked at them in turn. But he was in another world, another time.

'I can see it now,' he said. 'I know what he wants.'

The boy translated for his father. Both looked puzzled. It crossed Quester's mind that they were not natural father and son. They shared not a single characteristic.

'Inheritance,' he murmured. 'A strange thing.'

The farmer looked worried.

'Vous faites quoi dans mon champs?' he said. 'Vous êtes à Rocherath et vous posez des questions. Pourquoi, hein? Les flics sont après vous?'

So he was being taken for a crook on the run from the police. It was logical. Why else would he have been bolting through a cornfield in the dead of night? Quester searched through his pockets. He pulled out a credit card, his car keys and 200 francs in 20-franc notes.

'No fortune,' he said wearily, waggling a finger. 'No robber.'

The farmer took him at his word and relaxed. He propped the shotgun against a drinking trough and squatted closer to the stranger on the straw. He offered a reassuring smile. Quester returned it. The farmer was a gentle man, and Quester was relieved. He had no strength to fight or squabble. In such surroundings, he felt like a newborn lamb.

'Alain me dit que vous voulez savoir où trouver le Café Magritte et Madame Troyes.' The farmer was friendly now, even sympathetic. Quester expected he would soon fetch food and drink.

'I told my father the things you were asking in the village,' the boy said.

Quester nodded in gratitude. The farmer put on a face of distress.

'Elle a été tuée pendant la guerre,' he said. 'Le café était complètement détruit par les Allemands.'

'Madame Troyes was killed in the war,' the boy translated. 'And the café was destroyed.'

'I know,' Quester said.

'Then why did you ask?'

'I didn't know then.'

The boy translated for his father, adding that, in his opinion, Quester was sick.

'Vous voulez un médecin?' the farmer said.

'Do you want a doctor?'

'Men in white? No!' Quester was shaken by the suggestion. Suddenly, he felt under threat. Why did they want to do this to him? What had he done to deserve it? They were being so pleasant – and now this.

'All in white in Rocherath!' he shouted. 'Phantoms, coming at me. Me! Me!'

Quester shuddered violently, his arms and legs flailing on the bales. The farmer and his son went to hold him. Quester panicked. He fought free of their grip and sprang to his feet. They tried to grab him but he bolted through the stable door and ran as if his life depended on it. There was a flurry of footsteps behind him and a cry of 'Arrêtez!'

'Pull back!' Quester screamed. 'They're behind us, coming after us. Shrapnel all around. Christ, what have they done to you, Madame Troyes? No more schnapps . . .'

The farmer was too confused to give chase, but Quester did not slacken his pace. Running as fast as his lungs would allow, he headed back to the cornfield and past the well where Christie was shot.

He cracked his shins hard as he climbed the gate, but he scarcely noticed. He jumped the ditch and followed the winding lane into Rocherath. The BMW was where he left it, covered with a fine film of droplets deposited by the mist. Quester leaped in, started the engine and spun the back wheels in his haste to get away.

He knew he would not feel safe until he was over Elsenborn Ridge.

Bren boarded the plane in Malta with his head bursting. He felt as if the inside of his skull had been scraped with a spatula and then filled with clay. It was not only his four excruciating days with Lambert that had brought it on. Since leaving the Tudor manor, he had been at the second address, near General Eisenhower's headquarters in Versailles, to be briefed in detail about Soviet explosives and to learn the rudiments of the Russian language. His tutors had been told he was to help a Soviet sabotage team behind enemy lines on the Eastern front, thus promoting an historic co-operation.

The American and British delegations for the Yalta conference had gathered in Malta for their final flight to the Crimea. This was at the suggestion of the ailing Roosevelt's medical advisers. The president had originally planned to take off from Caserta, in southern Italy, but his doctors considered the high-altitude flying involved, over several mountain ranges, an unnecessary risk.

Bren found himself one of 350 in the US delegation of politicians, chiefs-of-staff, lower-ranked military men, bodyguards, advisers, pressmen and secretaries. There was a similar number of Britons. Bren was relieved. He would be able to achieve the prime precondition for a killer – anonymity.

Transport planes took off at ten-minute intervals. Bren travelled on the Sacred Cow with Roosevelt. It lifted off in the early hours of the morning and the president spent much of the five-hour flight sleeping. When he awoke, he tried his damnedest to inject himself with vitality. He kept quoting from a letter sent to him by Churchill.

'No more let us falter! From Malta to Yalta! Let nobody alter!'

Roosevelt chuckled. Churchill always made him feel lighter at heart, he said. Which was just as well, everybody thought, considering the dire state he was in.

Bren came face to face with Roosevelt as he returned to his seat from the toilet. But not a flicker of recognition crossed the president's face.

It was as if he was saying: 'You're on your own, now, buddy. Just do it.'

The plane touched down at Saki airfield just after midday. It was a bleak and cold place, but bustling with activity. Huts and barracks had been erected for Red Army troops and RAF men drafted in to prepare for the invasion. Large marquees flapped in the fierce, biting wind. Aircraft of every kind peppered the field. Soldiers unloaded supplies from cargo holds and carried them to waiting trucks. Jeeps burbled here and there, leaving muddy tracks in the wet grass. A huge flotilla of cars stood by, ready to despatch the 700 new arrivals to the Black Sea coast.

Churchill had landed minutes before. Bren watched as Roosevelt was carried down the steps of the Sacred Cow to greet him. Together, they inspected the guard of honour, Roosevelt riding in a jeep, Churchill walking beside. Then it was on into the grandest of the marquees, where Molotov and a smattering of other Russian officials offered refreshments and the hand of Soviet friendship. Already, Bren could feel a sense of occasion coursing through his veins.

Formal speeches were delivered and acknowledged. Then, one by one, cars drew up outside the marquees to scoop up four or five passengers and a hillock of luggage. Three men without uniforms climbed in with Bren. They were secret service, part of Roosevelt's protection squad.

'I don't know why we're bothering,' one said in a cynical Texan drawl. 'The old man's going to die anyhow.'

Bren visualized the Big Three standing side by side. Roosevelt, Churchill and Stalin. Soon, only Churchill would be left.

The journey was interminable. There were 100 miles to travel and for the first two hours, the roads were so bumpy and slushy that the convoy could not better 20mph. The Crimean countryside, arid in summer, featureless in winter, offered little distraction from the monotony. The only respite came from village streets and bridges, where rows of soldiers and Red Army girls stood to attention shoulder to shoulder as the convoy passed.

At first, Bren took them for isolated pockets. But it soon became apparent they were lining the entire route.

'Jeez! They must make up at least two infantry divisions,' the Texan gasped.

Bren swallowed uncomfortably. He was beginning to realize the odds against him. He made small talk to retain an unconcerned air.

'But where are the Russian people? I've only seen a handful of peasants. Surely the Crimea cannot be that sparsely populated.'

Another of the trio spoke. He introduced himself as Jonathan Pruett and was less bullish, more refined than his companions. He spoke matter-of-factly, displaying either wide-ranging knowledge or ability for painstaking research, or both.

'Two reasons,' he said. 'One. The fighting here only ended a few months ago. Two. Stalin deported the Crimean Tatars eastwards before the Nazis got here. The Tatars have a reputation as stubborn nationalists. Stalin thought it wise to transport the whole damn population, to be absolutely sure there would be no fraternizing with the enemy.'

The two other secret servicemen laughed. Bren did not. Pruett looked at him suspiciously. He had piercing green eyes and Bren was unnerved.

After what seemed an eternity, the convoy passed through the Crimean Mountains and began the descent into Yalta. Oppressive cloud gave way to brilliant sunshine. The air became warmer, almost spring-like, and the Black Sea, despite its name, was a vivid shade of blue. From a distance, Yalta had the appearance of a resort on the French Riviera. Clusters of white houses near the harbour, giving way to larger villas set in woodland as the ground rose towards the snow-capped range which swept

179

dramatically behind the town like a windblown cloak. But the truth was far less picturesque. Close up, every house was a jagged, open shell. Cubes of naked masonry reached to the sky. There were no roofs, no windows, no doors. The destruction had been methodical. Before evacuation, the Germans had seen to it that if they could not have Yalta, no-one would.

The American section of the convoy was directed on for another mile, until the delegation reached its conference quarters, the dazzling limestone Livadia Palace. The British trundled another few miles to the strangely styled palace at Alupka, a bizarre cross between a Scottish baronial castle and a mosque. The Russians had already set up house in the Yusupov villa, further up the hills from their guests in the hamlet of Koreiz.

Bren climbed stiffly out of the car, stretching his limbs with relief. He felt a piece of crumpled paper pushed into his left hand and glanced around to see Pruett standing behind him. Bren walked to one side and unravelled the paper. A note was scrawled on it, reading: 'Turkish gazebo. Palace grounds. Two o'clock tomorrow morning.' Bren looked up, searching for Pruett, but he was nowhere to be seen.

So, Bren thought, it has begun.

He was shown to his room by an NKVD major and a Russian interpreter.

'You may walk in the grounds,' the major said. 'They stretch from the palace to the sea and there are many places of beauty. But you must stay on the paths. Do not stray on to the grass. It has not been cleared of German mines. Very dangerous.'

'Mr Roosevelt said he wanted the conference to go with

180

a bang,' Bren said. But the joke was lost in interpretation and the major did not smile.

Bren was left to unpack. His room was no bigger than a shoe cupboard, but he had it to himself. Larger suites were being shared by five or six men, including senior officers.

It was being orchestrated, that much was clear. Bren knew he had been left to his own devices to prepare for his mission in privacy. But who was the conductor? Was it Pruett? Did he know of the plot to kill Stalin, or was he simply running errands with no idea of their real purpose? Bren did not expect any answers.

There was a small sash window beyond the foot of his bed. Bren looked through it. Darkness had closed in quickly and reflections of the pale lights of Yalta flickered up to the palace from the choppy sea. He opened the window and leaned out. He was on the second floor, but only six feet above an external staircase, decorated by fantastic stone chimeras, that led down to the ground.

'Perfect,' he muttered aloud. 'Full marks, Pruett.'

'Thank you, colonel!'

Bren spun round. Pruett smiled and cocked his head to one side, satisfied that his surprise had been total. He wandered up to Bren's shoulder, gazing past him to the harbour.

'It is a place for heroes, this,' he said pensively. 'It is a place where brave Soviet torpedo boat captains broke through nets and booms to attack Nazi ships anchored in the port.' Pruett turned to face Bren and added: 'Are you a hero, colonel?'

Bren did not reply. Pruett went on: 'Don't be too sure. The grounds are crawling with NKVD.'

Bren played the innocent. Lord knows, he felt isolated

181

enough. And an ally at such a time would be Heaven-sent. But there was something about Pruett he could not trust.

'I don't know what you mean.'

'You have an appointment. You'll have to get past the NKVD to keep it.'

'I'll manage.'

'Not without my help. What are you up to, colonel?'

'Nothing that concerns you.'

'Wrong. My brief is to protect the life of the President of the United States. That's a wide brief. Means I'm concerned with just about everything.'

Pruett's remark raised Bren's hackles.

'He's my president, too, asshole.'

'Yeah, but you're up to something. I know. I've been given some very strange instructions by some very strange people. They add up to spoon-feeding you, colonel, but no-one knows why. It would help us both if you'd tell me.'

'Keep your nose out – and it won't get bloodied.'

Pruett leaned on the wall nonchalantly.

'Threats. Must be something important.'

Bren changed his approach. He sighed, clicked his knuckles as if he was deep in thought and finally spread his arms in a gesture of conciliation.

'It's an exercise, that's all,' he said.

'Go on,' Pruett urged.

'It's classified. You know I can't tell you more than that.'

'You'll have to.'

Bren lost his temper.

'I don't have to tell you a damn thing, Pruett. Who knows, maybe I might be here to test you guys. See if you're up to scratch. Now take a walk!'

Bren showed Pruett the door. The secret serviceman gave him a numbing look, but left without further protest. Bren knew he was trouble.

Stalin came to welcome Roosevelt that evening. Almost the entire American delegation waited amid the blue-veined white marble of the palace's vast reception hall to catch a glimpse of the great man.

As he left, Stalin stopped to talk to officers who caught his eye. Bren was one of them. Roosevelt's interpreter, Bohlen, scurried to his aid. Bren stood stiffly to attention. Stalin told him to relax.

'And how old are you, colonel?' he said.

'Thirty-one, sir.'

'Ah, so young for such awesome responsibility.'

Stalin asked if he had seen active service. Bren told him of his part in the Battle of the Bulge – and Stalin was impressed.

'I admire young military fighters,' he bellowed. 'Of late, I have acquired a new interest in life. An interest in military matters. In fact, it has become my overriding interest to the exclusion of all others. I can understand why such a noble officer as yourself has become a part of your president's superb tactical force. I, too, will honour your achievements. I am to be the host at a great banquet in the Yusupov villa. Many revered people will be there. What is your name, Colonel?'

'Bren, sir.'

'You, too, will be my guest, Colonel Bren.'

Bren accepted gratefully. He studied Stalin as the dictator shook his hand. The invitation had been warm, but his eyes were as cold as ice. Bren was not surprised. He knew all about Stalin. He had a dossier of his atrocities locked away in a secret compartment in his brain. He could not forget. He would not forget.

Look down, Uncle Joe, he was screaming inside, you have hold of the hand that will kill you.

Over supper, Bren asked the NKVD major about the Livadia Palace. The major gushed with pride.

'It is beautiful, yes? It was built in 1911 as a summer residence for the tsar by the great architect Nikolai Krasnov. He was rewarded with the title of Academician in Architecture.'

'I hope to follow a career in architecture once the war is over,' Bren said. 'There must be many treasures here that will inspire me.'

'Hundreds! The galleries, the ornamental wells, the spectacular forged metal gates made by Ural masters, the exquisite Italian patio, the belfry. And, of course, the breathtaking White Hall, where the plenary sessions of the conference will take place. You will marvel at its painted ceiling.'

'Someone mentioned a gazebo. A Turkish gazebo.'

'Turkish in style, yes. It is in the grounds, near the far edge of the park. Find it tomorrow if you have time. Follow the pergola which begins at the corner of the palace beneath your room. It leads to a marble fountain and then on to the gazebo. You'll recognize it by its silver cupola. It has a wonderful view of the bay.'

'Thank you,' Bren said with a smile. 'I'll do that.'

Bren waited impatiently for the hands of his watch to move round to 1.30. He had considered simply walking to the gazebo out in the open, as he had every right to do. But he rejected the idea on the grounds that he would draw attention to himself, if only as a man who went for walks at absurd hours of the morning. This was a time for subterfuge.

He pushed a pistol into his pocket, opened the window and dropped lightly to the staircase below. It led through a colonnade gallery to the junction of the palace's south and east facades. He squatted behind a thuya hedge to survey the way ahead. The NKVD had set up a crude network of lights powered by a generator hidden in an outhouse, turning the garden into a patchwork of silver-blue and black.

Pruett had been right. The grounds were crawling with guards. Every two minutes or so, Bren caught a glimpse of greatcoats, peaked caps and rifles, usually in groups of three or four. None were static. Each patrol, it seemed, was under orders to cover every square inch of the parkland. There were important people to protect. Bren had to find a way to get through to the most important of them all. The answer, he hoped, would be at the Turkish gazebo.

The pergola was away to his right. Bren could not fathom any regular pattern followed by the night prowlers, so he chose his moment at random. Keeping low, he scurried towards the trellis tunnel glancing neither left nor right. Once there, he felt safer. Enmeshed by creeping plants waiting for the spring, it was a dark, comforting haven.

He waited for a moment – watching, listening – before making his way through the tunnel in short, sharp bursts. From the other end, he looked out over a terrace, set out regularly with gravel paths, clipped shrubbery, pavilions covered with wistaria and tecoma, lookout platforms and, as its centrepiece, an elegant marble fountain.

He chose to carry on in the same direction and followed one of the paths. After walking for thirty yards, he came to a bend made blind by a thicket of laurel. Experience told him to stop. He squatted on his haunches, trying not to be distracted by the raucous squawks of a flock of seagulls overhead. He waited for the silence that would tell him all was well. It never came. Instead, as the gulls banked away, he heard voices and footsteps in the gravel, approaching fast from around the corner.

A patrol!

Bren scanned the ground around him. There was only one refuge . . . a small gap between two laurel bushes. He dived into it, bouncing on his chest and sliding on the wet grass.

He saw the landmine even as he sped towards it. A small dome poking up through the ground, a dull, almost hesitant light reflecting from its metallic surface. Bren knew what it was immediately – he had stepped to one side of so many. He was gripped by panic and dug his toes into the soil so they acted as a brake. He came to rest with his nose directly above the dome. Three more inches and he would have been blown apart.

He wanted to cry out to purge his fear, but the patrol was on him, crunching the gravel beneath heavy winter knee-boots. How many? Four, at least. Perhaps five.

Bren wondered if the soles of his shoes were sticking out of the laurel. The mine had forced him to stop prematurely. Perhaps he had left skid marks in the grass. Perhaps he was not concealed at all.

All he could do was pray and wait, though even that was excruciating. He could not rest his head on the ground because of the mine. Nor could he use his hands or arms to support the dead weight of his body. He arched his back away from the mine and his breast-bone became the fulcrum for his bulk. The pressure on it was immense, and Bren knew he could not stay in such a position for long.

He could hear the patrolmen talking. But though the volume of their conversation had grown louder as they approached, it was not fading as they marched away. They had stopped – directly beside his hiding place. Had they seen his ankles? Were they pointing their rifles at him, ready to slice his back with bullets?

Bren felt a heavy sweat breaking out on his forehead. Beads merged to form rivulets running down to the tip of his nose. Droplets fell one by one on to the mine, carving narrow channels as they wound down its dusty dome.

A roar of laughter rose up from the patrol, signalling the end of a joke. The pungent stench of cheap, illicit cigarettes drifted through the laurel leaves into Bren's nostrils.

They were so close.

Bren took shallow, panting breaths for fear of making the slightest noise. He did not move, though his weight was bearing down on his chest like lead and it felt ready to crack open.

Come on, damn you!

More laughter, then a man spoke out in more serious tone. From what Russian Bren had learned, he guessed it was the patrol leader, reminding the others there were deadlines to meet, reports to make.

A discarded cigarette butt, still burning, landed a few inches from his head. There was a brief cacophony as they adjusted their greatcoats and hitched up their rifles – and then they were gone.

Bren waited as long as he could, concentrating on the metal canister of death beneath his nose. But his chest was hurting too much and he had to move. He stretched his arms and pushed his palms into the ground as far away

187

as possible from the edge of the mine, firmly but gently, praying that the small exposed dome did not have any companions hidden beneath the surface.

Keeping his feet where they were, he lifted himself slowly as if he was demonstrating a press-up, then swung back on his ankles and used them as a pivot. He felt safe only when he was on his feet and stepping back on to the gravel path.

He looked to left and right. A shadow loomed from nowhere and a powerful hand was clasped across his mouth to prevent him crying out. A knee crashed into his spine and he was jerked off balance so that he toppled to the ground on his back. The shadow leaped astride him and pinned him to the path.

'Better be more careful who you call asshole,' Pruett hissed. 'Could be your last insult.'

Bren felt an itching on his upper lip.

'Now who's the one with the bloodied nose?' Pruett said. 'Better not get my hands too dirty.' He released his grip on Bren's mouth. Bren heaved in large gulps of air. Pruett, his face blackened, took pleasure from the Colonel's panting.

'Creatures of the night,' he said. 'The hunter, pouncing proudly on his quarry, ready for the feast. The hunted, breathless and helpless below, waiting for the end.'

'What the . . .'

'Fuck am I doing?' Pruett interrupted. 'Making you aware, Colonel. Just letting you know.'

'Know what?'

'That I'm equal to any of your little schemes, that's all.' Pruett climbed off and helped Bren to his feet.

'I've been watching,' he said. 'Nearly got snared by the NKVD, didn't you? Now you're late for your appointment.'

Bren brushed Pruett's hand from his elbow.

'There'll be another patrol any minute,' he said. 'So I'll tell you what you want to know in a few brief words. I'm not here to spy on or assess the presidential guard, OK? It was just a remark.'

Pruett grinned from ear to ear and said: 'Off you go, then, soldier.'

'Are you going to follow?' Bren asked.

'Hmm . . . maybe.'

'Curiosity killed the cat.'

Pruett licked the side of his hand, drew it across his face and said: 'Miaow.'

The silver cupola of the Turkish gazebo shone in the vivid moonlight of what had become a clear Crimean night. The door was not locked. Bren walked in cautiously. A slight figure in a hooded cape rose from a bench and was silhouetted against the panoramic window overlooking the bay.

'Excuse me,' Bren said. 'I am ten minutes late. I am grateful and relieved that you are still here.'

The silhouette took a step forward. Small, slender fingers pushed back the hood to reveal the fresh face of a girl on the verge of womanhood.

Bren was taken aback. He froze where he stood and stared.

'Is something wrong?' The girl spoke in English with a heavy Soviet accent.

It was several moments before Bren could respond.

'Forgive me. It's just that I was expecting someone . . .'

'Older?'

'More senior.'

'Ah, a gentleman soldier.'

She smiled – and Bren was enchanted. Even in this

half-light, he could tell that the girl possessed a rare quality. It was not just the purity of her young beauty, though that was obvious enough. It was the sparkle in her eyes that captivated him. There it was again, as if the moonlight was dancing on her irises. A sparkle that reflected a strange combination of vitality, fear – and determination.

Bren returned her smile and asked her name.

'Morozova,' she replied. 'Lydia Morozova.'

14

Dawn was breaking as Quester skirted Liège on a deserted autoroute. Even at the lower altitude the mist had not lifted and his speed was restricted to 40mph. It was cool, yet Quester was covered in sweat. He was racked by the knowledge of what he had already learned, terrified of what he might learn in the future.

Time after time, he turned it all over in his head, hoping against hope for a full explanation. Why, for example, did the pain in his thigh keep returning, as it was now? In Kashmir, it had been a nuisance, but bearable. As he drove along the autoroute, it crept up on him mercilessly until he could barely press down on the accelerator.

Another pair of headlights loomed through the mist behind him. Quester glanced in his mirror. The car had come up on him so quickly, but showed no sign of passing. Closer and closer it came, until Quester felt a jolt as it gave a glancing knock to his rear bumper.

Quester swore. The headlights retreated into the gloom. But seconds later, they were back, drawing closer, until there was a second collision, harder than the first. Quester felt the BMW lurch to one side as it was pushed, but kept control with a flick of the steering wheel.

'Stupid prick!' he shouted aloud.

He wanted to pull over, to let the idiot through before he did any more damage. But the other car was too close. To slow would be to invite another collision. He gathered speed to move away. He watched the needle climb to

50mph and held steady, worried that his visibility was too restricted even for such a modest speed.

The headlights came again and the pursuing car thudded hard into the BMW's boot.

It was deliberate. It had to be. What in God's name . . .

Quester accelerated to 55mph, trying to fathom the identity of the invisible assailant. In his mind, he wondered who could be driving the other car. Had the Rocherath farmer set the police on him? The mist was too thick for him to identify any police markings in his mirror, but surely ramming was not their style. It only happened in the movies. Perhaps it was the farmer himself. Had he felt betrayed after offering help? Even if he had, he was not the type to stomach such dangerous tactics. If only it was clear . . . if only he could see.

The headlights burst through the grey cloud. This time, the impact was brutal and Quester finally realized what was happening.

The assassin had returned. This time his weapon was a ton of metal on wheels.

Quester floored the accelerator, letting out a gasp of pain as his thigh protested. The BMW was fast. It showed 140mph on the clock. Quester shot up to 100 and pressed his face close to the screen in a desperate attempt to peer his way ahead.

It was madness, suicide. But it had to be done. A slab of black came at him at full tilt. The back of a truck, its tail-lights lost in the gloom. He pulled at the wheel and swerved. The BMW's wing mirror was ripped off by the truck's fender. The crinkled steel of a guard rail appeared from nowhere. Quester was at an angle to it, hurtling towards a crash. He pulled the steering wheel the other way. The tyres of the BMW screamed and the car spun

192

like a top. The truck sped by on the inside, missing the back of the BMW by inches.

Quester dipped the clutch to keep the engine running. He was stationary in the fast lane, pointing the wrong way. He banged the BMW in first gear and twirled at the wheel until the front of the car swung round.

Where are you, you bastard?

He was behind again, matching Quester's increasing pace. Quester stayed in the fast lane and shot up to 120mph, but it made no difference. Still the headlights were there. Still he could feel the jolts in his back as metal met metal.

They shot under a sign indicating a turn-off to the centre of Liège. As they came to the junction, the headlights veered away, heading for the slip road. On the far side of the junction, they were back again.

'Games,' Quester muttered under his breath. 'Always games.' It was as if he could hear the assassin laughing. Laughing behind his back.

The headlights faded once more, then returned at tremendous velocity. The BMW was hit hard and Quester was forced into a skid. He tried to control it, but he was going too fast. The car careered across three lanes to the inside of the autoroute and shot up a grass bank. The stump of a tree tore a gash in its underside and launched it into the air. It landed heavily on its nose and Quester's head was catapulted against the dashboard. He was stunned, but held on to his senses. The rough ground rubbed off speed quickly. Quester saw the concrete stanchion of a bridge, felt a dull thud as the BMW slid into it and heard the manic hiss of a jet of steam.

He leaped from the car, stumbled to the top of the

bank and hid behind a hedge, waiting for the assassin to appear through the murk to check for a body.

But no-one came.

Bren took Lydia back to the safety of his room. She managed it without difficulty. She was agile and light on her feet. Bren could not take his eyes off her.

He sat her on his bed. She kept her coat on and crossed her arms tightly as if for self-protection. They spoke in furtive whispers.

'Tell me about yourself,' Bren said. 'Are you from Yalta?'

She shook her head and smiled.

'I have come here from Moscow,' she said. 'Everything has come here from Moscow. The furniture, the food, everything. There is nothing left in Yalta.'

'And what is your role in the Soviet delegation?'

She smiled again – a broad, ironic smile accentuating her high angular cheekbones.

'I am not in the delegation.'

'Excuse me?'

'I am a maid. Most have come from Moscow hotels. I come from a household.'

'Whose?'

'That of the woman who is helping you on this mission. Polina Molotov.'

Bren whistled.

'The wife of Molotov, the Foreign Affairs Commissar?' he asked with an air of disbelief.

Lydia nodded.

'My duties are many. But of course the main reason for my presence is to attend to her husband's welfare.'

Bren was taken aback. He had expected that the Soviet

contact mentioned by Churchill would be of high rank. But not that high.

'Is she here?' he asked.

'No, but I am,' Lydia said, trying to inject her voice with authority. 'I would do anything for her. She has been like a mother to me in Moscow. She took me as a peasant girl from the Ukraine, dusted me down, sent me to lessons in ballet, in French and in English. She has allowed me to make something of myself. Now, she has asked *me* to help *her*. And I will.'

'Why does Polina Molotov wish to be rid of Stalin?'

Bren knew the answer, but wanted confirmation. Lydia laughed as if he had asked a stupid question.

'Many reasons,' she said. 'But mainly because she is afraid.'

'Of what?'

'She is Jewish and she is afraid that Stalin will accuse her of plotting against him. She is afraid because Stalin is still jealous of her friendship with his wife, Nadya. She is afraid Stalin will send her into exile, or even kill her. She is afraid Stalin will kill her husband, just as he has killed many of his closest colleagues. And she is afraid for Russia.'

'She probably thinks her husband can do a better job . . .'

'Perhaps she has ambition for him and for herself. It is sure, however, that Comrade Molotov would follow the ideals of Lenin more closely than the class traitor Stalin.'

'Ah . . .' Bren tried not to sound cynical. Lydia reacted immediately. She looked at Bren with a hurt expression and said: 'You think I am naïve.'

'No . . . it's not the right word for you.'

'Then what is?'

'Vulnerable.'

195

'Pah! You don't understand the Soviet Union.'

'I'm not talking about Russia. I'm talking about you.'

'You still don't understand.'

'Then help me.'

'How can I do that?'

'Tell me why *you* are helping me.'

'I told you. For Polina Molotov.'

'But you are being put in great danger. She knows it. You know it. There must be another reason, apart from blind loyalty.'

'I am not blind!' Lydia snapped. 'I know why I am here.'

'Why . . . ?'

'To get Beria.'

'*Beria?*'

'We kill Stalin. Beria is blamed. He is despised by the others. This will be their excuse. Beria dies.'

Her voice was full of hatred – and Bren demanded an explanation. At first, she refused.

'It is personal,' she said.

She cast her eyes to the floor, but could not disguise her anguish. Bren saw her head shaking on a taut neck. She was wringing her hands, tapping her feet, exhibiting every sign of mental torture.

'Lydia, look at me.' It was the first time Bren had spoken her name. His invitation was gentle and warm. 'We are alone together here. We only have each other. There must be no secrets.'

Slowly, she responded. Once their eyes met, and she saw that genuine affection, and not mere idle curiosity, was prompting him, she could not stop herself.

She told him of the night she danced at Molotov's dacha and how Beria had come to her room.

'He forced me to do it,' she said bitterly. 'It is disgusting. I feel so much shame.'

Bren found himself holding her, wiping away her tears. She pushed her head into his shoulders for comfort.

'You must not be ashamed,' he said. 'Beria is a ruthless man. If you had not obeyed, you would not have been here now.'

'I was afraid . . .'

'With good reason.'

'No. I was afraid that he would make me hate all men.'

Bren took her shoulders and eased her back so she was sitting upright. Her ballet schooling gave her spine the curving grace and delicate poise of a piece of valuable porcelain. Bren held on to her firmly, but lightly, lest the porcelain should break.

'And do you hate all men?' he said.

They both knew it. The right time. The right place. A lonely man scarred by the womanless carnage of war. An abused girl waiting for someone who cared.

Bren could not help kissing her. She did not resist.

She was inexperienced, but compensated with a fierce passion. She wanted, needed, love. Bren gave it to her. He lost his breath every time he stroked the lushness of her young flesh. He touched her in places where she had never been touched before, made her sigh with lingering curls of his tongue. She asked him what she should do in return.

'Just let me love you,' he said. 'It is a privilege.'

'I am a maid, that's all.'

'You are the most beautiful creation on the face of the Earth. I thank God I've met you.'

He entered her little by little so she would not be hurt and would not remember Beria. He had been without a

197

woman for so long and had to fight a bestial urge to climax immediately. But he wanted her to see there was another way. The man giving to the woman. This, more than any other, was the night she would remember.

Before she dressed, Bren combed her long, chestnut hair. It reached down almost to her buttocks. Bren drew it aside to marvel at the splendour of her back, small and compact like her breasts.

'What time must you return?' he asked.

A note of regret entered her voice.

'I must leave soon, before dawn. I will hide for an hour and then walk openly in the daylight to the Yusupov villa.'

'Don't you have to serve breakfast?'

'We have been split into two shifts. From five in the morning to three in the afternoon. And then from three until one in the morning. I am on the second shift.'

'We have to talk about Stalin.'

'I know . . .'

'He will rarely leave the Yusupov villa, except for the plenary sessions of the conference. I will have to kill him there.'

'I will help you to get inside.'

'No need. I have been invited to a banquet there three nights from now.'

'I will be waiting at the tables.'

'Good. You must find out where Stalin is sleeping and draw a guide.'

'Anything else? It seems so little.'

'I will give you a case.'

'A case?'

'A small travelling suitcase.'

'What will be inside?'

'Nothing that can harm you. You must take it into the Yusupov villa and return it to me after the banquet. And I'll need an NKVD uniform. Can you get one?'

'From the laundry, yes.'

'The higher the rank, the better.'

'You will be a general.'

They agreed to meet once more before the banquet to exchange the guide and the case.

'Once more,' she said.

'That's right.'

She fell back on the bed, stretching, relishing her nakedness.

'Not that,' she said. 'Love me once more, Bren.'

15

In the bay, a great shoal of fish was under dual attack from porpoises beneath the waves and a swirling flock of gulls above them. Bren, drawing deeply on a foul Russian cheroot, watched the slaughter for more than an hour from the window of his room. It was a terrible sight, the more so because the shoal's only answer was to pack itself tighter as the unfortunates on the outside of the circle were picked off one by one. Porpoises snapping. Gulls dive-bombing. And all the time, the silver cloud of fish, so awesomely proud just a short time ago, was being dissipated until there was virtually nothing left.

For an instant, it reminded Bren of the 2nd Division's fate on the Ardennes plateau. Blood and slime and death. There was no end to it. Now it was time to slaughter another man. One more life snuffed out. What difference would it make?

He turned his attention to the largest of the two suitcases he had brought with him to Yalta. He emptied it of clothes and used a small penknife to carefully unpick the seam joining lining to leather. The case had a false bottom, and Bren pulled out the ten slats of wood it contained.

His object was to build a replica of a Soviet TMD-B anti-tank mine, recently introduced by the Red Army and the only common mine using wood as its body material. Once exploded, its nation of origin could be simply identified by the scorched splinters and pine ash left behind.

Bren was following his instructions to the letter. Stalin would be killed by a Russian device. And as Beria was combining his duties as head of the NKVD with his wartime role as procurer of armaments, it was not difficult to add two and two.

The TMD-B could be adapted as a time-bomb and was ridiculously simple to construct, having been specifically designed as a crude mine that could be assembled in the field as well as industrially.

Before leaving for the Crimea, Bren had cut the slats to the exact dimensions required. He arranged six of them in box shape until they made a cube measuring 12½ inches long, 11 inches wide and 5½ inches deep, which he secured together with Russian screws. Using a pocket saw, he cut a large square hole in the top of the box, covering it with three smaller slats placed side by side and grooved at one end. These acted as the pressure plate of the TMD-B in its mine form.

Bren screwed a hinge on to the centre slat so it could be lifted up and down like a lid, giving access to the hollow box. The other two slats were screwed down tight. The final piece of wood, amounting to little more than a stick, slipped into the grooved end of the slats and acted as a fastener. Once lined with a Russian newspaper Bren had stolen from the palace lobby, it was ready to accept its charge.

Bren tipped his personal belongings from the second suitcase, a small, compact affair. Nothing was as it seemed. Everything – books, metal soap holder, shaving stick, toothpaste tube, hip flask and so on – had been either hollowed out or emptied of its usual contents. Each item contained as much TNT powder as Bren could pack in. In all, he tipped just under 8lb into the TMD-B box, more than enough to kill a man. The Red Army blew tanks off their tracks with a 15lb payload.

All that was needed to complete the bomb was a booster charge of an eight-ounce block of TNT, a timing mechanism, a pull fuse and a detonator. Bren had them all in his pocket. He planned to keep them there until the last moment.

After midnight, he put the bomb inside his small suitcase and handed it over to Lydia at the gazebo.

'Take it and hide it,' he said.

In return, she gave him a roughly scribbled plan of the Yusupov palace detailing halls, lobbies, corridors, libraries, staircases and rooms on three levels.

Two rooms were marked in red ink. One was sandwiched roughly midway between the main banqueting hall and the kitchen – and was where the two conspirators agreed to meet after the banquet.

The other was on the second floor. Lydia had written across it in capitals: STALIN'S BEDROOM.

Kelly was told to go home. Exhausted by lack of sleep, torn apart with worry about Quester, tormented by her confrontation with the assassin, she was clearly unable to perform her duties.

'Go now,' the ward sister told her, forcing a pair of sleeping tablets into her taut fist. 'Get some rest. You should be in time for the last Tube.'

The train was about to pull out from Westminster station as Kelly ran on to the platform, but the guard opened the doors to allow her on. She felt uneasy. It was past midnight and there was no-one else in the carriage. She talked to herself in an attempt to fend off the insecurity of isolation.

'At least the train will take you home, Kelly,' she

repeated under her breath. 'Once there you can lock, bolt and barricade.'

At Cannon Street, she got to her feet, intending to hop out and find another, more populated, carriage further up the train. But before she moved another inch, a door hissed open and the trousered leg of a new passenger appeared. She sat down again with a sigh born out of both irony and relief. She glanced across the carriage to get an early glimpse of her companion. The assassin smiled and lifted a hand of recognition.

Kelly screamed, but the doors rattled shut behind him and no-one heard. The train moved off into the next tunnel. The assassin approached with a glint of triumph in his eye. Kelly could not move. She could have been welded to her seat. The assassin sat beside her and took her hand. He felt the same sensation as that which had startled him in the shopping precinct.

'Don't touch me!' Kelly snapped, pulling her hand away.

He was not concerned. He had the air of a man at peace with the world.

'I followed you from the hospital,' he said. 'Didn't you see me?'

Kelly could not bring herself to look at him. She stared straight ahead, focusing on a gaudy advertisement for secretarial temps without absorbing its message.

'I never look behind,' she said.

'Oh, but you should, my dear,' the assassin chuckled. 'You never know who may be lurking there.'

'You didn't get on the train at Westminster. I was the last.'

'I did not follow you all the way. There was no need. I know your route home – and your means of travel. District Line to Mile End. A short walk from there to your flat in a converted Victorian school. So much more surprise if I join you halfway.'

'What do you want?'

'To let you know I am with you. I will always be with you . . . until the end.'

'I thought you were going to the Ardennes.'

'I have been – and I have returned.'

Kelly looked at him for the first time. There was something she had to know.

'Tom . . .' she said. 'Did you find Tom?'

'The Colonel? Oh yes, he went back to the scene of the battle at Rocherath. Amazing . . .'

'Battle? What battle?'

'They called it the Battle of the Bulge.'

'That was years ago, during the Second World War.'

'Yes . . .'

'You're mad.'

'No!' he said sternly. 'It is you who cannot see.'

The train slowed for Monument station. The assassin grabbed Kelly's wrist and held it tightly. She tried to pull free, but he was too powerful.

'No sound!' he warned, his tone suddenly menacing. 'Or I will finish you off now.'

The train came to a halt. Kelly prayed for someone – anyone – to appear. She heard the wheezing of compressed air as passengers pushed the buttons of doors closer to the front.

But no-one chose her carriage. The train droned away and she was left alone with the assassin again. He smiled smugly – and she let out a whimper of anguish. She knew he was in control and she was helpless.

'What did you do to Tom?' she said, her voice laden with resignation.

'The same as I am doing to you. I let him know I was with him.'

'Did you hurt him?'

'Not physically.'

'But you want to kill him, don't you?'

'Eventually, yes. It is inevitable.'

'And me?'

'You will die, too, when the time is right.'

'*Why?*'

The assassin did not answer. He gave Kelly a contemptuous look, as if she was a form of inferior being who could never understand. It made her irrational.

She jumped up, held out her arms and shrieked: 'Why wait until the time is right? What is wrong with now? Kill me, why don't you?'

There was a jolt as the train's brakes were applied. Kelly was thrown off balance and had to grab a handrail to prevent herself falling. The train pulled into Tower Hill station. The assassin rose to his feet, ready to get off.

As he brushed past Kelly, still lurching on her heels, he smiled and said: 'My dear, one thing I have learned is that I have time. All the time in the world.'

Bren considered the banquet little more than a pantomime. Laughter and bonhomie over twelve sumptuous courses, throwing a smokescreen over the dismay and suspicion that four days of talking had unearthed. Already the Yalta conference was awash with rumours of bitter disagreement over the future of Poland. Stalin, it was said, was adamant that Poland should be 'strong' after the war, so it would not be a 'weak' corridor through which Russian enemies could pass to attack the Soviet Union.

Bren looked across his table to a pair of British bigwigs from the Foreign Office. They had mixed too much wine with too much vodka – and their loud conversation revolved around how the Reds, as they called the Russians, had responded eagerly to every chance remark overheard in the Alupka Palace.

'Sir Robert was admiring a large glass tank with plants growing in it. He mumbled that it was all very well having plants, but really they were tedious and what the tank needed was fish. Within the blink of an eyelid, the tank was alive with scores of goldfish.'

'And what about the lemon tree?'

'Do you know the full story?'

'Donald complained casually to a waiter about the lack of lemon peel in the gin-and-tonics. Next day there was a complete bloody lemon tree growing in the middle of the conservatory, dripping with lemons. Apparently the Reds flew it in overnight from somewhere down south.'

Their tone was patronizing and they took no account of the English-speaking ability of the Russians seated at their shoulders. Bren despised their chauvinistic arrogance.

'Gentlemen, you are being offensive,' he said firmly. 'I believe the incidents of which you speak were simply demonstrations of Soviet hospitality.'

They told him to mind his own business and called him a Yank. But they quietened down and the Russians discreetly nodded their gratitude. Bren responded with a smile, hoping it did not betray the irony he felt inside.

He turned his attention back to Lydia, scuttling between the tables as she had been all evening. She looked flushed and her eyelids were heavy with fatigue. Bren felt an urge to take her in his arms and rock her to sleep.

She came towards him, a bowl of sugar-coated almonds in one hand, a box of cigars in the other. A waiter followed with bottles of French Cognac.

'Sir . . .'

Bren, full of suckling pig, turned down the almonds but accepted a cigar.

'Thank you, miss.'

She turned to his neighbour without delay. Bren admired her nerve on such a tumultuous night. Polina Molotov had been wise indeed to trust her.

It was time for the after-dinner speeches and the general hubbub gave way to a monastic silence. Churchill rose to his feet. Bren was at the back of the hall with other lesser lights and could not hear clearly. But the snatches that drifted across the tabletops made him retch.

'. . . It is no exaggeration or compliment of a florid kind when I say that we regard Marshal Stalin's life as most precious to the hopes and hearts of all of us . . .'

'. . . I earnestly hope that the Marshal may be spared to the people of the Soviet Union and to help us all to move forward to a less unhappy time . . .'

'. . . I walk through this world with greater courage and hope when I find myself in a relation of friendship and intimacy with this great man . . .'

Stalin was less gushing, more circumspect in his reply.

'. . . Possibly our alliance is so firm because we do not deceive each other; or is it because it is not so easy to deceive each other?'

Bren felt strong before Stalin's speech. Now he felt invincible. You're wrong, Uncle Joe, it *is* easy to deceive. You will find out within hours.

The banquet, like all grand events, came to a sudden and unexpected end. As the guests filed out to collect their coats, Bren excused himself and headed for the bathroom. On the way, when no-one was watching, he slipped into a corridor and on towards the room near the kitchen.

Lydia was waiting for him. She handed him the case containing the bomb and the uniform of an NKVD general. Her face was blank, as if she was in a trance.

'I cannot be long,' she said quietly. 'I must not be missed.'

Bren bent to kiss her, but she ducked under his arms and hurried to the door. As she reached it, she stopped, spun round and faced Bren with an expression of terror that took him aback. He could not believe the change in her. So cool and composed as she served the dinner. Now, away from prying eyes, alone with him, she had thrown away her mask.

She ran headlong into his arms and held him as if she was clinging to a rope above some awful precipice. Bren felt the trembling that had erupted throughout her body.

'I am not afraid for myself,' she said. 'It is you who must be careful. Please. You must be careful. I must see you again.'

Bren pressed his lips against her temple and squeezed her. In his mind, he vowed that if all went to plan, if he was allowed to hold Lydia in his arms again, he would never let her go.

Stalin made straight for the war room. It had been set up on the second floor, a short distance from his bedroom. Antonov, the Deputy Commissar for Defence, was already there. Molotov joined them soon afterwards.

'Back to the real world!' Stalin exclaimed, slapping his thigh. 'Away from all the gas-bagging. I thought Winnie would never sit down . . .'

Antonov's chuckle was cut short by Stalin's strident demand.

'Our positions. Show me.'

A vast map of Central Europe had been laid on several

tables pushed together. Wooden markers showed the positions of rival armies, facing each other on a straggly line west of Berlin. Stalin, hands on hips, studied it intently.

'The Germans are vanquished,' Antonov said proudly.

'Never underestimate a cornered animal,' Stalin said without looking up. 'It has teeth. It can bite. It can still draw Russian blood.'

Antonov decided to concentrate on facts. They were safer.

'Konev has pushed the 1st Ukraine up to the Oder along a wide front in Silesia, and has isolated Breslau. Cherniakovsky has encircled Konigsberg, on the Baltic, with the 3rd Belorussian.'

'Cherniakovsky. Fine officer,' Stalin murmured. 'I have never ceased to be amazed by his military genius.'

'He has taken many prisoners. They had orders to defend Konigsberg to the last. But they were too tired. They have spoken about panic among civilians. Schools, theatres and railway stations packed with wounded . . .'

'And Rokossovsky?' Stalin interrupted.

'Moving on Pomerania with the 2nd Belorussian, just south of Cherniakovsky's army.'

'And Marshal Zhukov? What of him?'

'He is about to march the 1st Belorussian over the Oder near Kustrin, only fifty miles from Berlin. He has signed a directive to his commanders and staff warning them to be ready tomorrow . . .' Antonov checked the line of clocks on the wall, each representing a different time zone, and corrected himself. 'To be ready later today to resume the offensive towards Berlin.'

Stalin suddenly slammed his fist into the map, so hard that the wooden armies jumped in the air.

'What is the fool doing, eh? Is he co-operating with

other marshals, or is he competing with them? I'll tell you. He is trying to race Konev to Berlin, to cover himself with self-seeking glory, the arrogant shit.' He pointed at a black wooden cube placed on the map above Zhukov's forces. 'And who are they, gentlemen? I'll guarantee they are not spectators.'

'The Nazi battalions pushed back from the Vistula river,' Antonov volunteered.

'I know!' Stalin snapped. 'I also know they are occupying all the territory around Kolberg. Look how Zhukov's flanks are exposed.'

'Rokossovsky will deal with them.'

'But he is 100 miles behind Zhukov. Do you think the Germans will sit around on their arses waiting for his tanks to appear over the horizon? No! They will turn south to attack Zhukov's flanks. Logic demands it.'

Stalin ordered Molotov to ring Marshal Zhukov on the telephone. Molotov tried, but the line was impossibly bad.

'Get the engineers to fix it,' Stalin said.

'The fault could be anywhere in Poland or the Soviet Union,' Molotov pointed out.

'I don't care *where* it is,' Stalin retorted. 'I want it fixed!'

Molotov tried his best, pleading with engineers in Yalta, Moscow and beyond, but there was no easy solution. As he waited, Stalin stomped from one end of the room to the other until he finally lost his patience and announced that there was nothing better for him to do than to withdraw to his bed.

Before he left, he told Molotov: 'You will stay in this room until the fault is fixed, do you understand? And you know what to do when it is.'

Molotov, desperately weary after a day of negotiation and a night of diplomacy, nodded with resignation.

'Of course, Supreme Commander,' he said quietly. 'Sleep well.'

Bren climbed into the NKVD uniform, sliding a pistol into a jacket pocket, and pushed his own clothes into the case with the bomb. He slipped out of the rendezvous room and stooped low into the shadows. The ground floor was still a hive of activity as the service staff cleared the banqueting hall. He considered being brazen about his presence. Blending in with the NKVD night shift. But he rejected the notion on the grounds that his face could be identified and decided to use his Russian clothes for emergencies only.

He had memorized Lydia's plan. The hallway in which he was crouching led to a small lobby, from which other corridors broke off in all directions. He waited for a maid to cross into the kitchen, then hustled into the lobby, disappearing around the corner and pinning his back to the wall. Behind him, a furious argument erupted between a chef and a waiter about who was entitled to the banquet's left-overs. It spilled over from the kitchen to the hallway. From the volume of their yelling, Bren estimated they were confronting each other at the very spot where he had crouched a moment earlier.

He chose a corridor leading to the rear of the villa, but was horrified to discover that it was entirely barren. No pictures on the wall, no floor vases, no tables . . . no hiding places. The Yusupov villa had been looted by the Nazis before retreat. And unlike the palaces in which the British and American delegations were staying, it seemed the Russians had not troubled to re-stock their own.

Bren trusted to luck, easing his way along the corridor

211

with a feeling of dread brought on by his helpless exposure. As he crept on, the lights went out. Someone had thrown a switch.

'Thank you, God,' he murmured under his breath.

But there was no divine help on offer at the end of the corridor. The window Bren had been hoping to find was not there. It had been blown out and bricked up. Only a lintel remained.

Bren retraced his steps to the lobby. The chef and the waiter were still arguing. It was becoming serious. One was threatening to knife the other. Bren prayed there would be no bloodshed. The last thing he wanted was an incident that would alert the entire villa.

He chose an alternative corridor – a long, twisting affair that seemed to go on forever. As he turned a corner, he heard voices behind him. Two men following in his footsteps, one shrieking excitedly, the other trying to calm him.

'Come help me swallow a bottle of vodka,' the chef was saying. 'Before I break it over the head of that bastard waiter.'

'He is a Crimean peasant,' the second man said. 'He does not understand the ways of Moscow.'

'He threatened to cut me from ear to ear.'

'You must report him tomorrow.'

Bren saw a glow as their candles approached. He looked around in desperation. A battered oak door was set in the wall to his right. What was beyond? A room full of people, ready to raise the alarm? He had to take a chance.

He turned the doorknob silently and slipped inside. There were five beds tightly packed inside the room, three containing sleeping men. Bren felt a flush of despair. Two empty beds – and two men on their way to fill them. He had chosen their room as his haven . . .

What to do? What to do? There was no choice.

He rested his case on the floor and hid behind the door. As the men entered the room, he took a knife from his waist belt. He had the blade across their throats before they took another step. They slumped to the floor heavily, making atrocious gargling noises as their life blood spurted from them. One of the sleepers stirred.

'Sergei? Yasha? Is that you?'

Bren dealt with him first, then the others, his arm striking out from an angle so that no blood squirted on his uniform.

He watched their final, fevered twitches and felt sick. Two dead on the floor. Three dead between their sheets. They had been on his side in this war – and he had killed them. Five good men. Six, for the threatening waiter was sure to be blamed and executed.

Bren hurried out into the corridor. It was useless even to try to purge his guilt and, though it shocked him, he found himself quietly reassured that the bodies would not be found until morning, long after he was gone and long after the greater goal had been achieved. Besides, time was pressing. He checked his watch and had to control a sudden surge of panic. His Lambert-inspired memory bank told him that Stalin always concentrated on the war effort until the early hours, no matter what. But the time at which he finally caved in to fatigue varied enormously. Sometimes it was 2 A.M., sometimes 4.30 A.M. It was now 1.42 – and the truth was that Bren did not know how much longer he had to plant the bomb.

A degree of relief waited for him at the end of the corridor. A sash window, letting in a narrow band of pale light from the NKVD field lamp outside. It was nailed

213

down, but the nails were on the inner frame in order to keep intruders out rather than vice versa. Bren freed the base of the frame with his knife and slowly, without a sound, raised the window with the palms of his hands. He had half-expected to see what confronted him, and congratulated himself on his foresight.

The window had been set in what amounted to a false wall. Between it and another window on the outer wall of the villa was the narrowest of staircases, often built in to palaces of the era as part of a network of secret passages, enabling the master of the house to make nocturnal visits to the servants' quarters for illicit carnal pleasure.

Bren squinted through the outer window. In the distance, he saw a patrol of three men, one being heaved along by a thick-coated shepherd dog, its nose pinned to the ground and steam cascading from its open mouth. He waited until they had passed out of sight before easing himself on to the staircase, dragging his bag behind him.

The steps had been crudely fashioned and squeaked under the slightest pressure, an irony considering the purpose for which they were installed. Bren felt his skin becoming moister with each sound that came from under his feet. Surely someone, somewhere, would hear him.

Another patrol forced him to pause before he crossed the window on the first floor. He pressed himself against the Gaspra limestone from which the wall was hewn. It was cold and raw, but he did not notice. By the time he reached the second floor, he was dripping with perspiration.

He looked down through the outer window. The coast was clear – and he set to work on the inner frame. Like that on the ground floor, it was nailed to the sill. And from the outside, it was a far tougher nut to crack. Bren used his knife as a jemmy, sliding it under the frame at key places and rocking it up and down. At first, he applied a gentle touch in the name of discretion. But as the minutes ticked by and his frustration grew, he exerted more force.

Every ten seconds, he glanced over his shoulder for patrols. His luck was holding, but for how long? He was there for the world to see, a manic figure now pushing on the knife with all the power he could muster. As he made what he swore would be his ultimate effort, the blade snapped clean in two and the severed tip clattered down the staircase with an echoing rattle loud enough to wake sleeping gods.

Bren gasped inwardly. He ducked down and waited in perfect silence for any reaction. He gave himself five minutes. Long, barren minutes in which his heart pumped and his legs trembled. As he was about to return to his task, he heard the clumping of jackboots on the bare wooden floorboards of the corridor on the far side of the glass. They stopped short of the window itself. The cylindrical beam of a torch passed over his head. More footsteps, fading into the night. He was still free, still alive.

He jumped up and tried to slide his fingers under the window frame, where his jemmying had created the tiniest of gaps. He broke three fingernails in the process, but there was a hint of movement. He rocked the frame up and down, whispering encouragement to it. He could feel the nails giving and finally, mercifully, they popped out in a rush as if they had been loose all along.

Bren climbed into the corridor. It was 2.05 A.M. So much time had been wasted, so little was left. Perhaps Stalin was already lying in his bed, sleeping like a baby. Or, worse, awake and ploughing through a pile of documents.

215

Bren threw caution to the wind. The layout of each floor was similar and he hustled quickly to the lobby at the end of the corridor. From there, another passageway, the main artery of the villa, ran the length of the building. Secondary corridors branched off it at right angles. One of them, half way along, led to Stalin's bedroom.

He peered around the corner of the lobby. What he saw took his breath away. Guards! Scores of them, positioned at twenty-foot intervals along either side of the passage, for as far as the eye could see.

Bren retreated into his thoughts and put himself on the rack. Now there was no alternative but to show his face, to bluff it out. Now was a time for supreme courage. He curled his fingers around the pistol in his pocket and made a silent vow to shoot himself if he was cornered.

So what would they find? A rogue American in a Russian uniform carrying a Soviet bomb. There was no way he could be connected with Roosevelt or Churchill. Suspicion would still fall on Beria.

Unless he was captured alive and tortured . . .

Bren pushed the barrel of the pistol against the roof of his mouth in a rehearsal of what he would do if the worst happened. He had to make sure he would die.

He dropped the pistol back into the pocket, but kept his hand on it. Clearing his throat to announce his imminent arrival, he marched into the corridor as an NKVD general.

The effect was stunning. The guards closest to him took one glance at his insignia and stood stiffly to attention. Others followed suit along the line, even those at the end who had not seen him. Right arm across breast. Left hand gripping upright rifle. Eyes front. None dared to move. None dared to blink an eyelid, or even flick a cornea in his direction. As he walked past them, all they saw was the blurred kaleidoscope produced by his medals.

He passed a room in which a furious man was raising the ceiling. The voice was unmistakable. Gruff and uncompromising. The voice of Joseph Vissarionovich Stalin.

'I don't care where it is. I want it fixed!'

So he is still awake. There is still hope.

Bren reached the corridor leading to Stalin's bedroom. There was a guard on either side of the great man's door. Bren kept to the main passage and did not stop, lest he gave them the opportunity to study him.

'You men, follow me!' he called out in Russian. 'The Supreme Commander is sleeping in another room tonight.'

It was not unreasonable. Bren knew from the picture in his head that Stalin bedded down in any one of ten rooms in the Kremlin. Sometimes, he simply tugged off his boots and slept on the sofa or chaise longue on which he happened to be sitting.

The pair of guards did as commanded and followed Bren's heels. He led them on a wild goose chase until he found a room with a half-open door situated on another branch of the main passage.

'Here!' he barked, slamming the door shut and ushering the guards behind him as he turned. He did not look back. They did not see his face. They took up their positions and watched him stride away.

Bren marched between the khaki banks with increasing confidence. They were frozen with fear, a prerequisite, it seemed, of being a member of the Supreme Commander's guard. Bren walked back to Stalin's bedroom and entered it without delay. He closed the door behind him and set to work.

He placed the pistol on the floor within easy reach. Only Stalin could interrupt him now. If he did, Bren calculated, he could shoot the great man in the head before killing himself. He took the bomb from the suitcase, flicked out the fastening strip and lifted the hinged lid.

From his pocket, he pulled out the paraphernalia needed to prime the explosive. He placed the booster charge on the TNT powder and pushed the detonator into it. Then he made two connections to a Russian MUV pull fuse and a clockwork mechanism with rubber-coated cogs to ensure silent operation. All that was required was the setting on the timer. Bren looked at his watch. It was 2.17 A.M. He set the timer to go off in two hours, forty-three minutes.

The bomb would explode, and Stalin would die, at 5 o'clock exactly.

He pushed the bomb under the bed, directly beneath the centre of Stalin's pillow. He took his pistol, left the bedroom and returned to the door at which he had left the two bodyguards.

'The Supreme Commander has changed his mind!' he called out in a voice conveying the impatience of a harassed general. 'Return to his normal quarters. Now! At once!'

Once again, they obeyed their orders without question. Bren saw them into position before leaving. He reached the secret staircase as Stalin stormed out of the war room.

'So the destiny of victory now rests with a faulty phone line!' Stalin shouted. 'If only Hitler knew, he would laugh his fucking cock off.'

He stomped angrily to his room, pausing only to exchange words with the guards outside.

'So what are you smirking about?' he challenged the man on the left.

'Nothing, Supreme Commander. I mean, I was not aware that I was smirking.'

'You were. I saw it.'

'It will not happen again, Supreme Commander.'

'That is correct. The next smirk will be wiped off your face with a bullwhip.'

'Wherever Stalin sleeps, I will guard him.'

'Guard your arse, too.'

Stalin stripped to his underwear and climbed into bed at 2.28. For half an hour, he read a report on Marshal Yeremenko's push with the 4th Ukraine north of Czechoslovakia. He threw the document on the floor at 3.01 and was asleep within three minutes.

Below him, the cogs whirred silently onward. If everything went to plan, he had one hour fifty-six minutes to live.

At 4.30, he was woken by a gentle push on his shoulder. Molotov, his eyes listless behind his round spectacles, stood above him.

'The line is ready – I have Marshal Zkukov,' he said.

Stalin yawned grotesquely, letting out a stench of stale tobacco that made Molotov wince. The Foreign Affairs Commissar left for the war room. Stalin insisted on putting on his uniform before following. Molotov held out the telephone with relief. Stalin took hold of it with a fierce grip.

'Zhukov! What is this crazy plan of yours to march on Berlin?'

'It can be taken in seven days, Supreme Commander,' came the enthusiastic reply.

'You are playing the fool . . . racing Konev.'

'It is an orderly plan, Supreme Commander.'

'And what of your right flank? It is exposed to the enemy. They will launch an offensive from Stargard and chop off your balls.'

There was a silence on the line as Zhukov considered the merits of committing himself. Stalin breached the gap.

'Marshal Zhukov, you are the most handsome of my commanders. A sharply defined nose and lively eyes. A jutting, strong chin. But nobody is perfect. In your case, you must carry the burden of having a brain the size of a walnut.'

There was another pause before Zhukov said: 'What do you wish me to do?'

'Remain cautious. Turn the projected axis of your front from Berlin to Kolberg, on the Baltic. Wait for Rokossovsky to lend you a hand. Then cut the enemy's East Pomeranian grouping in two. Otherwise you will be swimming in a sea of Russian blood.'

'But . . .'

'But then Konev may beat you to Berlin. Yes, that is possible. Goodnight, Marshal Zhukov.'

Stalin slammed down the receiver before any further conversation. He looked at Molotov, scowled and said: 'You look tired. What time is it?'

Molotov checked the clock.

'4.42,' he said.

'And what time is our first appointment?'

'7.30, with Admiral Zaikin.'

'Well, then. Like me, you will be sleeping like a baby by 5 o'clock. Plenty of time to recover.'

Stalin slapped Molotov on the shoulder and stepped from the war room into the main passage.

There was a blinding flash from around the corner followed instantly by the roar of a massive explosion. Stalin was knocked off his feet by a shock wave and slid backwards until his head thudded into the foot of the war room's door frame.

The blow knocked him senseless. He struggled to his knees, heard screams and saw the rag-doll bodies of his bedroom guards, flung the length of the branch corridor by the blast, crumpled and purple against the wall. Another guard, a great wooden stake spearing his stomach, staggered towards him, arms outstretched and pleading for help. Stalin could not understand. He rocked sideways and crashed to the floor an instant before losing consciousness.

16

Stalin took hold of the telephone as if it was Beria's neck.

'How many guards? How many dogs? How many rifles? And yet the NKVD could not save the man they were protecting above all others!'

'Russia rejoices that you were not killed,' Beria gasped, his Kremlin office already taking on the aura of a cell in the Lubyanka.

'Answer the question!'

'I . . . I am sure . . .'

'You are sure of nothing! Chandeliers crashed. Men's guts were sent flying. Where my bed once stood there is nothing but a gaping hole in the floorboards. My brass tablelamp is now to be found in the room below.'

'It was indeed a disaster, Supreme . . .'

'A disaster for you, Beria! Your ham-fistedness has let you down for the last time. Do you know what was found in my room afterwards? Splinters. Tiny splinters of scorched wood. And a small, jagged piece of metal, which I am told was once an MUV pull fuse.'

Beria did not understand.

'Antonov has spoken with a field general. His opinion is that an attempt was made to blow me to pieces with a derivative of a Soviet TMD-B anti-tank mine. What does that tell you, shithead?'

'I do not . . .'

'That a *Russian* was responsible. Perhaps a Russian whose interests would be served if I was to die.'

Beria caught the drift – and froze.

'Surely you don't think . . .'

'And what else am I to think? Strange that the NKVD allowed this outrage to happen. Who takes the reins of the great Soviet stallion if I fall off?'

'No! No!' Beria's voice was shrill, frightened. 'I beg you, Supreme Commander. Do not allow such thoughts to enter your head.'

'You are a killer, Beria. A mass murderer. A man who has committed genocide. Why stop there?'

'No! I would not . . . I could not. My loyalty to the great Stalin is unquestioned.'

'I am questioning it.'

'Please, I beg you. It is not so.'

'Then *prove* it, Beria. Find out who was responsible. If you do not, I shall know – and you will suffer.'

Stalin took the telephone in both hands and hurled it against the wall so that it smashed to pieces. He issued orders that every soldier, every member of staff who either saw the explosion or helped to clear the debris should be returned immediately to Moscow.

'Tell them there was a leakage of gas which went undetected until it exploded,' he said. 'Take them to their barracks and to their homes – and watch their every movement.'

He arranged a private audience with Churchill and Roosevelt in the White Hall of the Livadia Palace. They had never seen him angrier. He clenched his fists so tightly that his knuckles were white. His face was dappled scarlet and reminded Churchill of a great thunderstorm at sunset.

'There are traitors at this conference!' Stalin roared. 'Those who are not with us. Those who deceive. Those who skulk in shadows in the dead of night. Those who would rape their mothers. From where do they come, gentlemen? From which filthy, scum-covered hole do they creep?'

Churchill disguised his dismay at the failure of the assassination plot. He gave an impression of being staggered by events and dabbed at his forehead with a handkerchief.

'The people of Great Britain, and . . .' He glanced at Roosevelt. '. . . those of the United States would be joyous at Stalin's escape from treachery.'

'Empty words!'

Both Churchill and Roosevelt were taken aback. Stalin the diplomat had always been careful not to offend.

'Who am I to trust?' Stalin went on. 'How do I know it was not the British or Americans who were responsible?'

'I must protest!' Roosevelt cried.

'But you must understand. The people of the Soviet Union are loyal to Stalin as they are to the memory of Lenin. They could not even countenance the thought.'

'A Nazi agent?' Churchill suggested. 'They tried at Teheran.'

Stalin paced up and down beneath the stone canopy of the vast marble fireplace which dominated one end of the hall. Churchill and Roosevelt watched him from the round conference table in the centre of the room.

Suddenly, with a screech from his boots, Stalin swung round to face them. He was visibly shaking with the purest fury they could have imagined. The veins in his face and neck, full and pumping with purple blood, stood proud of his skin. His teeth were grinding, the muscles in his cheeks were twitching. He looked like a man on the brink of a massive heart attack. The uncompromising vow he made, there and then, chilled them to the bones. For they knew he meant every word.

'I will find those responsible. And when I do, I swear I will take complete and utter revenge!'

17

Quester called at the hire car firm's office in Brussels, paid the excess and told them where they could find what was left of their BMW. He took a train to Ostend and booked into a hotel for a week's stay. He alternated his time between long walks by the sea and secret, introspective hours locked away in his room. He needed both. The walks gave him space, time and room to manoeuvre. His intense, private thoughts gave him a vital opportunity to unravel the tangled ball of string in his mind.

It was a week of contrast. At first, Quester plunged into dark hours of suspicion, paranoia and fear. He did not shave, barely washed and took on the appearance of a vagabond. He felt shame, but was powerless to reverse the decline. He was plagued by visions, both by day and by night. In the most vivid, repeated time after time, an empty bed rose up from a floor and disintegrated into a billion molecules. Quester did not know why, or how. But he was aware that something had gone badly wrong.

Now, five days on, he was fighting back. He felt an inner strength beginning to build, a strength he had not possessed before.

There *were* answers. He knew that now. And he felt close, so close, to the final solution. His mood grew less morose. He shaved, bought himself a new pair of jeans and a shirt . . . and thought of Kelly.

He pulled back a curtain and gazed down to the street below. Kelly was everywhere. Arm-in-arm with ferry crewmen marching to the quay. Laughing with a teenage boy who mockingly pushed her towards every lamp-post, yet held her back just before a collision. Sumptuously dressed for a night out with a dinner-jacketed suitor. Walking by herself, content for now with her own company.

Every girl he saw was Kelly. Shining, golden Kelly.

He dreamed of her that night. He was with her – and they were both naked.

They were making love on a carpet of snow, yet it was not cold. Kelly was on top of him. He was deep inside her. She dug her fists into his shoulders and moved gently up and down. He stroked the firm curves of her buttocks, feeling the warm button of her anus on his fingertips. She reached forward to allow her breasts to brush his face. He kissed them as they passed.

Suddenly the snow was moving, flowing down the side of a mountain. They were on the crest of an avalanche. Tumbling down, tumbling down. There was no roar, not even a murmur. The only sound was Kelly's voice, thick and throaty with desire fulfilled and pleasure taken.

'You and me,' she said. 'You and me.'

'I'll come back to you wherever you are,' Quester said. 'I'll find you and love you.'

Beria contacted Rostochev, his mole in the NKGB, the espionage and counter-espionage arm of the Soviet secret service. Rostochev had been entrusted with two tasks. Overtly, he controlled the cabinets containing dossiers on foreign agents, contact men and Soviet sympathizers. Covertly, he kept files on the attitudes and opinions held by other senior NKGB officers. Beria had need of both fields of expertise.

They met discreetly in a park on the outskirts of Moscow and faced each other across a public chessboard.

Beria pulled some unostentatious wooden pieces from the pocket of his greatcoat and they played. Like their neighbours, gathered in a cluster on a small patio beneath the barren branches of magnolia trees, they wore woollen gloves cut away at the fingertips and covered each other in steamy breath every time they talked.

'Why so frantic, Lavrenty Pavlovich?' Rostochev asked as soon as he saw the state of Beria. 'Which little girl's father is after you this time?'

Beria made an attempt at laughter. He did not want to arouse Rostochev's suspicions.

'I have seen off more of them than the number of warts on your face.'

'Such a cutting humour.' Rostochev, a vain man acutely conscious of the shortcomings of his complexion, thought of Beria with increasing bitterness. 'Then my initial question remains to be answered.'

'I am not frantic.'

Rostochev took Beria's attacking knight with a free bishop.

'Not frantic, perhaps,' he said. 'But certainly preoccupied.'

'A clumsy move, that was all.'

'Since when do you make clumsy moves, Lavrenty Pavlovich?'

'I seem to have made one or two lately, without knowing about them.'

'Then how can I help? I assume you have asked me here for a reason.'

'Yes. Of course.'

'Which is?'

'You must tell me of our agents in Britain and America.'

'Every detail?' Rostochev chuckled. 'It would take a

year. You know how enthusiastic Comrade Stalin has been recently about infiltration of our allies. Groundwork for the future, he called it.'

'I will be specific.'

'Well then, are we talking of scientists on the trail of Western atomic technology, or those engaged in more subtle espionage?'

'I am looking for any of your men who may be with the negotiating parties at the Yalta conference.'

'Why?'

'You know better than to ask such questions, Rostochev. Let us not forget your purpose in life, and who you serve.'

'But if I am to help, I must know –'

'Nothing!'

Beria trapped Rostochev's queen in a pincer movement with a castle, a bishop and his surviving knight. Rostochev looked up from the board, his jaws heavy with submission, just as they had been so many times in the past.

'There is a man,' he said quietly.

'And . . .' Beria hurried him along.

'We have manoeuvred him close to Roosevelt. He is now among the President's personal bodyguard.'

'Name . . .'

'Pruett. Jonathan Pruett. Born Alexei Fedrovitch Novchenko, in Omsk.'

'I must see him.'

'Now?' Rostochev asked incredulously.

'At once.'

'It will be difficult. The Yalta conference has only two days to run at most. And Pruett's cover must be protected. Are you sure it is so important?'

Beria sliced his queen diagonally across the board.

'Checkmate,' he announced dryly. 'Either I see Pruett,

228

or you will be found with a broken neck at the foot of a steep staircase.'

Beria rearranged the chess pieces and said: 'Another game? Now, about your colleagues in the NKGB . . .'

It was dangerous – even foolhardy – to meet after the explosion, but neither Bren nor Lydia could resist. They had their reasons. Bren was devastated by the failure of the bomb, yet as he lay entwined with Lydia in his bed, he was besotted by her need to love and be loved. It helped.

'Show me how to pleasure you,' she whispered as she urged Bren to pass on his experience. At first, he was reluctant. Somehow, though he knew it was what she wanted, he felt as if he was taking advantage. She sensed his reservations.

'What is wrong? Am I asking too much?'

'No, no, no.' He reassured her quickly and firmly. For him, she could do no wrong.

'You are troubled.'

'Of course, but it has nothing to do with how I feel for you.'

'It exploded before 5 o'clock.'

'Something to do with the timer. Perhaps it was running fast. But Stalin should still have been in bed, asleep. He wasn't. It was bad luck. The worst luck.'

'Polina Molotov will be sad.'

'Other people will be angry.'

'Perhaps you will have another chance. I can help. There is still time.'

'No. His guard is formidable now. Impossible. You have seen it yourself. He is too strong for me . . .'

'So Stalin is still alive. And Beria is still alive.'

'I'm sorry, Lydia.'

She kissed him on his cheeks and on his lips with a tenderness that took his breath away.

'It is not so important to me, now I have you. Now I have discovered that not all men are like him. Show me how to thank you, Bren. Show me how to make love to you. I want you to relax, to do nothing. I want to be the one who moves. You must promise to stay as still as a lily leaf on the surface of a lake. Do you promise?'

'I promise.'

He rolled onto his back and guided her down on top of him. At first, she wiggled her hips from side to side like a Tahitian dancer. Bren laughed and she looked dismayed. He put a teasing finger on the tip of her nose and she broke into a smile. Then he placed his palms around her waist and lifted her an inch before easing her down again. She needed no further tuition.

Bren thought he would die as he climaxed. She felt it and pressed herself into his groin, arching her back so her hair tumbled down her spine, her breasts stood erect and her ribs forced her pure white skin into parallel ranges of sharply defined hills and valleys.

They made love through the night, intoxicated with each other, welded to each other, tasting each other, smelling each other, clawing each other, their bodies the more sensuous the hotter and stickier they became. An hour before dawn, they both knew they would never find another passion, another love, like this.

Bren felt as if his chest was about to burst open.

'I don't want to go,' he murmured. 'I can't leave you. I want to be with you for the rest of my life.'

Her tears tumbled on to his shoulder. Warm and soft, like tropical rain.

'You must go where you are sent. I must go back to

Moscow. That is the way of things. Perhaps when the war is over . . .'

'Everything is over for me if I don't have you.'

'You and me,' she sang. 'You and me.'

If only, Bren told himself. How he wished he believed it could come true.

'I'll come back to you wherever you are,' he said. 'I'll find you and love you.'

Beria moved quickly after seeing Pruett. Within three days, he ordered the arrest of an elderly NKGB major who had been working undercover at Yalta as a groundsman. Two of the major's Moscow staff, both lieutenants, were also held, along with three known leaders of the Crimean Tatars. Beria lined the men up in his office. 'The charge,' he bellowed, 'is that you did carry out a plot to assassinate the Supreme Commander of the Soviet Union, Joseph Vissarionovich Stalin, thus committing the highest and most despicable treason imaginable. You, major, were the perpetrator of this crime, aided and abetted by your miserable lieutenants.'

Turning to the Tatars, he went on: 'You were the spiteful instigators and paymasters of the plot, nationalistic-minded traitors disloyal to the Union of Soviet Socialist Republics.'

The NKGB trio, mindful of Beria's methods, admitted guilt there and then. The Tatars succumbed under torture, signing confession statements with what strength they had left after metal clamps were removed from their testicles. The six were shot through the back of the head in the Lubyanka the following day.

An hour later, Beria faced Stalin in the Kremlin. Stalin studied the last statements of the executed men.

'Inconclusive!' he roared. 'I can almost hear their screams of protest.'

231

'Surely not,' Beria said with a self-satisfied smile. 'An attempt at revenge by the Tatars has always been on the cards.'

'This was not it!' Stalin hurled the statements into the air. They flapped noisily before splitting up and fluttering silently to the floor at Beria's feet.

'I can assure you that the correct procedure was followed from beginning to end,' Beria said. 'The major has admitted that he was the mysterious NKVD "general" seen near your bedroom on the night of the bomb.'

'It could have been anyone.'

'As his file shows, he did not hold you in the greatest esteem.'

'Many millions feel the same way.'

'The major was paid for his deed from the proceeds of Tatar robberies. He was nearing retirement. He wanted some comfort in his old age. He was living above his means even before Yalta. It was his suspicious behaviour that alerted me to his crime. A great deal of money was found hidden in his dacha.'

'Planted,' Stalin said uncompromisingly. 'You probably put it there yourself.'

The two men glared at each other. For once Beria did not relent, returning Stalin's stare with equal tenacity. A battle of nerves broke out. Not a word was spoken. Each man thought the unthinkable – and let the other know with eyes that penetrated every crevice of their opponent.

Stalin, his gaze pummeling Beria about the head and chest, was screaming: *'You know who tried to kill me. It was not you, but you know who it was. And yet you are choosing to keep this knowledge from me. How dare you! Don't you know I can snuff you out for such defiance? You are but a sparrow to an eagle.'*

Beria, his face free of the anguish that usually paralysed

it in Stalin's presence, was screaming back: '*For once I am your equal. I have something you want, but I will not give it to you. Just as you were confused by your wife, Nadya, so now you will be confused by me. Don't you see, Stalin, you bastard, you fucker, this knowledge is my passport to a longer life. Without it, who knows when you would have ordered my death? Sooner rather than later, that is for sure. Now you cannot kill me without losing all hope of discovering who tried to kill you. And that would be too much for your curiosity – and your infernal arrogance – to withstand. For once, the sparrow is flying higher than the eagle.*'

'Get out of my sight!' Stalin barked. 'And take your fake confessions with you. They are littering my study.'

Beria picked up the papers and shuffled them into some semblance of order.

'What are you waiting for?' Stalin shrieked. 'Get out! Get out!'

'Of course, Supreme Commander.' Beria dipped his head in deference to his leader, to further infuriate him. This was a moment to savour.

Bren left Yalta with one last withering look from Roosevelt – and his return to Patton's HQ was no more forgiving. He was immediately posted back to the front. Even the man who handed over his orders, a catarrh-ridden general named Rogerson, could offer no explanation.

'If you ask me, son, you made a damn fine strategist,' he said between phlegm-laden snorts. 'But the orders came on down from high. Now who the fuck did you upset at that conference thing? Must have been something you said. You didn't suggest that we carry right on from Berlin to take Moscow, now, did you?'

Rogerson waited for an answer. Bren was obliged to offer him a 'No, sir.'

'Ah, maybe you did, maybe you didn't,' Rogerson said obscurely. 'Anyway, you're going to get a chance to finish off the Nazis *and* stop the Reds from marching into Denmark and Scandinavia. You'll be fighting in the north with the US Ninth Army, alongside the British and under the wing of Montgomery.'

Bren saluted formally and said: 'If I am to be transferred again, sir, I'd prefer to return to my old unit. The 2nd Infantry Division.'

'No,' Rogerson said abruptly. 'They had a hard time in the Ardennes, but they're coasting now. It's felt you are needed more in the north. There's the Ruhr to tackle. It is very heavily defended.'

Bren did not need telling – and felt a furnace of indignation inside his ribcage.

Damn you, Roosevelt! Damn you, Churchill! You want me dead now, don't you? God, I did my best, but it wasn't good enough for you cowards. Always letting others clean up your shit. Now you're going to let the Nazis take care of me. Why don't you do it yourselves, eh? Get some blood on your fucking fingertips. You'd probably enjoy licking it off. . .

Bren survived the crossing of the Rhine and the struggle for the Ruhr, but died of shame.

He found himself more cautious than before, always hanging back from the thick of the action. His soldiers, their respect waning, found him unapproachable and wrote him off as a 'headquarters man'.

An argument broke out after a fierce battle outside Hannover. A black sergeant named Carey stormed into Bren's tent late at night.

'It's not over yet. The men want a leader. A bold leader, like they hear tell of how you led your soldiers at Rocherath.' His tone was challenging – and caught Bren off guard.

'They're trying to kill me,' Bren said in a daze. 'Don't you see that?'

'They're trying to kill all of us!' Carey shouted. 'And they'll do it unless you can push one last stick of dynamite up our asses.'

'But Lydia. I must go back for Lydia.'

'We've all got girls back home, Colonel. What makes yours so special?'

Bren was tempted to tell Carey just how special Lydia was to him, but the sergeant's threatening scowl forbade it. It was relentless. Bloodshot, woebegone eyes, accentuated by the deep colour of Carey's skin and a hood of eyebrow twisted in anger and bitterness. It was as powerful as a slap in the face – and forced Bren to face up to his responsibilities.

'You're a brave man, Carey, confronting me like this.'

'It's nothing compared to confronting the Panzers.'

'I'll lead you, sergeant. I'll be at your side tomorrow.'

Carey's scowl gave way to an unrestrained smile. Bren felt a wave of relief sweep over him and realized just how much guilt he had been suppressing.

The next morning, Bren spearheaded an assault on a line of machine-gun posts protecting the rear of the German retreat. The operation was carried out with few casualties – and Bren's spirit was lifted to new heights.

Word came through that the war would be over within days. Nazis were surrendering in droves, leaving little resistance to counter the Allied onslaught.

Bren gazed across the countryside. Abandoned, free countryside, sparkling in the sunshine after a heavy spring

235

shower. Fresh air. Fresh hope. No enemy troops or tanks for as far as the eye could see. In the distance, the silver ribbon of the Jeetze river, a tributary of the Elbe, wound through deserted meadows. To the right, the pockmarked road that led to the town of Dannenberg disappeared over a crest. To the left, columns of British soldiers sang bawdy songs as they tramped past the remnants of a German field cannon. And in the centre of the landscape a small tumbledown farmhouse announced its presence with a charcoal curl of smoke that rose from a cracked chimney pot.

'There's someone there,' Bren said.

'Maybe they'll cook us a hot lunch,' a young GI chirped.

'Maybe they're Krauts with one last machine-gun,' another pointed out.

'One way to find out,' Bren said sternly.

The farmhouse was at the foot of a wide, sloping pasture churned into mud gullies by retreating armour. Burned-out jeeps and mangled mortars littered the ground and provided adequate cover against any small-arms fire. Bren ordered his men to fan out into a semicircle. They jogged towards the farmhouse, shoulders crouched and rifles at the ready, sheltering from time to time behind jagged metal. But there was no attack, no spitting of flame, no sign of movement in the farmhouse.

Bren crept to within twenty yards of the door. Suddenly, the calm was shattered by a cry of pain. A sharp, high-pitched cry. The cry of a woman, coming from inside the farmhouse. Bren stood erect and shouted: 'Storm it!'

He led the way, breaking into a sprint before anyone else moved.

He saw the pressure plate of the mine an instant before

236

he stood on it, but could do nothing to twist his body away.

The mine exploded and he was hurled into the air. He landed heavily on his back. His right leg was torn off at the thigh and a fountain of blood flowed from the wound into a puddle of mud that lapped at what was left of his limb.

Blood and slime and death. Now it had happened to him.

He was surrounded by soldiers, looking down, mouths open, eyes aghast. A civilian in braces pushed through the crowd and knelt at his side. He was hysterical and did not appear to notice the bloody stump poking from the tatters of Bren's uniform. He was German, but spoke in broken English.

'You are the officer in charge, yes?' he demanded.

Strange, but Bren felt no pain. He was drifting away. He could feel it. Going somewhere or other. It really did not matter where. He looked at the German, saw that he was sweating and dribbling like a mad dog.

'You must take us to England!' the German said feverishly. 'All of us! My wife is having a baby. Now, right now, in the farmhouse. You must take us all to England, just as you promised. We have been helping the English soldiers. Hitler is wrong. He has always been wrong. Not far from here is Belsen. Have you seen it? Terrible, terrible. We have been helping the English soldiers. Now you must repay us, just as you promised. The war is over, but collaborators will be remembered. We will all be killed. Me, my wife, my baby.'

Bren was bemused.

'What is your name, sir?' he managed to ask breathlessly.

'Quester,' the German said. 'Klaus Quester.'

'Well then, Mr Quester,' Bren said. 'I am an American. You will have to ask someone else.'

He could not say any more. There was no strength left for words. No strength left for anything. It had ebbed away through the hole in his leg. His head flopped to one side and he stopped breathing.

A long, wailing scream pierced the walls of the farmhouse.

'My wife!' the German exclaimed. 'My baby!'

18

'Father!'

Quester screamed as he woke. He was in agony, a searing pain shooting up his right leg from knee to hip. He twisted frantically on the bed and became entangled in his topsheet. He rolled off the mattress and landed on the floor with a thud. The sheet wrapped itself around him until he was cocooned.

'Get me out!' he cried. 'Push, mother, push! Pull, father, pull!'

He hooked his thumbs around the edge of the linen and forced it down until it was tight around his ankles. Then he thrashed his feet from side to side until it finally came loose. He rose to his knees, turned and gathered the sheet with his fingers, spreading his hands so the material between them became round and stretched like a rope. Working as swiftly as he could, he wrapped it around the top of his excruciating thigh like a tourniquet and tied it tightly with a secure knot.

'Stop the blood,' he jabbered. 'Birth and death. Much the same. Blood and slime.'

There was a rattle at the door, accompanied by the frenetic voice of the hotel manager.

'Monsieur! Monsieur! Mon Dieu, qu'est-ce qu'il vous arrive?'

'Go away, I'm OK!' Quester shouted. He wanted to face this alone.

It was two hours before the pain subsided. Quester pinched his skin above and below the tourniquet, and felt nothing. He untied the sheet and stared at it blankly. Was it saturated with blood or merely soiled with dirt lifted from the floor? He could not tell. He threw it to one side and drifted into the bathroom, washing his hands maniacally to remove any trace of a stain.

Exhaustion overcame him before he could return to his bed. He fell limply on to the cold tiled floor beside the shower and slept for fourteen hours.

He came to in darkness, but it did not matter. He did not need light to see.

He rose slowly to his feet and shook his head, then prodded himself all over with his fingers as if to make sure his flesh and bone were still intact, especially his thigh. He walked out of the bathroom and across the sheets on the floor, pushing open a window and relishing the cool coastal air that swept into his nostrils.

He had no doubt he was a changed man. For the first time in his adult life, his mind was *clear*. No clouds, no disturbances. No visions. It was as if he was standing on a cliff looking out to sea on a bright summer's dawn. He could see everything without interference, without pollution.

'Born again,' he muttered to himself. 'Thank Christ . . .'

Now, at long last, he knew the truth, the amazing, incredible truth – and was eager to share it.

Kelly!

He wanted to see her at once and to tell her everything.

He checked out of the hotel and caught a night ferry to Dover and a train to London. It was mid-morning when he knocked on the door of Kelly's flat.

As soon as she saw him, she fell into his arms. He held her tight and whispered: 'Lydia, my love, I'm back.'

Kelly did not hear him.

'God, where have you been?' she uttered.

'In another time,' he replied.

'I missed you so much. I need you. Something awful has happened.'

'I was a soldier called Bren. I fought in the Battle of the Bulge before I was sent to Yalta.'

'The man you said was trying to kill you. He has been following me, too.'

'He smashed my skull in Kashmir. Carved open my brain. Released my soul. That's what did it. Everything that was stored in there came rushing out, like a river bursting through a breeched dam. My world, my *entire* world was opened up for me to see.'

'He said he would kill me, but he wouldn't tell me why.'

'My dreams, my visions. All memories. Images of experience. Retained suggestions. Some locked inside my head by Lambert and his hallucinogens. Some filed away by me as they happened.'

'He'll come back again, Tom. I know it.'

'Oh yes. He wants you, too, Lydia. We are both in grave danger.'

Kelly heard this time. She freed herself from Quester's grip and took a step backwards, saddened that she was looking at him in the same old disbelieving way. She crossed her arms over her breasts, as if matronly formality was appropriate. She asked her question breathlessly.

'Why did you call me Lydia?'

'Because that's who you are . . . were. I was Bren.'

'What are you talking about?'

'The National Gallery, remember? Your love of vast rolling landscapes. Cornfields stretching to the horizon.

241

They were your childhood in the Ukraine before you went to Moscow.'

'The Ukraine? Moscow?'

Kelly's face was twisted in bitter confusion. Quester felt hurt that she could not see, but her expression made him realize he was going too far, too soon. He sat her on a chair, poured her a vodka and took her step by step through what had happened to him since he collapsed in the field outside Rocherath.

At first, she did not want to listen. She sat poker-faced, hands on her knees, staring straight through him as if he was not there. But he persisted with his story. His struggle for survival on the Ardennes plateau. His rendezvous with Churchill and Roosevelt. His attempt to kill Stalin. His death outside the German's farmhouse. And his birth inside.

'There's a word for it,' Kelly said.

'It may be right, it may be wrong,' Quester replied.

'You are saying we have all lived before.'

'Perhaps all of us. Perhaps some of us. Perhaps it is not a question of *living* again. It could simply be some form of powerful spiritual connection between a person who is dying and an infant who is being born. I don't know . . .'

There was something about Quester that softened Kelly's hostility. His sincerity, perhaps. Or his honest doubt. She found herself split in two. One half of her felt foolish, ashamed even to consider the notion. The other half, the half she was desperately trying to make dominant, wanted to believe.

'I thought that kind of thing was baloney,' she said. 'The sort of stuff touted by strange old Victorian ladies in dingy rooms with lace curtains.'

The words of Lambert flashed before Quester's eyes.

'*The brain's resources are enormous, Colonel Bren. But*

we are far from being able to mine its more glittering treasures . . .'

Quester passed the professor's thoughts on to Kelly.

'What we don't know as fact, we dismiss. But then how much do we know about the human brain? Nothing. Absolutely *nothing*. And yet it exists, it functions, in a billion different ways. How much do we know about life and death? The whys and wherefores. *Nothing*. We're born, we live and we die. For what purpose? What the hell is happening to us? We're as ignorant as the first cockroach to crawl on the Earth. So who are we to say something cannot be possible?'

'I still think it is baloney,' Kelly countered. 'What makes you think I am – was – Lydia?'

'The way you felt for me when you first saw me, even though I was a bundle of bandage. The way we made love on our first night together. The chemistry has not changed. I have held you both. I know. The assassin knows, too.'

'It's too much of a coincidence. I mean, two people separated by war, who never saw each other again, an American and a Russian, being reunited decades later as an Englishman and a Canadian. How do you know Lydia is dead? She was only eighteen or nineteen when Bren last saw her. She could still be cleaning rooms and washing dishes in Moscow. It is preposterous!'

Quester clenched his fists in frustration.

'I don't pretend to know all the answers,' he said. 'Who knows, the whole thing could be a circus orchestrated by some form of superior being for its bloody entertainment. I have no way of telling. The only thing I know is that, somehow, we have all been thrown back together by history.'

'All?'

'You, me. Polina Molotov, maybe, wherever and whoever she is. Churchill and Roosevelt, perhaps. And the assassin, hell-bent on revenge.'

'You mean – '

'Stalin! He was with his father at Gori. He was with his troops at Stalingrad. He was with Bren at Yalta. And he is with us now!'

Kelly shuddered, though she could not tell if it was through fear or because of the chaos in her mind.

'But how could he know about Bren, Lydia and Polina Molotov? Second sight? Sixth sense?'

Bren wished to God he could deliver clear, concise answers, but found himself struggling. He looked at Kelly guiltily, as if he was asking her forgiveness for his ignorance.

'I'm not sure,' he said quietly. 'Perhaps our spirits or souls – call them what you like – mix or exchange information, sort out the lies from the truth. Perhaps, after death, we can see things we could not see before. Or perhaps someone else found out about us – and told him. The only certainty is that he knows – and that he will not rest until he has our blood.'

The Kuntsevo dacha. 28 February 1953.

Stalin bolted his meal, making disgusting sounds from a full, but open mouth. Even Beria, watching from the other side of the walnut dining table, was revolted by his gluttony. Malenkov, Bulganin and Khrushchev ignored both and talked among themselves.

Stalin turned to his neighbour, Molotov, and grinned vacantly. A shred of venison hung down from the corner of his lips, glued to the edge of his moustache by spittle. Molotov returned the smile dutifully.

'Yes, Vyacheslav, we have come a long way,' Stalin

244

said solemnly. 'Do you remember when we worked together on *Pravda*, long before the glorious revolution? What year was it? I am seventy-three – my memory is becoming feeble.'

'1912,' Molotov said.

'More than forty years ago! Ah, yes, we have come a long way.' Stalin lost his train of thought and gazed over Molotov's shoulder towards a drinks cabinet. The room appeared hazy and he could not make out whether the cabinet was near or far. He shook his head to regenerate his concentration.

'Have you seen your wife?' he asked.

Molotov wondered why Stalin, of all people, had asked after Polina.

'Yes,' he replied, looking downcast. 'Three weeks ago.'

'And?'

'She feels the air of northern Kazakhstan is good for her health. Before she was exiled, she suffered a series of mysterious ailments.'

'How long has she been there now?'

'Don't you know?'

'My memory . . .'

'Three years. She has been away from Moscow – and from me – for three years.' Even Molotov's voice ached.

'You know I had to do it. For you and for me. She was with the other fucking Jews. A Zionist conspirator, threatening me, spying on you.'

'Polina was Minister of Fisheries, a member of the Central Committee. She founded the Soviet perfume industry.'

'She was a threat to the state and she had to be punished.'

Molotov stayed silent, hoping Stalin would change the subject. He did not.

'She was found guilty, Vyacheslav,' he said sternly.

'Her trial was held in secret. Even I was not permitted to attend.'

'Do I detect a trace of bitterness in your voice?' Stalin challenged. 'Are you now defending your treacherous wife? Are you suggesting justice was not done?'

Molotov sighed. 'The answer to all of your questions is No,' he said.

'But you are hurt. You feel pain.'

'No more than when you took away my post as Minister of Foreign Affairs. It is painful to be mistrusted.'

Stalin slapped Molotov hard on the shoulder.

'Don't be ridiculous!' he chided. 'You are still one of the deputy Prime Ministers of the Soviet Union, which is indeed a great honour . . .'

'Yes, but –'

'. . . And you are here at my side. Granted, you are not invited to my dacha as often as some of the others. But, tonight, you are dining with Stalin!'

More than ever before, Molotov wanted to confront Stalin with the truth. That his poor, wretched wife had been the closest friend of Stalin's poor, wretched wife. That Stalin had never got over Nadya's suicide. That he could not bear to be reminded of Nadya by Polina. And that, in his warped way, he thought it was Polina, and not himself, who had caused Nadya to shoot herself. And that was why Polina had been condemned to the wastelands of Kazakhstan. Her 'treachery' had been a sham. Her 'trial' had been a sham. She had warned him it would happen. And it did.

Molotov stared at Stalin. Inside, he was urging himself: *Tell him! Tell the brute! Tell him I will fight to my last breath to gain my beloved wife's release from her inhuman ordeal!* Stalin leaned back in his chair and waited for the words he knew would never come. Molotov's gaze sunk to his feet. He was filled with self-disgust. *Worst of all*, he told himself, *I am a sham*.

Stalin filled Molotov's glass.

'More wine, Vyacheslav?' he smiled.

Molotov forced himself to look benignly at Stalin and said quietly: 'Thank you, that's very kind.'

The following night Beria took a call at his dacha from the panicked duty officer of the Kuntsevo guard.

'No-one has seen Comrade Stalin for nearly twenty-four hours,' he blabbed. 'It is most irregular. I fear something has happened, but, as you know, it is forbidden to disturb him and I dare not enter his room.'

Beria arrived at Kuntsevo to find Malenkov, Bulganin and Khrushchev already there. Voroshilov and Kaganovich were also summoned. Together, the six broke through the armoured door of Stalin's bedroom. He was lying fully clothed on a rug. They tried to rouse him, but he was in a coma. While Malenkov loosened his tunic, Khrushchev called a team of doctors. They diagnosed a severe brain haemorrhage brought on by chronic high blood pressure. Stalin was hauled into bed and the doctors packed the room with medical equipment as they began a battle to save him. The six members of the Politburo organized guard duty, taking it in turns two at a time to watch over Stalin and the doctors.

In the dead of night, while Voroshilov went to fetch more coffee, Beria dismissed the doctors for half an hour and knelt beside Stalin's bed. He leaned forward until his mouth was less than an inch from Stalin's left ear.

'Can you hear me, old man?' he said. 'You're dying. At last, you fucker, you're dying. Do you hear?'

There was no response. For once, the great leader was as helpless as a baby.

'I'm glad you're dying,' Beria continued. 'But first we have to talk, Joseph Vissarionovich. It is important. Hey, fucker! We must talk.'

Stalin's eyes flashed open as if someone had thrown a switch. Beria, taken by surprise, jerked his head backwards. He saw the beginnings of a smile on Stalin's lips.

'I'm still here. You won't have my guts yet, Beria.' The voice was strained and croaky, but it did not yet possess the rattle of a dying man. 'What happened? Did you put something in my wine? Is that why you bought me those bottles of my favourite kinzmarauli, so you could lace them? What did you put in? Some sort of stuff that would increase my blood pressure still further and finish me off? You knew about my blood pressure, didn't you?'

At first, Beria hesitated. But there was no movement from Stalin apart from his lips, and it was clear paralysis was setting in. It gave Beria confidence.

'There was no need to lace your wine,' he said. 'You are finished in any event. You are about to join the millions you have already sent to hell. Strange how life – and death – turns out. For years, you have been threatening to kill me. And yet it is I who will outlast you. Ironic, isn't it?'

'The only way for you to escape me, Beria, is for you to strike first.'

'As I said, there is no need.'

'If I cannot take care of you, have no doubt that others will. Khrushchev and the rest. They hate you, Beria. You are hated by everyone. That is why I have kept you in high office all these years. I knew there was no chance of you joining any subversive group, because none would have you.'

'And yet I know who perpetrated the greatest subversion of all. Those who tried to blow you to mincemeat in Yalta . . .'

248

Even in the half-light given off by the room's solitary bulb, Beria could see Stalin's skin turning purple with fury, and momentarily thought he would die there and then.

'I knew it,' Stalin gasped.

'We had an agent at Yalta. A man called Pruett. He saw quite a lot there, as it turned out. And from what he knew to be fact, he was able to put a name to the conspirators.'

'*Who?*' Stalin was frantic. 'Who has escaped justice all these years?'

'Curiosity killed the cat,' Beria said, a smirk crossing his face. 'And I want it to be a slow death. Just think about it while you're lying there these next few days, if you're capable. It will drive you to distraction.'

'You are a coward. Even now you dare not tell me.'

'Oh no, I will tell you, but only at the very moment of your death. That way, you will have no time to work out why they did it, or who they were working for. And you will have no time to even *think* of revenge. For a man such as you, that will be the ultimate suffering.'

Stalin was on the verge of losing consciousness again, but managed one final question.

'Which cesspit did you creep from, Beria?'

'The same one as you did, Joseph Vissarionovich,' Beria replied. 'Sweet dreams.'

Stalin's daughter, Svetlana, held his hand. From time to time, he opened his eyes, but saw nothing.

'He has done well to last four days,' a doctor announced. 'Something must have kept him going. But the bleeding is spreading . . .'

The news went round that the end was near and the six from the Politburo gathered in the bedroom. Briefly,

Stalin regained consciousness. A nurse gave him a drink from a spoon. He pointed to a blown-up photograph he had pinned on the wall months earlier. It showed a lamb being fed by a young peasant girl.

'He is the lamb, the nurse is the girl,' Malenkov said. 'Stalin keeps his sense of humour to the last.'

Stalin choked on the drink. It triggered the death throes. His face became contorted as he fought for every shallow breath. The doctors could only stand back and watch.

Beria stepped forward and brushed them aside. He bent to kiss Stalin's cheek and cried aloud: 'I will be the first to take leave of my supreme leader.' The others could not see him whispering in Stalin's ear.

'An American Army colonel called Bren. Polina Molotov, wife of your former Foreign Minister. And one of her loyal maids, Lydia Morozova. They tried to kill you in Yalta.'

Stalin's entire body shuddered and his skin turned black. His left arm shot into the air. For an instant it stayed there, erect and supporting a tightly clenched fist, as if Stalin was putting one last curse on all his foes.

It only flopped on to the bed after he took his last breath.

19

Kelly wanted proof, something to hold on to, before she would go any further. Quester promised to provide it.

'But you'll have to leave your job,' he warned. 'You can go back to nursing any time. But, for now, you have to concentrate on staying alive. We must travel to find the answers.'

'Where do we start?'

'At the time of birth and the time of death.'

'What do you mean?'

'That is when things happen. Strange things. Do you remember when I was on the very brink of death at the hospital? I saw Rosanne. She was there, waiting for me to die. She was smiling – and now I know why. She was happy that I was about to join her in whatever world she was in.'

'You could have imagined it . . .'

'No! It was real. Just as I died an American soldier and was born the son of a German collaborator an instant later.'

'How do you *know*?' Kelly shrieked.

'I'll show you,' said Quester. 'Come with me.'

They went to the orphanage where Quester was raised, an ivy-covered hall overlooking the North Sea on the outskirts of Harwich. The principal, a dishevelled but kindly man called Stockton, greeted Quester's plea for help with uncommon enthusiasm.

'A Quester on a quest, making a request,' he said with

251

a self-congratulatory smirk. 'Do you know on which date you came to live here?'

'I did not ask – and no-one ever told me.'

'And did you ask for details of your parentage?'

'No. I thought my parents were either dead, or I had been abandoned by them. Either way, there didn't seem to be much point in knowing. I was here, and I had to get on with it.'

'Perhaps you know the date you left the orphanage.'

Quester smiled at the memory. 'I remember it well. I ran away on my fifteenth birthday. I had made a pact with myself to skip as soon as I was fifteen. Try 12 April 1960.'

Stockton, muttering darkly about how children should not leave the orphanage without proper preparation, documentation and permission, took them to a neighbouring office and leafed through drawers full of plain manila folders.

'Such a catalogue of tragedy,' he said as his fingers worked away. 'Ah, here it is. There's bound to be only one Quester, I should say. It's not a common-or-garden name like Smith or Brown, now, is it?'

He pulled out a folder, its corners curled and its edges ragged, and handed it to Quester.

'I'll leave you to it,' he said. Then, glancing at Kelly, he added with a wink: 'I'd have run away for her, too.'

Quester waited until Stockton was out of the room before examining the folder. His name was written in black ink towards one corner:

QUESTER, Tomas
(No known middle name)

'German spelling of Tomas!' Quester exclaimed. 'I didn't know. For as long as I can remember, I have been just plain Tom.'

'Look inside,' Kelly urged.

Quester flicked through a sheaf of papers, dropped loosely into the folder. Most of the documents dealt with his behaviour, attitudes and schooling. But there was a typewritten preface dated 16 January 1946 and headed: TO WHOM IT MAY CONCERN. Quester read it aloud.

'Tomas Quester was abandoned as a baby, having been left in a porch at Harwich general hospital on 1 May 1945. Doctors who examined him diagnosed severe malnutrition. It was clear the infant had been fed little since birth. A note attached to the child's clothing gave his name and date of birth – 12 April 1945. Thus he was approx. three weeks old. The note was written in German. Further enquiries revealed that a German refugee (not Jewish) and his infant child were given passage in a Royal Navy vessel sailing from Hamburg which berthed briefly at Harwich quay on the day before the discovery of the baby. The father was said to have been in a disturbed state. He is believed to have jumped ship and was not seen again. Attempts to trace him have so far been fruitless.

'In view of the chaotic circumstances and the state of war that still existed at the time, and in view of certain facts known about his father, the Home Office decided to issue the child with a birth certificate stating his name as Tom, and his parents' (false) names as Gwendoline and Sidney to avoid any anti-German prejudice that the blameless child may have suffered. His place of birth was registered as Harwich. In other words, he is a bona fide British citizen and should always be treated as such.'

There was a postscript.

'Please note: A letter in an envelope addressed to the child was left at his side. In view of its contents, it is

253

suggested that it should be handed over to the boy on his 18th birthday.'

Quester rifled through the rest of the papers. It was there. A crumpled, stained envelope, clumsily re-sealed and bearing the handwritten name: 'Tomas.' He ripped it open, but the message was written in German.

'There's an old friend of Rosanne's, Claire, back in London,' he told Kelly. 'She taught in Munich for three years. She'll tell me what it says.'

Claire, already in an emotional state through being in the throes of divorce, had tears in her eyes after reading the letter.

'Are you sure you want to hear this?' she asked Quester sincerely.

'Of course.'

She read self-consciously like an actress rehearsing her lines for the first time.

'My dear little Tomas, I hope one day you will forgive me for what I am doing, and will understand the reasons. Your mother died while giving birth to you and I find myself in a strange country with a baby I cannot feed. This is a terrible time, which I hope and pray you will never have to experience. You must believe me when I say that my heart aches at our parting, but I feel sure that this is the best way for you. All my love for ever more. Papa.'

Quester turned to Kelly and said: 'Convinced?'

She saw the hurt he was masking and pulled herself into his arms.

'He may be still alive,' she said. 'Do you want to try to find him?'

'Not now.' Quester's cracked voice betrayed the wavering in his mind, but he knew there was no time.

'Come on,' he said, taking Kelly's hand. 'Next we have to find out about you.'

They flew to New York by Concorde the next day and went straight to the Bureau of Vital Records in Albany's Empire State Plaza. They had Kelly's birth certificate with them, detailing her birthplace as a hospital near Prospect Park in Brooklyn.

'We'll go through the deaths for the same day,' Quester said. 'Ignore the surnames. Just look for a Lydia and hope to God she never changed her Christian name.'

Kelly pulled a massive volume of death records from a crowded shelf and dropped it heavily on a wooden lectern. The flight had made her tired and irritable – and no matter how she tried, she found it impossible to shake her scepticism.

'Why the same day?' she asked coldly. 'And how do we know Lydia died in New York?'

'Because that's where you were born.'

'So?'

'I was born only a short distance from where Bren died, at the same time he fell.'

'That doesn't mean the same will apply to Lydia and me.'

'I am trying to establish a pattern.'

'You're grasping at straws.'

Quester forced himself to retain his temper. The monastic atmosphere of the records hall helped – and he kept his voice low and calm.

'It is all I have to go on,' he said. 'This phenomenon, this transference of spirit or whatever between the dying and the newborn seems to take place over a short distance, that's all.'

255

'What if someone dies alone in the middle of the desert?'

'I don't know. Maybe the spirit withers and dies itself. Maybe it travels for hundreds of miles until it finds someone . . . a recipient. I don't know. You don't know. No-one knows.'

They concentrated on running a finger through the names of all the New Yorkers who died on the day Kelly was born. There were hundreds, and without a surname to look for, each entry had to be studied with a fine toothcomb. It was two hours before they found it.

'There!' Kelly followed her cry with a sigh of relief. There had been only ten more names on the list. She pointed triumphantly to her discovery.

Dolores Lydia Zuhat. An American first name. An Arabic surname. But an unmistakably Russian filling. Quester was sure it was her. His eyes flicked between Kelly and the stark entry of death on faded, yellowing paper. He could not fathom his emotions. His heart was torn in two at the thought of Lydia's premature end, thousands of miles from her homeland. Yet the girl who stood beside him was real – and no less enchanting. He felt a wave of dread like that experienced by lovers who suddenly remember how easily they could have missed meeting each other. He took Kelly in his arms, kissed her and whispered: 'I'm glad you're here.'

Kelly's doubts had been finally crushed and she, too, was overcome with sorrow. She could not take her eyes off the little typed paragraph denoting the end of a precious life.

'I can't describe it,' she said, her voice stuttering with anxiety. 'It's as if part of me is in that book. This paper . . .' She flicked the corner of the page with a finger. 'My flesh . . .'

Quester pulled her into him and held her tightly.

'In a way, it is,' he said.

Lydia's last known address was recorded as a street off Atlantic Avenue in the heart of Brooklyn. Quester and Kelly went there the next day. They had made love as soon as they woke in the hotel, as if to cement their growing sense of unity, but their resultant headiness was dampened by the sight that confronted them.

They turned the corner from a bustling avenue of Lebanese restaurants and Egyptian grocery stores to find a street left to the dogs, stinking of decay and neglect. A shaded collection of rusted iron railings, overflowing garbage cans and jaundiced blocks of tawdry tenements. Few were inhabited. Windows were boarded and gates chained. Paint peeled away from doors to reveal slabs of grey, rotting wood. The whole place, it seemed to Quester, was in limbo. Waiting for the day when the bulldozers would move in to put it out of its misery.

The address in the deaths catalogue was a basement apartment, lurking at the foot of crumbling concrete steps. Quester heard shuffling footsteps inside and the stench of spilled beer wafted from an open window.

'At least someone still lives here,' he said.

'Thankful for small mercies,' said Kelly.

Quester knocked on the door.

'Whaddya waiting for?' The hoarse voice was that of a heavy smoker. The accent was a strange concoction of aggressive New Yorker and the more circumspect rolled tongue of the Middle East. 'Come in. Every other fucker does. Door's always open, you know me. Bring the drink with you.'

The man was as shambolic as his room. Frayed braces held up black trousers stained with ketchup and frying

257

fat. His faded collarless shirt was torn under both armpits. He had only remnants of hair on his head and his sunken olive face was hidden behind the stiff silver stubble of four or five days. His eyes were listless, his body bent and undignified, making him look even older than his seventy-odd years. Around him, spent beer cans littered a threadbare carpet. He looked blankly at his visitors. They were not who he had been expecting. He turned slowly, eased himself down on to a mattress pushed into one corner of the room and rested his chin on his knees.

'So who are you?' he growled. 'Where's Lenny? Where's the beer?'

The man reminded Quester of Stalin's father, the drunkard Vissarion Dzhugashvili. He shuddered as the vision of the young Joseph's beating swept across his mind.

'Mr Zuhat? Are you called Zuhat?'

'You should know. You're from the welfare, aren't you?'

'My name is Quester.' He motioned to Kelly. 'This is my . . . er . . . wife. We have come to talk about Lydia.'

The name slapped Zuhat out of his stupor. His eyes lit up and he leaped to his feet with a sudden energy that took Quester by surprise.

'Jesus! How'd you mean? Are you Russians, you bastards?'

Quester thought quickly. He pulled a sheaf of notes from his pocket and handed them over to Zuhat.

'You were right first time,' he said. 'We're from welfare – and we've been going over our records. We have discovered you are still owed a small amount of money, a tax refund, that was never paid to you after your wife's untimely death. She was your wife, wasn't she?'

Zuhat counted the notes before replying.

'In a manner of speaking. I mean, we were married. Though we sort of led our own separate lives. But she has been dead twenty-odd years . . .'

'We must apologize for the delay,' Kelly intervened. 'It is unforgivable, but the payment in your hands includes interest.'

Zuhat looked at them quizzically. He was still suspicious, but the money – more than 400 crisp dollars – had mellowed him.

'I'm sorry I yelled,' he said. 'Only you used her real name. Lydia. She was born in Russia, you know, but she called herself Dolores over here in the States. Dolly. Everyone knew her as Dolly.'

'Lydia is the middle name on her death certificate,' Quester said. 'That is how we knew.'

'I insisted on it. I thought it was only right when she died, even though she made me promise never to call her Lydia in public while she was alive.'

'Why?'

'She was frightened of something.'

'What?'

Zuhat shrugged his shoulders.

'I never knew exactly. All I know is that she was a maid in Russia, but was smuggled out towards the end of the Second World War by her mistress, someone called Polina Molotov. Like the fire-bombs, you know, Molotov cocktails.'

'Why smuggled?'

'I tried everything to make her tell me. Everything. But she was as stubborn as a mule. No matter how many times I asked, she wouldn't tell me. I just got the impression that she had done something awful bad – so bad that she was convinced the Russians were after her. Stalin was in control then. She was scared as hell of him. She half expected him to come for her in person.'

Quester glanced at Kelly and saw a shiver escape down her spine.

'Shit!' Zuhat slapped himself on the face. 'All that stuff about smuggling. I didn't mean she was an illegal immigrant, or anything like that . . .'

Quester grinned. 'Don't worry. I won't take the money back. I'm just curious. I've found the people round here have some great stories to tell. How did you meet Lydia?'

'Two lost souls, that's all. She was fresh in from Russia. I came from Palestine. We met. We kept each other company. We married.'

'And yet you said you lived separate lives . . .'

Zuhat looked away. A melancholy air swept over him and he began rummaging through the beer cans with his feet, searching against expectations for a full one. When he spoke, he kept his gaze directed at the floor. He did not want to display his wounds.

'I fell in love with her the moment I first saw her . . . and I went on loving her with a power that could light up this city. But, if the truth was told, she never really loved me. Perhaps because I was a Palestinian content enough to live in America. Perhaps because I was never the romantic hero who would die rather than give up the struggle for his homeland. I don't have any answers. All I know is that throughout our life together, I had the impression that I was not her first choice. That she would rather have been married to someone else. That somehow, somewhere – maybe back in Russia, I don't know – she loved another man.'

Quester felt a pounding in his chest. It was fierce and resonant with the force of Lydia's love. He yearned to tell Zuhat the truth, that he was the man. But he knew it would sound both ridiculous and cruel. Instead, he asked quietly: 'How did she die?'

Zuhat looked up, his eyes suddenly full of shame and degradation. He cast a hand around the filth of the apartment and shouted: 'It wasn't always like this. Oh, it was never a palace, like some of the places Lydia worked at, but it was a home. Until she died. *Until I let her die!* I had left her a couple of weeks before, you see. Moved in with a woman four blocks away. Hell, I was due some affection, wasn't I? How was I to know Lydia would catch pneumonia?'

'You mean . . .'

'She died alone. Lydia died alone.'

Quester and Kelly left. They did not let Zuhat see their tears.

20

They obtained holiday visas from the Russian Embassy in London and flew to Moscow the following week.

As the Aeroflot jet circled Sheremetyevo airport before landing, Kelly was gripped by a sudden terror.

'This is suicide,' she said through clenched teeth. 'We're putting our heads inside the lion's mouth. I know it. I feel we're like cancer patients who look over their shoulders as they are wheeled into hospital. They know, too.'

'Know what?' Quester asked.

'That they won't be coming out again. Just as we won't be coming out of Moscow. We're going to *die* here, Tom. You know it, too.'

Quester stroked the back of her neck, underneath her hair, to relax her. 'I thought we had agreed this was the best way,' he said quietly.

'I must have been mad,' Kelly replied without hesitation. 'I think we are both mad.'

Quester gazed out of the window at the stark criss-cross patterns of the workers' suburbs below, new high-rise blocks dwarfing the five-storey economy flats that shot up in the early sixties. As the plane banked, the city centre came into view. Quester's lips thinned in determination.

'You're down there, Stalin,' he muttered. 'And I will find you.'

He turned to Kelly, who was chewing frantically on a sweet to ward off earache – and fear – as the jet descended.

'Would it help if I went through the reasons one more time?'

She nodded without looking at him. He noticed her hands, bleached of pigment and clinging on to each other for strength and support. It crossed his mind that he should have come to Moscow without her, but there were no easy solutions. In London, alone, she would have been even more vulnerable. He tried to explain.

'We could let him come to us, but there is a good chance he will kill us before we know it. Even in the dead of night, as we sleep. We would be none the wiser – just dead. No, it is better for us that we bring ourselves to him. Confront him. Talk to him. Tell him that what happened was in another time, another place. That we cannot be held responsible. Reassure him that we mean no harm now. Persuade him to leave us alone. It's the only way we will ever have peace. The only way.'

'The ramblings of a naïve man,' Kelly said boldly.

'But you agreed . . .'

'I must have been mad,' Kelly persisted. 'The whole expedition is mad. We don't even know he is here.'

'He must be!' Quester said it like a man obsessed. 'Look, we know who he is, where he came from, how he was born. Stalin died in his dacha near Moscow. The assassin was born nearby.'

'Russia is a vast country. He could be anywhere.'

'He lives in Moscow. If he is following in the footsteps of his predecessor, he has to. He will be on his way into the Russian hierarchy by now. He travels abroad freely. A government man, perhaps. Or more likely an officer in the KGB.'

Kelly gripped Quester's wrist with all her might. He saw the haunted look in her eyes, the tautness of the muscles in her face. He had never seen her in such a panic.

'Please!' she pleaded. 'There's still time. All we have to do is stay at the airport and catch the next plane home to London. Please, Tom, I beg you . . .'

The airliner touched down heavily, its jets screaming into reverse thrust. As it came to a standstill, Quester unbuckled his seat belt, rose slowly to his feet and looked down at Kelly.

'Are you coming?' he said softly.

She stared ahead for a moment, then said: 'You're determined, aren't you?'

'Yes,' he replied.

A look of defeat crossed her face, but she could not fight the love that bound her to him.

'Then I won't let you go alone,' she said.

Intourist, the state travel agency, had booked them into the Rossia Hotel, a mammoth rectangle of concrete and glass placed at one end of Red Square and sandwiched between the curling Moskva River and a cluster of small churches, each topped with gaudy onion domes.

At first, they played tourists. They joined other foreigners and Russians of sharply contrasting shapes and sizes – swarthy southern oilmen, windblown Arctic fur-trappers and slight Oriental librarians – for a guided tour of the Kremlin. They braved interminable queueing and bullying by gruff policemen to catch the briefest glimpse of Lenin in his mausoleum. They watched men playing dominoes amid the red autumn glow of Sokolniki Park. They bought ice cream from street stalls. They drank kvass, grimacing slightly at its fermented flavour of black bread.

And all the time they assumed that while their eyes were on Moscow, Moscow's eyes were on them. That like most Western visitors, they would be scrutinized and their identities and intentions processed through police headquarters.

Once on file, there was every chance that a pair of steel-blue eyes under a canopy of spiky blond hair would pick out their names and track them down. According to Quester's calculations, the assassin would be consumed with curiosity – perhaps even admiration – about their presence in Moscow. And he would be unable to resist meeting them in his home city before resuming his maniacal offensive.

That would be the chance Quester needed to talk.

The plan did not work. After three days, the only man they had attracted was a French tourist called Giroix – elderly, travelling solo and desperately using his schoolboy English in an attempt to latch on to them. The few Russians they encountered to any degree included a smart teenage boy who made persistent attempts to buy Quester's watch and a bedroom maid who told them in alarmingly fluent English how the Rossia was despised by Moscovites because its construction had ruined the view at one end of Red Square.

Quester scolded himself and reasoned that the assassin was too highly placed, too important in the hierarchy, to see their names on any list of mere tourists.

'We have to do something more,' he said.

'Rob a bank,' Kelly suggested.

'Don't be facetious.'

'Don't be pompous.'

Quester wanted to yell at her, but stopped himself. He knew her attitude had been coloured by what had happened to her since they arrived. The growth of a warm, comforting feeling deep inside her that she was home

265

again. She had told him as much that morning as they watched strings of seven-year-old children walking the streets, holding on to their parents with one hand and clasping huge bunches of flowers in the other – gifts for their teachers on their first day at school.

'I must have done that once,' Kelly said. 'It's familiar, but new. Real, but unreal.'

'How do you mean?'

'I mean . . . I'm still frightened to be here, but I like it. I think I must have always liked it.'

They spent the whole of the next morning at Dzerzhinsky Square, parading up and down in front of the Lubyanka. Attracting attention. Being provocative.

From time to time, they caught glimpses of men in grey suits, looking at them curiously from behind smoked windows. Security cameras whirred in their direction. Pointing, probing. But there was no challenge.

They joined a group of four men resting side-by-side on a bench, each with a pram containing a sleeping baby at his knees. Quester reckoned at least one was a KGB plant – and launched into a diatribe of anti-Soviet propaganda. But there was no reaction, no hint of an arrest. To all intents and purposes, they had not understood a word.

After half an hour of sharing mutual moans and groans, two of the men rose to their feet. They nodded at Quester and Kelly in recognition of their foreign nationality before pushing their prams casually towards the crowded expanses of Marx Prospekt, pausing to window-shop on behalf of their infants at the colonnaded Children's World toy store that stood incongruously across the road from the Lubyanka. The other two headed without a backward glance for the entrance to Dzerzhinskaya Metro station.

Quester was overcome by a feeling of being a helpless amateur on such a stage and was forced to agree with

Kelly that his behaviour was at best eccentric, at worst ridiculous.

'What do you expect them to do?' she challenged. 'Come out here and haul us in? Risk an international incident involving two strange but harmless tourists who could merely be fascinated by the Lubyanka?'

'All right, all right! Come with me.'

Quester took hold of Kelly's hand with a firmness that angered her. He dragged her through the streets back to the Rossia, ignoring her squeals of protest. Once there, he searched the bars and the dining rooms until he found the lone Frenchman, Giroix.

He was sitting at a table with a young Russian couple clearly embarrassed by his presence. Quester prised him away and bought him a 200-gramme flask of vodka. Kelly smiled guiltily at the Frenchman, suspecting some sort of deception was afoot.

Giroix had mentioned that he had driven himself to Moscow – and Quester turned the conversation to the topic of cars. Giroix, it transpired, had a Mercedes.

'More strong than French autos,' he said.

'Where is it?' Quester asked enthusiastically.

'Hotel parking,' Giroix said, thrusting a thumb over his shoulder.

Quester pointed first at the Frenchman, then at himself, saying, 'You show me?'

Giroix, sensing a chance to finally befriend the Englishman, was happy to oblige. He took Quester and Kelly to the Mercedes, a new model automatic, and allowed them to sit inside to enjoy its comfort.

'Engine quiet?' Quester asked.

Giroix, leaning on the driver's open door, passed Quester the keys and, with an outstretched palm, invited him to start the motor.

267

Quester did so. Then he looked up at Giroix and said: 'Understand this, monsieur . . . I am stealing your car.'

He flicked the door shut from underneath Giroix's elbow, selected forward drive and accelerated away, leaving the Frenchman rooted to the spot, gaping in disbelief and gesticulating wildly with his arms.

Quester swung the Mercedes into Moscow's late afternoon traffic of pale-coloured Volgas, Ladas and Moskvitchs. He worked his way around the inner city to Gorky Street by blindly tracking a tourist bus, keeping close to it so he was not left to his own devices at traffic lights.

'Where are we going?' Kelly said.

Quester pointed to a map in the glove-box and said: 'You tell me.'

Kelly unfolded it and tried to find landmarks. The first she picked up was the Pushkin memorial.

'Well?' Quester asked.

'Towards the Leningrad Highway.'

'That'll do us.'

The bus turned off into a side-street. Quester steered across the junction with the Garden Ring Road and on along Leningradski Prospekt. The first police car picked him up as he swept past the floodlights of Dinamo Stadium. A second joined the chase outside the Aeroflot terminal.

Quester was jubilant.

'Giroix reported us,' he said. 'I knew he would.'

Kelly glanced over her shoulder at the flashing lights of the two pursuing cars. A policeman in the passenger seat of the first waggled his finger at her as if he was scolding a naughty child.

'What now?' she said.

'I go faster – they get angrier,' Quester said.

Kelly glanced at Quester, but did not like what she saw.

Every feature of his face – his eyes, his nose, his mouth – was twisted in a feverish concentration that bordered on frenzy.

'Stop now,' she said. 'The police will pull us in. You'll have what you want.'

'No!' Quester yelled. 'I want to make sure of getting inside the Lubyanka. I want to see Stalin!'

He pressed the accelerator and the Mercedes responded without hesitation. The sirens of the police cars faded along with their reflections in his mirrors. Others took up the chase at intervals. But one by one they, too, were dropped.

As Quester reached the open road of the Leningrad Highway, he pressed his foot down harder. Soon, the speedometer needle was touching 120 mph.

There was no further challenge from behind, but within minutes a helicopter roared low above them, taking up station thirty yards ahead. A man in a uniform, his hair blasted back by the slipstream, leaned out and waved his hand stiffly in an unmistakable gesture of authority.

'He's telling us to stop,' Kelly said.

'No!' Quester shouted. 'Not now!'

He accelerated again, momentarily taking the helicopter pilot by surprise and shooting under the machine's belly.

'You're going too fast,' Kelly protested, frightened now by the sheer speed of the car.

'I have to,' Quester said.

'The helicopter's got guns and rockets.'

'They won't be used.'

'The pilot can shove us off the road.'

'He won't.'

'He can try to swoop low in front of our bonnet to slow us up.'

269

'Too dangerous for him.'

'He can radio ahead.'

'Yes.'

'They'll set up a roadblock.'

'That's what I want.'

It came sooner than Quester expected. Shadows loomed through the gathering gloom of evening and suddenly he was roaring past two lines of slower cars. From the corner of his eye he could see police trucks parked on the verge of the highway. Men with peaked caps and epaulets were gesticulating at the Russian drivers, telling them to keep to one side and to slow down. Quester sped past the head of the two lines, where cars were at a standstill behind a human barrier of police standing side by side across the inner lanes. Scores of officers were there, but they watched him go.

Now, apart from the ever-present helicopter, he was on his own again, all three lanes of highway stretching out before him, pine forest to one side and flat, deserted scrubland to the other.

The uniformed man in the helicopter made one last futile attempt to persuade Quester to stop before the machine arced up into the sky and banked away to the right. At the same time, Quester crested a rise and saw what awaited him.

Two hundred yards ahead, at the foot of a dip in the road, a barrier had been thrown up across the entire width of both carriageways. It was made up of three layers. The first consisted of interlinked wooden fences like athletes' hurdles, painted in diagonal red and white stripes with flashing orange lights hooked over their perpendicular posts. The second was a line of men – police and military – armed with sub-machine-guns pointing upright towards the sky. The third was a cordon of police cars parked end to end.

Quester took stock of the situation. He slowed to a crawl, peering ahead with eagle eyes for any sign of a weakness. He found one near the central reservation – a gap four feet wide between the fenders of two of the parked cars.

Kelly realized what was going through his mind and panicked.

'You can't do it!' she screamed.

'I can – and I will.' Quester was like a starving wild animal desperate for a kill.

'The fences . . .'

'Wooden. Like matchsticks.'

'The men.'

'They'll shift.'

'But why break through? There's no need.'

'There is!' Quester insisted. 'You know what it is.'

'We'll be killed. I told you we would die in Russia.'

Quester braked until the Mercedes stopped. A man in an ankle-length raincoat stepped forward from the barrier, ready to accept the surrender. He was a brave man, approaching without guards, without arms. Quester let him come, let him come, until the man was twenty yards away. Then he switched his foot from brake to accelerator and floored it.

There was a scream of resistance and a burst of blue smoke from the rear tyres, but the Mercedes gathered speed instantly. Kelly saw the terror on the approaching officer's face as the car hurtled towards him. Quester flicked the steering wheel to one side, brushing the man's raincoat, before aiming directly at his target.

'Hold on!' he shouted to Kelly. 'Brace yourself.'

The men in the second line of defence pulled their

triggers and a volley of machine-gun fire ripped up into the clouds with the crackle of burning wood. Kelly screamed, but nothing could deter Quester.

It all happened within a second. The car smashed through the wooden barrier, sending a cascade of splinters into the air. Soldiers and policemen leaped for their lives. Quester, seeing only a blurred flurry of ankles and elbows, punched the Mercedes through the hole they left and rammed its bonnet into the gap between the two police cars, banging them apart amid a shower of lamp glass and a thunderous sound of gouging metal.

Once through, he carried on for thirty yards before deliberately yanking on the handbrake and spinning the car through 180 degrees, lurching to a halt against the buttress of a bridge.

Kelly, panting and on the verge of passing out, peered over the dashboard to see a group of thirty soldiers creeping cautiously towards the stranded Mercedes, their submachine-guns balanced on their hips and thrust menacingly in front of them. Kelly shook, waiting for the death rattle of the guns to erupt.

'They're coming, but they're not firing,' she said.

'They want to talk to us,' said Quester. 'That's good.'

The man in the Lubyanka introduced himself as Yuri Rats.

'A funny name in English, yes?' he said with a wry smile. 'And it is true, to a certain extent, that I must spend much of my time in the company of garbage. Happily, that does not appear to be the case on this occasion.'

Quester was impressed. Not only by the man's humour, but by his sheer presence and obvious stature. He was

272

tall, suntanned, and his sharp green eyes exuded alertness. His silver crescent of hair, curling around a bald crown, was complemented by sideburns grown deliberately long and bushy. He wore an expensive dark brown three-piece suit with magnolia pinstripes. Despite his age, which Quester estimated at around fifty-five, he was the face of modern Moscow. When Quester asked his rank, he simply grinned and said, 'High enough.'

Rats blended in naturally with his clean, carefully sculpted surroundings. He faced Quester and Kelly across a low glass coffee table in a sumptuously furnished, glass-panelled room looking on to a vast openplan office filled with air-conditioned policemen in shirt sleeves. Policemen on the telephone, policemen peering into computer terminals and policemen laughing over cups of lemon tea.

Rats observed Kelly's surprise and said: 'Hardly the international image of the Lubyanka, is it now? Where are all those wretched souls waiting against a wall to be shot through the head? No, no, my dear. That sort of thing went out with Stalin.'

He offered cigarettes, which both Quester and Kelly accepted.

'Do you want to call the British Embassy?' Rats said. 'It is, of course, your right.'

'It won't be necessary,' Quester replied without hesitation.

'You are sure?' Rats said with raised eyebrows. 'You were less than an inch from killing many Russian citizens. This is something we cannot take lightly.'

'If I could explain . . .'

'No. You will answer questions.' Rats asserted his authority quickly. 'First, why did you steal the Frenchman's car?'

'A misunderstanding,' Quester said. 'Monsieur Giroix had become our co-tourist and friend in Moscow. We spoke together in broken, awkward English. I thought that when he showed me his Mercedes in the hotel car park, he had told me I was welcome to drive it around Moscow for the evening.'

'He denies he said anything of the sort.'

'Yes . . . he is probably right. As I said, a question of language. A misunderstanding.'

'But why did you not stop when you were challenged by the police?'

'I was afraid. I did not have any papers authorizing a car journey. I knew that was a serious offence. I thought if I could shake off the police cars, I could return to the hotel and there would be no harm done.'

'You did shake them off. Yet you kept going, even when a helicopter, of all things, was brought in to stop you.'

'I was lost. I panicked. Things just went from bad to worse.'

'Even when you came across what was clearly a road-block to halt your progress, you carried on in a violent fashion, putting many brave Soviet citizens at risk.'

Quester did not reply. He had been distracted by something – someone – he saw in the open-plan office. A fleeting glimpse of a man with spiky blond hair. He stared open-mouthed through the window, hoping against hope to see him again.

'Mr Quester . . .'

Quester did not hear Rats. He did not matter. Only the assassin mattered now.

'*Mr Quester!*' Rats was abrupt, uncompromising, forcing Quester to attend. 'Has something disturbed you?'

'What?' Quester's mind was in turmoil. 'Er, no. No. Not at all. Please carry on. I apologize.'

Rats glanced out of the window for a clue to the distraction. When he found none, he turned back to Quester and repeated his previous question.

'Why ram the roadblock?' Quester said. 'I was out of my mind.'

'Had you been drinking?'

'No. Not that. It's just . . . just that you don't know how frightening it is for Westerners to come face to face with Russian police, helicopters, soldiers, things like that. For us, it is sinister, alarming. We watch too many films. But you must understand. I was out of my mind with fear. I just did not know what I was doing. I cannot tell you how sorry I am. The last thing I wanted on this holiday was any unpleasantness or ill-feeling.'

'Ah, a missionary of peace from the West.' Rats' tone was sarcastic, but even so he did not appear unduly suspicious.

Quester kept glancing out of the window. *Show yourself, Stalin*, he was shouting inside. *Come on, you bastard, let's see you*.

Rats cleared his throat to attract attention. Quester looked at him guiltily.

'Your face, I feel, reflects the veracity of your astonishing story,' Rats said.

'No!' Kelly interjected. 'What he told you is true. I tried to stop him many times, but there was nothing I could do. He just kept going because he was scared.'

Rats studied her with a finger on his chin, weighing her up in his mind.

'So,' he said suddenly. 'We are left with an impasse. I accuse. You deny. Who shall be the judge?'

'That, sir, is up to you,' Kelly said with all the courtesy she could muster.

'May I make a suggestion?' Rats had the profound air of a man who knew what he was about to say would meet no opposition. 'I could begin criminal proceedings, but such a case could become a cause célèbre without deserving to be so. You know how it is. No-one in Britain would believe you are guilty of anything, whatever you have done in reality. It's the same for everyone arrested in the Soviet Union, eh? A British murderer could kill twenty Russians and the newspapers in England would still have headlines proclaiming his innocence. No, if I prosecuted you, diplomats would poke their noses in and the whole episode would become a messy, unnecessary distraction.'

'So what are you suggesting?' Quester asked.

'That I allow you to leave this building on condition that you finish your holiday as scheduled, without embassy contact, as if nothing had happened. But I must inform you here and now that you will never be allowed to revisit the Soviet Union. That, lady and gentleman, is the deal.'

'And Giroix's car . . .'

'. . . Is already under repair. This office will meet the expense.'

'I don't understand.'

'No, Mr Quester, it appears not.' Rats flashed another of his disarming smiles in Quester's direction. 'What I am trying to make you see is that I am a busy man, engaged in rather more serious disputes between our nations. I *know* that neither of you are spies. So tell me, why should I be bothered with a pair of foolish adventurers who wanted to see the inside of the Lubyanka?'

'You saw us outside this morning?' Kelly said.

'Of course. You were taped also. You are the stars of

the most boring film since *Last Tango in Paris*. Now, I will fetch someone to see you out. He is an adventurer also. He will be far more interested to meet you than I.'

Rats opened the door of the room, leaned out and shouted, 'Viktor!'

The assassin appeared moments later. Quester could not believe his inner reaction. Full of restless aggression just a moment ago, he was rendered impotent on the spot by the man's casual smirk. Kelly could not help trembling. The assassin, calm and collected, showing no trace of recognition, offered his hand for shaking. His invitation was ignored. Rats watched the confrontation with interest.

'May I present Mr Viktor Lavochkin,' he said. 'He knows England well. He returns from his little trips full of enthusiasm for London, eh Viktor?'

Lavochkin nodded and smiled. He used the hand he had offered to brush back his hair, making its spikes stand on end.

Neither Quester nor Kelly could speak. Before them, less than three yards away, stood the most evil man the world had known.

'What's this?' Rats said with a chuckle. 'What is it about you that frightens people so, Viktor?'

Lavochkin joined in the laughter, but there was no mirth in his eyes.

Rats smiled at Kelly and said: 'I have to tell you that he frightens us also. His mere progress through the ranks has been frightening. So swift, so sure. Who knows, I have possibly given you the honour of meeting the future Soviet leader. That would be something to tell the grandchildren about, eh?'

Quester looked at Lavochkin. He expected the assassin

to dismiss Rats' suggestion with a blush or a modest shake of the head. But he did not. It was clear that he, too, was sure of his destiny. He motioned to the door and said: 'Let's go,' before spinning round to lead the way. Rats called a reminder to Quester and Kelly.

'Stick to your schedule. Enjoy Moscow. Catch your plane as planned. And remember . . . I have the power to re-arrest you.'

They were left alone with Lavochkin, but he took no notice of them. They followed his stumpy, bulldog body as he led them to a lift, striding briskly so they had no chance to walk alongside him without running to catch up. In the lift, he made it his business to strike up a conversation with a colleague, ignoring them totally. It was only when they reached a back exit that Quester had the chance to face him.

'We're here,' he said simply.

Lavochkin pointed to a gate in a brick wall off to the right. 'Beyond that is Kirov Street. It will take you back to Dzerzhinsky Square and from there you can find your way to the Rossia Hotel.'

'We're here,' Quester repeated.

'And soon you will be gone.' Lavochkin turned on his heels in military fashion and walked back into the Lubyanka without another word.

They waited for him for three days. In hotel bars, restaurants and cafés. But he did not come. They had been denied their chance to reason with him – and he had made it clear he did not care. All they had left was their memory of a two-minute meeting and their imagination.

It began to play tricks.

Their fear grew. Their suspicion grew. Their paranoia grew.

By day, they walked the streets of Moscow. Always in

278

public view, yet looking over their shoulders. At night, they took it in turns to rest. While one slept, the other stood guard with a heavy brass table-lamp shaped like a ballerina. Against Lavochkin, it felt as slight as the genteel figure it represented. They knew he could be there, yards away. Perhaps even shuffling up and down in the corridor outside. Stalking his prey. Waiting for the right moment. Ready to pounce when it suited him.

They realized they had failed, just as Bren and Lydia had failed before them. Defeated by a stronger man, a man who always did things on his own terms.

Their spirit had sunk to new depths by the time they reached Sheremetyevo airport for the journey home to London. They had two hours to kill before their flight – and spent their last roubles and kopecks at the airport bar on glasses of vodka, determined to get drunk and to forget.

A man hoisted himself on to the stool next to them and offered to buy them a bottle.

Quester recognized the voice immediately and turned to glare at the new arrival. Lavochkin smiled and said: 'Welcome to Moscow, Colonel.'

21

Lavochkin sat them at a table away from flapping ears and for ten minutes delivered a monologue that left them breathless. It was his absolute conviction that was most frightening. He *knew* who he was, who he had been. He *knew* his place in history was assured. He *knew* his capabilities far outstripped those of his peers. He *knew* that if he continued on his current course, climbing the ranks of the KGB one by one, he would rise to become the new Supreme Commander of the Soviet Union.

'Of course, it is not as easy as it once was,' he said, puffing out his cheeks in mock exasperation. 'The bureaucracy is so big, so cumbersome. Bastard Brezhnev saw to that. But I am cultivating political friends, some in the Politburo itself. They are beginning to see my point of view. They will have to take it on board soon. I cannot wait forever. There is so much to be done.'

He filled a Georgian pipe with makhorka tobacco kept loose in the pocket of his jacket. Before he lit it, he poked it roughly into Quester's shoulder. Quester saw Captain Ronsky in the Stalingrad trenches, being poked in the shoulder by his Supreme Commander.

'You see, Colonel, I have a knack of getting my way,' Lavochkin said. 'It was not difficult for me to persuade Rats that I should see you off personally, just to make sure the troublemakers caught their plane. It gave me a chance to meet you and the girl again.'

'I have a name,' Kelly said pointedly.

Lavochkin smiled and lit his pipe.

'Ah yes. My apologies, Lydia Morozova.'

'My name is Kelly Warren. I am a Canadian nurse working in England. I am not a Russian housemaid working for Polina Molotov. Lydia is dead. Polina Molotov is dead.'

'I know Polina Molotov is dead,' Lavochkin said. 'I killed her.'

Quester and Kelly were struck dumb. What did he mean? Their bleached faces demanded an explanation. Lavochkin was happy enough to provide it.

'Strangely enough, Polina Molotov went back to Kazakhstan. Who would have thought it after she spent so many years in exile there? But there she was, in her neat little room, being well fucked by a fat Russian called Grigori Golikov. Always the charming hostess.' Lavochkin broke off for a chuckle at his own joke. 'She called herself Aleksandra. It was a front, of course, designed to throw me off the scent. And I must admit that at first, I felt guilty at interrupting her fun. I mean, she had precious little of that with the old bore Molotov. But then I thought of her treachery, her connivance, her whispered words of hatred that made my poor Nadya shoot herself. And then came Yalta, the final insult. She had been quite prepared to have me killed – it was only just that I should return the compliment.'

Kelly was overcome by a wave of sympathy, though she could not fathom if it was for Aleksandra or Polina Molotov. Almost in a whisper, she asked Lavochkin what he had done.

'One shot – it was all that was necessary.' He slapped his hands together to emphasize the point. 'It cleared the decks. Enabled me to concentrate on finding the two main protagonists of the bomb plot.'

He stared directly at the couple confronting him, his lips curling with contempt as if he was about to spit.

'We are no threat to you.' Quester spoke calmly, deliberately and with sincerity. 'What happened has long since ceased to have any significance to anyone. I am not involved, I am not your colonel. Kelly is not involved, she is not Lydia. And you are not involved, because you are Viktor Lavochkin . . . and not Joseph Stalin.'

The final remark offended Lavochkin to the point of outrage. Quester saw blood pumping into his face as his temper frayed.

'How dare you!' he hissed. 'How dare you even suggest such a thing. There has only been one Stalin. There will only be one Stalin. And I am that man!'

'We are no threat to you,' Quester repeated firmly. 'So why do you threaten us?'

Lavochkin's voice took on the harsh quality of sand rubbing against glass.

'I will do more than threaten you,' he warned. 'Have no doubt, I will end your lives once and for all. You cannot try to kill Stalin and expect to survive.'

'But you have had your chances. Why did you not take them? Are you afraid of something? Tell me . . . is the great Stalin afraid?'

Lavochkin brushed aside the challenge with a sneer.

'I could have killed you in Kashmir, Colonel. Or in your hospital room. Or at the fairground. Or on the autoroute in Belgium.'

'Then why didn't you?'

'To prove my superiority to you, over and over again, until your pea brain absorbs such an obvious fact. When you finally die, when I finally kill you, I want you to be sure of that. Has it not crossed your mind that I knew exactly which part of your head to damage to ensure that

282

you would suffer for six months, but would not die? Has it not crossed your mind that when I removed your ventilation mask, I knew it would soon be replaced? Has it not crossed your mind that I have the ability to torment you, to taunt you, to drive you to the edge of insanity? Because that is exactly what I have done. I am a trained professional, Colonel, the finest in my field. You are weak. A speck of dust under the sole of my shoe.'

Quester listened with a growing awareness of a bad taste in his mouth. He was convinced there was another motive for Lavochkin's delaying tactics.

Cruelty, that was it. Cruelty beyond belief.

Lavochkin confirmed it with his next comment, delivered with an arrogance that was itself insufferable.

'I am a hunter, Colonel. I have a nose for it. I sought out Polina Molotov, I found you, I am close to others who crossed me. My only chance encounter was with you, Lydia. That was your bad luck, but I would have tracked you down sooner or later in any event. You can ask any hunter, he will tell you the same. That once he has unearthed his prey, he does not like to go for the kill immediately. He enjoys the thrill of the chase. It gives him time for his confidence to mature.'

'Dangling life on a string,' Kelly said.

'I really do not care what you call it. The end result is the same. Death for the prey. Triumph for the hunter.'

'You will not triumph!' Quester snapped.

'Oh . . .' Lavochkin said with an indifferent air. 'And who will stop me?'

'Stalin's ways have been rejected. And your ways will be rejected.'

'You really believe that?' Lavochkin checked his watch. 'Come with me,' he said with a sudden urgency.

'Where?' Kelly demanded.

'To a small bar close to the airport. I'll show you.'

Neither Quester nor Kelly moved an inch. Lavochkin laughed and opened his arms in a gesture of innocence.

'I will bring you back for your plane, I promise,' he said. 'You don't think I would kill you here and now, do you? Your names are on the passenger list. Whatever would Rats think if you did not climb aboard?' He checked his watch again. 'Come,' he urged. 'We just have time.

He drove them to a village four miles from the airport. On the way, he told them what he was going to do.

'The village has one factory, producing pistons for tractor engines. Its workers go to a dirty little bar run by a Georgian. He keeps kinzmarauli wine, Stalin's favourite. To this day, the people associate kinzmarauli with Stalin, like cigars with Churchill. And they use it to toast the greatest leader they have known.'

Quester scoffed in disbelief, but Lavochkin rounded on him.

'The pathetic laughter of ignorance. Stalin is still loved. He is still revered. The people want a *strong* leader, someone who will show them the way so they know where they stand. Someone who will control the slackers, the drunks and the drug-takers. Someone who will make other countries treat the Soviet Union with fear and respect. And what have they had instead? A succession of bunglers who have created chaos in agriculture, industry and the economy. After suffering such a herd of fucking boars, the people deserve a knight in shining armour. And I will not let them down.'

It was raining when they reached the village, a dismal collection of old houses set on a dismal plateau. The bar stood on the only through-road, 200 yards on from the slabby greyness of the piston factory. It was little more than a wooden shack, advertised solely by a small metallic strip above the door proclaiming the name of the licensee. But the trail of footsteps in the mud outside demonstrated that it was well patronized.

The arrival of the newcomers was greeted by indiscreet stares from the thirty or so drinkers gathered in groups around gnarled trestle tables. Lavochkin did not delay. He bought a bottle of kinzmarauli and asked for seven glasses.

He chose a table around which six unshaven men in boiler suits were playing cards amid a haphazard collection of vodka glasses and pepper pots. He greeted them in a friendly manner, poured each a glass of thick red wine and then served himself.

Raising his glass to the level of his chin, he barked: 'Joseph Vissarionovich Stalin!'

To a man, they leaped to their feet, one knocking over his chair in his haste to get up. For one silent, dignified moment, they stood firm and erect, like soldiers awaiting inspection on a military parade. Then they punched their glasses high in the air and chorused: 'Stalin!' before downing their first gulp.

Lavochkin, glowing with pride, turned and walked away. Case proven. No need for elaboration. He strode straight past Quester and Kelly and out into the rain. He did not speak again until they were back in the airport terminal, ready to filter through passport control.

'Look at me now!' His voice was commanding and demanded their attention. 'Remember who I am. Remember what you did to me. Above all, remember that the next time you see me will be the last.'

285

22

They lived on Quester's houseboat but were paralysed by indecision. Day after day, they found themselves asking questions to which there were no answers.

Should they run – flee to another country to throw Lavochkin off the trail? If they did, would he be able to find them? Should they stay and fight on home territory? With what weapons? And when? How could they know when he would come? Would it be by day or by night? And would there be a warning?

Should they be defiant – or should they be afraid?

It made them withdraw into themselves. One by one, friends began to reject invitations to dinner. The telephone stopped ringing. Quester was no longer concerned with finding work. Kelly forgot about the hospital.

They were trapped in their own timeless world, a world shared by only one other. The assassin who wanted to kill them.

They made love most days, sometimes staying wrapped together in bed until evening. Caressing, stroking, comforting. Reassuring the other that everything would be all right, each doubting there was a future beyond the next dawn.

When they walked beside the river, they saw no-one else. They ignored the 'good mornings' and 'good evenings' from passing strangers. In the middle of suburban London, they had become hermits.

They missed meals and grew thin. They drank too much

vodka. They watched hours of television, but every storyline of every film and every play seemed the same – and every news bulletin was irrelevant.

As the days, the weeks and the months rolled by, it slowly dawned on them what they were doing.

Waiting. Waiting to die.

On a morning that felt no different from the last, Quester shuffled into the kitchen and cast a bloodshot eye at a pictorial calendar hanging from a hook. It had become a symbol of their non-existence and he scowled at it as if it was his worst enemy. Something, though he was not sure what, demanded his attention. He had a hangover and found it difficult to focus. Making a supreme effort, he tried to absorb what he was seeing, nodding his head as he counted off the days in his mind. It was not until he reached 28 December that he discovered why he felt nauseous.

'We've missed Christmas,' he uttered aloud, scarcely believing his own words. 'It has been and gone – and we've simply missed it.'

The realization snapped him out of his stupor. He told Kelly – and she burst into tears, weeping uncontrollably into the bedsheets.

'It's my fault,' Quester offered. 'I don't understand it.'

'It's both of us,' Kelly sobbed. 'We can't go on under such pressure.'

Quester rammed a frustrated fist into a pillow.

'I need strength!' he shouted. 'I need Bren's courage.'

'It won't be enough.' Kelly sounded as convinced as she had ever been. 'He's coming for us now. I can feel it in my bones.'

Lavochkin watched the man play football under flood-lights. He was one of the oldest in his company team and was struggling through a poor game. But he was still athletic, which Lavochkin found amusing given the man's previous obesity.

After the match, he followed him to the home of one of his many girlfriends. A slender and innocent-looking seventeen-year-old, with shades of Mongolian olive in her appearance, she lived with her parents on the outskirts of Moscow. They disapproved of her relationship with a man many years her senior, but could do nothing to prevent her infatuation. The man drove her to his dacha near the town of Ryazan. Lavochkin followed.

He burst in on them as they made love in front of the glowing embers of a robust log fire. The girl was on her hands and knees, grimacing with pain. The man was pushing hard behind her, the tips of his fingers lost in the soft flesh of her buttocks.

'Unplug her!' Lavochkin ordered.

The girl screamed with indignation. The man stopped thrusting and looked up at Lavochkin. His eyes clouded with fury as he recognized the smiling spectator.

'You!' he cried.

'Me,' Lavochkin confirmed calmly.

'Who are you?'

'An old friend or an old enemy. The choice is yours.'

'What are you? Some sort of pervert?'

'No. I don't have the need.'

'Then why come here, now? Why have you been following me? On every street corner. In every shadow. You were even at the football match tonight, weren't you? I saw you in the crowd.'

'You did not play well.'

'That's not surprising. Are you police?'

'Who knows?' Lavochkin said, shrugging his shoulders.

'I have done nothing wrong.' The man flicked his head towards the girl and said: 'She is old enough.'

'I know,' Lavochkin said.

'So? So? If you have no further business I suggest you get out. Now! This instant! Get out!'

Lavochkin shook his head slowly and tucked his hands into the pockets of his greatcoat, making it plain that he was not ready to leave. The man growled with disgust and pulled out of the girl crudely. She scurried behind a sofa on her knees, gathering her clothes on the way as best she could. The man was not ashamed of his nakedness. He sprang to his feet and stomped towards Lavochkin with the intention of punching him. But there was a chilling aura around the unwelcome guest like some sort of magnetic force field, and he stopped short. Lavochkin absorbed the man's hesitation.

'You were always afraid, Lavrenty,' he said quietly.

'My name is not Lavrenty,' the man replied. 'It is Sergei. Sergei Ermanoff.'

'But you are still Beria. In a better body, perhaps, but still the same swamp reptile.'

'Beria?' The man knew the name from legend, but could not fathom its relevance. Lavochkin did not give him time to understand.

'You let them try to kill me!' he shouted.

Lavochkin took a pace forward. The man instinctively withdrew by the same distance.

'And you would have been in ecstasy if they had succeeded.' Lavochkin suddenly moved with the speed of light. He whipped a shining, immense hunting knife from his pocket, lunged forward and sliced it backhand across the man's right eye. The man screamed in agony, cupped his hands over the saturated wound and shouted: 'No, God, no! I can't see.'

'You found out who they were.' Lavochkin slashed the man on the shoulder. He staggered backwards, barely able to keep his balance.

'But you did not tell me.' Lavochkin carved him across his chest from nipple to nipple. Globules of scarlet seeped from the horizontal line and spilled over into channels running down his front. He screamed 'No! No!' until his voice cracked.

'You wanted me to suffer.' This time the blade dug into the man's right flank, above his hips. He was staggering now, lurching from side to side.

'You were the only one to smile as I lay dying.' The man tried to shield himself with his arms. Lavochkin cut them both beneath the elbow.

'Last time it was Khrushchev who got you, just as I said he would. How did you cope with being executed in the Lubyanka, Beria? Did you feel a sense of irony?' The man could only croak. Lavochkin gouged the knife into his remaining eye and twisted the blade.

'This time it will be your true leader who ends it, though it is more than such a buffoon as yourself deserves.' Lavochkin drew the blade in a diagonal stroke from right shoulder to left hip. The man, choking as warm liquid filled his lungs, slipped on his own blood and toppled backwards into the fire, sending up a cloud of ash and sparks. The room was filled with the stench of burning flesh and the last screams of agony. Lavochkin bent forward, dug the knife deep inside his victim's gut and, with a wrench of the wrist, opened up his stomach.

'It was all for nothing,' he muttered. 'You told me their names in your poisonous whispers. I have killed Polina Molotov already. Lydia and the colonel will follow within days. Then, for a while at least, I can rest.'

Lavochkin watched as the fire was slowly extinguished

by the leaking corpse. As the hissing subsided, he became aware of another noise. A constant intake, in rapid succession, of the shallowest of panicked breaths. Lavochkin found the girl still cowering behind the sofa, rigid with fear. She had dragged her panties over her feet to her ankles, but her limbs had been seized by what she had witnessed and she could not move another inch. Lavochkin dropped to his knees beside her and pressed his face close enough for her to smell his last pipe of tobacco.

'I should have cut off his prick for you, my dear,' he said. 'He was always a donkey with his women.'

The girl could not respond. She found herself praying she would pass out, but even that was denied her. Lavochkin looked her up and down. She was a rare beauty. Thick black hair tumbling over skin with the quality of polished china.

'Such a shame,' he said. 'But there are important things in life you must understand, little one. Sacrifices must be made for the greater good. The Soviet Union needs me, but it will not have me if you tell the authorities what happened here. It is a question of time . . . and identity.'

He raised the knife and drew it firmly across her throat. She barely seemed to notice. Lavochkin carried on talking to her as she slumped to the floor.

'Time, because I am not yet powerful enough, though it will not be long now. Identity, because, well . . .' Lavochkin chuckled as he folded her hair behind her ears. 'Ah, but you're too young to remember.'

They went to see in the New Year at Trafalgar Square. In a way, it was an apt place, a magnet for those without friends or family, desperate for company on the most sociable night of the year. But Quester tried to persuade Kelly it would be a new beginning.

291

'It's not just for lonely hearts,' he said as they walked along Whitehall towards the gathering throng. 'It attracts the young, the free and the flippant. It is an occasion that bursts with vitality and energy. It will be what we need. An injection of adrenalin.'

'And then?' Kelly felt Quester was forcing his enthusiasm, but did not say it.

'Then we start the New Year with a new outlook. We leave Stalin behind. In history, where he belongs. We'll go abroad. America, if you like. We'll find new work, new horizons.'

'It's not so easy. Lavochkin won't give up.'

'I think he has. It has been three months since we were in Moscow. We've seen nothing, heard nothing. Whatever else he is, he is not stupid. He will see the futility of this mad chase.'

'He's a barbarian. Barbarians always seek revenge.'

Quester grew impatient. He tugged at Kelly's wrist, pulling her back so she was forced to face him. He kissed her lightly on the tip of her nose.

'You said so yourself,' he said. 'It's a cliché but it's true. We can't go on like this. We've got to try.'

At first, she refused to respond. But he held on to her and would not let her go. Every time she flicked her eyes away to avoid his gaze, he sought them out again. She realized he would not let it ride. And the more she thought about it, the more convinced she became that perhaps, maybe, he was right. When she spoke, she tried not to sound reluctant.

'I'll do it for you, Tom. I'll try.'

Quester could not stifle a sigh of relief and felt a surge of hope bursting inside him.

'America?' he said.

'America.' Kelly smiled with a radiance that Quester

feared had been lost forever. 'We'll buy the tickets tomorrow.'

Quester had been right. The night was the tonic they needed. There was singing, chanting and laughter. As midnight approached, Trafalgar Square became a sea of people. Heaving, swaying. If Nelson could have looked down from his floodlit perch high above, he would have seen not the waves of the ocean, but currents of humanity. Surging this way and that, covering every inch of tarmac and flagstone.

Kelly enjoyed it. The air, sharpened by an earlier fall of snow, was freezing. Yet the atmosphere amid the steam cloud of 60,000 instant friends was warm and comforting. She babbled incessantly about the beauty of the giant, twinkling Christmas tree proudly soaring above its festive domain. She made jokes about the stern expressions on the square's immovable stone lions. She posed for a TV crew filming the event, puckering her lips and thrusting out her chest in a mocking impression of a model.

Quester watched her – and fell in love with her all over again.

The cacophony was too loud for the chimes of Big Ben to be heard from the other end of Whitehall, yet somehow everyone knew when midnight finally arrived. A mass countdown began. The entire crowd, pressed shoulder to shoulder, yelled 'Ten, Nine, Eight' and so on until the unity was broken by a myriad of individual cries of 'Happy New Year!'

Each joined hands with neighbours for a chorus of Auld Lang Syne and then it was open house for kissing, cheering, whooping, shakes of the hand and slaps on the back. Pretty girls threw themselves around the buttoned

shoulders of policemen and left bright circles of lipstick
on their cheeks.

Quester turned to Kelly and took her in his arms. He
folded himself around her and held her tight. She looked
up at him, her laughter suddenly overwhelmed by a need
to give and receive all the love and hope in the world.
Their lips came together slowly, and when they met it was
as if each was a part of the other's flesh. They stayed as
one until it seemed they would never be prised apart.
They kept their eyes open, exploring emotions, finding
nothing but love. It was only as the kiss finally came to an
end that Kelly's lost look of contentment was replaced by
a sudden scowl.

'What is it?' Quester asked.

'I don't know,' Kelly replied. She glanced at her elbow,
lifting her arm to examine it. 'I felt a jab. I'm sure of it.
Something sharp – a needle or something. It came right
through my coat.'

'It did indeed!'

They spun round in the direction of the voice.

Lavochkin smiled at them from underneath a fur hat.
Amid the pushing and the shoving of the crowd around
him, he was standing stock still. He raised his hand.
Between his thumb and forefinger was a miniature hypodermic syringe.

'Ricin,' he said. 'The protein of the castor oil seed and
one of the five most toxic substances known to man. In
fact, one gram is enough to kill 36,000 people.' He looked
at Kelly and shrugged his shoulders. 'You have minutes
to live, my dear, before your red blood cells turn to
poisoned jelly. You should never have become involved –
the water was too deep for such a novice swimmer. Great
national leaders are seldom overcome by mere
maidservants.'

He turned to face Quester.

'Better say it was a heart attack. It is not uncommon at events such as this and ricin can only be detected in the body by the most expert toxicologist. Besides, what else are you going to tell the poor British police? That your sweetheart was killed by Joseph Stalin?'

Quester went for him, but Lavochkin pushed backwards into the crowd and was swallowed up in seconds. Quester could not see him, but heard his voice above the mayhem.

'You're next, Colonel! Any day now.'

Quester barged his way back to Kelly. She felt ill already and beads of sweat were breaking out on her forehead. She did not say a word. She just looked vacantly at her elbow, trying to find the invisible hole in her sleeve.

Quester slung his arm around her shoulder and tried to haul her through the crowd. He was sure it was another nightmare – and prayed to God he would wake up soon.

'Don't die!' he pleaded. 'Please don't die. I'll find an ambulance. You'll be all right.'

Kelly could no longer walk. Her feet dragged along the ground as Quester pushed on. In his panic, he lost all sense of direction. All he could see were legs, feet, torsos, heads. Human walls, standing in his way.

'Move!' he yelled. 'Get out of the way!' But no-one could hear him.

Kelly's weight grew on his shoulders. He could feel her through his coat, trembling and as hot as a furnace.

He burst through the outer perimeter of the throng and found himself on the steps of the National Gallery. He scanned the area for an ambulance or a first-aid man, but there was none. Kelly was gripped by palpitations. He laid her flat on one step and gave her the kiss of life. A small group of onlookers gathered. They quickly saw that what he was doing was useless. Kelly's whole body was shuddering. There was no return now.

Quester, desperate, tried heart message, pumping his palms into Kelly's chest with all the force he could muster. Her skin turned dark as if someone had cast a shadow over her. Terrible sounds came from her throat as air was denied entry by constricting muscles. She managed to raise a hand – and stroked Quester's face as tenderly as she had ever done. Then she went into one final, awful spasm before her body became still.

Quester cried out like a wild beast, striking his fist on the concrete steps no matter the pain. The sense of grief was instant. There was a pounding in his chest like rolling thunder and tears spilled down his cheeks as if a giant dam had been breached. When he had shouted all he could, when he realized that it was over, he cradled Kelly's head in his arms and gently rocked her from side to side as if he was trying to soothe a baby to sleep.

He told her he would always love her and repeated her name over and over again.

'Lydia . . . Lydia . . . Lydia.'

23

He slipped away from the hospital without telling anyone. There was no point in staying. Kelly was dead. There was nothing he could do to bring her back. There was nothing anyone could do. Her body had been taken to hospital as a formality. Soon, it would be transferred to a mortuary – and Quester did not have the stomach to see her in such a place.

He felt the onset of madness, just as he had before he collapsed in the middle of a field in a remote corner of Belgium. He talked to himself – trying to stave it off yet recognizing its merciless power.

'Quester is weak, Bren is strong. Which one am I?'

He said the words time after time, forcing himself towards a decision.

He reached Taggs Island at dawn, creeping over the bridge with the guile and silence of the hunted animal that he was, eyes flicking in all directions through the morning half-light, ears pricked up for the slightest snap of a twig.

'Are you here, Stalin?' he whispered. 'Have you come to get me?'

There was no sound, no movement. Even the ducks and the geese were quiet and still.

'The calm before the storm,' Quester muttered. 'So peaceful. So violently peaceful.'

He took one step at a time until he reached his houseboat. Still there was no challenge. No-one lunged from the shadows. No-one swooped from behind. He opened his door, pausing for a moment before entering in case it was a trap. Once inside, he searched every room, every cupboard, every corner, expecting to find the smirking face of Lavochkin in each.

'You're not here, but you're here, Stalin. Man of steel. Steel ghost.'

He found his passport and stuffed a case with winter clothes. Lavochkin had given him time and a plan was formulating in his head. He knew Quester could not carry it out alone. In these modern days, Bren could not carry it out alone. But together, there was a chance.

He scribbled a note and pushed it through the letterbox of his neighbours, the Amanious. It told them he was going to Switzerland and they should not expect his return for a week.

'Leave clues,' he muttered. 'Leave a trail for Stalin to follow. An easy trail. Now is the time for the final conflict.'

At Heathrow Airport, he arranged for the entire contents of his bank account to be transferred to a branch of Crédit Suisse in Geneva. Then he caught a scheduled Swissair flight to the city. Lavochkin watched the plane take off from the comfort of a coffee lounge.

In Geneva, Quester withdrew his money and used it to buy plastic explosive, detonating cord, detonators, pull fuses, wire and a radio control pack from a wholesale store he knew in the Old Town. He also paid for a revolver and six rounds of ammunition.

'That's for Quester,' he told himself. 'Now for Bren.'

He shopped around the markets to build up a kit of US Army combat clothing. By evening, he had a collection of boots, socks, pants, shirts and jackets. All he lacked was a helmet, but that could wait.

He went to a travel agency and asked them to find him a cottage in the Swiss Alps.

'Away from the ski pistes,' he said. 'Away from tourists. Somewhere completely on its own. Isolated. I don't want to hear a feather drop.'

After an hour phoning around, after he had rejected several suggestions, they found him one above the town of Martigny, in the shadow of the Matterhorn. He hired a four-wheel-drive Fiat and drove there the next morning.

It was called Les Érables and was set in thickets of maple trees. The whole terrain, for as far as the eye could see, was dazzling white, the purest Quester had seen. A blanket of thick, soft snow had been unfurled over pasture and meadow. Tell-tale humps in criss-cross patterns hid stone walls denoting the borders of the fields. Thick hoarfrost sparkled on the maples, turning them into crystalline statues like witches with long, arthritic fingers. The only sign of human activity came from two parallel tracks made by cross-country skiers, a foot apart and meandering across the contours until they disappeared over the horizon. But the edges of the channels were ill-defined and dusted by a fresh snowfall, indicating that it had been days since they were last used.

The cottage itself was set on a ridge, the rear terrace plunging down into a valley filled with wispy cloud turned silver by glaring sunlight, the front giving out on to a small patio leading into the maples. Beyond, the ground soared steeply upwards, first through a copse of pine trees and then on to virgin snow-covered rock.

Quester jerked his neck back as far as muscle and bone would allow, but even so he could not make out a specific peak to the mountain. Either he was too close, or it was simply too far away. The huge, dominating slab of white was hostile to his gaze, as if it was challenging him to a

299

duel. Climb aboard, it said, you'll see just what an infinitesimal speck you will become. Quester took a deep breath of the sweetest air and muttered: 'Perfect.'

He turned and marched purposefully into the cottage. It was 300 years old and built of two-foot-thick stone to ward off the cold. Each entrance had a double door, each window had two frames – one placed at the outer edge of the wall, the other lining the inner. The interior was all pinewood. Floors, ceiling and wall-panelling. There were ceramic furnaces in each room, cracked and distorted with the passing of heat and time. Quester's first task was to light fires in them. He needed warmth to keep his muscles supple, his brain alert. He needed smoke from a chimney to tell Stalin he was there.

Enough logs to last a winter were neatly stacked to the roof in an outhouse. Quester collected what he needed in large straw baskets, chopping some into smaller sticks to start the fires. It was not long before the outer tiles of the furnaces were warm to the touch and the pungent smell of burning wood filled the cottage.

It was time for his second task. He changed into the US Army fatigues he had bought the day before, looking at his reflection in a mirror to see if they would have the desired effect. They did. He felt ready to fight, ready for war. He felt like Bren.

He filled a back-pack with explosive and detonating cord, and tied the cottage's path-clearing shovel and broom to it with rope. Then he heaved the complete, awkward bundle over his shoulders and struck out into the snow. He walked through the maples and on through the pines, his heavy boots crunching deep into windblown drifts. On the outer fringe of the pine copse, he stopped and studied the hillside to find what he was looking for: a slope leading up the mountain that was steep enough to be a challenge, yet gentle enough to be climbed without aids like ice picks and crampons. He found it fifty yards to his right. At first, it followed a twisting path, avoiding protrusions of rock and jagged-edged gullies. But the higher it climbed, the more it straightened out, until it became a simple case of plotting a course directly up the incline.

Quester found he could manage by punching his toes into the snow for each individual step, though the toll on his limbs, particularly his calves, was excruciating.

He tried to ignore the pain and scanned ahead for his next target – a more acute angle of ascent topped off by an overhanging ridge of snow. The end of the line for all but well-equipped mountaineers.

It took him another hour to reach it, by which time he was exhausted and had to rest. He sat in the snow and looked down to the cottage below, now just another dot in the distance. Beyond, a half-cleared road, looking like a strand of cotton, wound towards Martigny, though, mercifully, neither the town nor its people were visible.

Quester wished he could sit there forever. It was an immaculate place, untainted by the grime, threat and fear of the real world. But he knew he could not delay long. If he was lucky, he had today – and today alone – to prepare the ground for Lavochkin. Any time wasted could only hasten his death.

He gave himself five minutes before easing himself stiffly to his feet. He was struck immediately by the vastness of the snow bank which confronted him. It was a thousand times bigger than it had appeared as he approached, and curled up and away in concave shape until it reached a windblown lip high above. Quester felt as if he was standing at the foot of a solid tidal wave.

He had no surveying equipment beyond the trained

lenses of his own eyes and cursed himself for not packing
a theodolite. He stood bending to right and left, comput-
ing down-loads, forces and pressure points lurking unseen
in the hulking mass. For a fleeting moment, it reminded
him of Mother, the great bulge of rock in Kashmir.

That is where it started, he thought. This is where it
will end.

He used the shovel to dig six holes ten feet apart along
the base of the snow wall. Then he fell on his knees to
scoop out deeper funnels in each hole with his cupped
hands. It was hard labour and soon he was steaming with
evaporating perspiration. As he worked, Quester talked
to Bren, and Bren to Quester.

'The air. So rarefied. It makes me light-headed,' said
Quester.

'It's not light-headedness,' Bren replied. 'It's insanity.'

'He's insane.'

'Who?'

'Stalin . . . Lavochkin.'

'He will be here soon. Tonight. Tomorrow.'

'And how will we defend ourselves?'

'Are you asking me?'

'You're the soldier, the strategist. Play a war game.'

'It has already begun. That is why we are here, doing
what we are doing.'

'But there's no logic. It is just a wing and a prayer.
Futile hope.'

'That's Quester talking.'

'Help me, Bren.'

Quester packed fist-sized cylinders of plastic explosive
into each funnel and connected them with detonating cord.

'To win a battle, one must first discover a weakness in
one's enemy,' Bren said.

'He has none.'

'He has one.'

'Which is?'

'His arrogance. His infernal, sickening arrogance.'

'That is a strength, not a weakness.'

'It is both. It gives him confidence, but it makes him blind.'

'Blind?'

'At Moscow airport, he told you he smashed your skull so you would suffer, but would not die. But he made a mistake and did far more damage than he meant to. Afterwards, he tried to keep you alive. He paid for all the best treatment. But in the end, it was he who signed your death warrant – the papers allowing the hospital to switch off your life-support machine. Your subsequent survival was sheer chance. He could not have known. Yet by the time you saw him in Moscow, he had fooled himself into believing he had done exactly as he had intended. You see, there is no room in his mind for the notions of failure or error. He is blinded by his obsession with his own infallibility.'

'So? How will that help us here?'

'It means he will not shoot from a distance like a sniper. He will come close. He will want to talk to us, to demonstrate his superiority one final time at close quarters. That is where you come in. Your talent and skill with explosives.'

'I left it in Kashmir.'

'No. Look at what you are doing.'

'It may not work.'

'It will. Believe it.'

'I won't have the courage to carry it out.'

'I will be with you.'

Quester taped two primer charges to the end of the detonating cord. He pushed a detonator into one and

303

connected its electric leads to a small radio receiver. He made a small mound of packed ice and placed the receiver on its crest, tuning it to the required frequency before dusting it with a disguising veil of powder snow.

'Where shall we stand?' he asked.

'All we can do is run to one side and hope that only the centre of the snow bank falls.'

'I'm not sure . . .'

'I watched you place the charges. It will work. It has to work.'

'To avenge poor Lydia.'

'And to save the world from another Stalin. If he succeeds in killing us, it will only be the start. He was a butcher. He will always be a butcher.'

'Blood and slime and death.'

'That is how it has always been.'

Quester left the charges in place and the radio receiver ready for its signal. He descended the mountain backwards, a step at a time, sweeping away his footprints with the broom as he went. He could not obliterate them totally, but was confident the wind and the frost would do the rest. At the foot of the slope, he used the shovel to hack a notch in the trunk of the nearest pine. When he returned to the cottage, he still had the bulk of his day's work in front of him.

For an hour, he collected logs from the outhouse and piled them haphazardly in the kitchen. When he was sure he had enough, he climbed a young maple tree growing outside the back door and kicked at its lower branches until they snapped off. Then he set to work with axe and knife. Chopping, cutting and slicing until he had 120 fresh stakes of equal size, about six inches long with one end sharpened to a point.

He pushed them into the snow in pairs, each stake six

feet from its partner. On one, he stuck a small chunk of explosive with detonator and pull-fuse. This was attached to the other stake by stretched wire with virtually no give. The end result was a trip wire capable of triggering a stun blast like that of the most potent firecracker.

Quester arranged each wire side by side to make three concentric circles around the cottage. Working from the outside in, he placed the first at a radius of twenty-five yards from the building, the second at fifteen yards and the third at ten yards. By the time the system was complete, it was dusk.

He locked himself inside the cottage and, as night fell, he used the logs from the kitchen to build thick wooden barriers against every door and every window.

The cottage became a fortress, an impenetrable refuge protected by three rings of explosive. Quester dragged a mattress into the lobby and dropped it beside the warmth of the main furnace, though he still wore several layers of clothing so he would be instantly ready to spend hours in the cold outside, should the need arise. He loaded the revolver with its six bullets, pushing the gun into one pocket and his radio transmitter into another.

Only then did he feel safe enough to sit and wait for Stalin.

The first crack of explosive split the air at 3 A.M., followed in swift succession by two more blasts. It was clear that someone – or something – was tangled in the trip wires. Quester prayed that it was not a fox or a rabbit.

There was a fourth crack. Louder. Nearer.

Quester jumped to his feet.

A fifth explosion rang out. It had the same intensity as the first three. The wire-tripper was heading back. Retreating.

Quester ran to a window in the dining room, carefully removing two logs from the barrier so he could see out.

There! The merest flash, but it was unmistakable. A shock of spiky hair, silver in the moonlight, speeding away from the house.

'Stalin on a reconnoitring mission,' Bren whispered.

'What shall I do?' Quester asked.

'Shout. Let him know that you know he is here.'

The silver hair vanished into the night. Quester took a deep breath and yelled: 'Try again, Lavochkin. In the morning. Try again then.'

Lavochkin's reply swept across the snow with piercing clarity.

'If you wish to die in daylight, so be it. It matters little to me one way or the other.'

Quester forced himself to wait until dawn before looking through the window again. Lavochkin was there in the midst of the maples, leaning nonchalantly against the nearest trunk, his greatcoat smeared with smoke stains from his encounter with Quester's firecrackers.

He did not change. He was the man enjoying the sun on the far side of the bridge at Taggs Island, the man flushed with pride in a bar near Moscow airport. Unruffled, unconcerned. To Quester, this was a time for the ultimate test of survival. To Lavochkin, it was just another day.

The early-morning glare reflected off his pale skin. Shadows thrown by the branches above him danced on his cheeks. As he watched Quester dismantling the log barrier at the front entrance, he waved his greeting as if he was meeting a long-lost friend at a crowded sea port.

Quester paused before opening the door, steeling himself for what was about to happen. Lavochkin did not move, absorbing without interest what had become another tiresome delay.

'Now?' Quester asked.

'Now,' Bren replied.

'Talking to yourself?' Lavochkin called. 'Such a pity you will not be able to make it back to the asylum.'

Quester pulled the revolver from his pocket and bolted out of the door, deliberately tripping wires to create noise and confusion. He fired the gun and Lavochkin thought it prudent to take cover, ducking behind the tree trunk he had been leaning on. He saw that Quester was dressed for combat and laughed out loud, sending a raucous echo bouncing back from the mountainside.

'What's this?' he shouted. 'The colonel on a charge?'

Quester fired again. A bullet ricocheted off a branch and sent a shrill whine down into the valley.

'Where to?' Quester asked breathlessly.

'Move out to the left,' Bren advised. 'You've got to get on the other side of him. Swing him round so his back is to the cottage.'

'I'm in the open. Exposed.'

'He won't shoot. You'll smell his breath before he tries to kill you.'

Lavochkin watched Quester veer away.

'Where are you going?' he yelled. 'France? Or back to Belgium, perhaps.'

Quester crashed against a maple tree fifty yards to Lavochkin's left. He fired the gun again, but the bullet dug silently into the snow behind the Russian's shoulders.

'Such a pity, Colonel,' Lavochkin called. 'You have lost your accuracy over the years.'

Quester hurried through the copse towards the pines.

'Run blindly,' Bren urged. 'Don't let him see what you are doing.' Even such muffled words picked up an echo and were amplified. Lavochkin could not hear every detail, but was amused at the sonic effect.

'I have done my work well,' he said. 'All that remains of you is a mad tin soldier.'

'Shoot!' Bren ordered. Quester fired the revolver for a fourth time, forcing Lavochkin to shuffle around the base of the tree to ensure his safety. Quester ran in a curve towards the foot of the mountain climb. Now Lavochkin was between him and the cottage.

'It's where we want him,' Bren said. 'Pin him down so we have a chance to run.'

Quester reached the far edge of the pines at the foot of the mountain slopes. Lavochkin cried, 'Coming!' as if he was playing a childhood game of hide and seek. Crouching low, he scurried a few yards towards Quester, but was stopped by another crack from the revolver.

'Six-five-four-three-two-one,' Lavochkin called. 'Really, Colonel, revolvers are simply not enough for today's punishing demands. Automatic pistols are favoured by all. Even if you could shoot straight, I'm afraid you only have one bullet left.'

'Make him wary,' Bren said.

Quester shouted: 'I have another gun in my pocket.'

'You're lying.' Lavochkin sounded so sure. 'Your folly is transparent. No-one advertises their arsenal.'

'No matter,' Bren whispered. 'He cannot be certain. It will delay him another few seconds. It's all we need.'

Quester fired his final bullet. It tore into the tree bark two feet above Lavochkin's head, sending a shower of splinters into the Russian's hair.

'Better!' Lavochkin called. 'But too little, too late.'

Quester threw down the gun and ran along the perimeter of the pines. When he came to the tree with the notched trunk, he turned sharp left and headed up the slope.

Lavochkin, puzzled for the first time, watched for a moment, then trotted through the copse to take up the pursuit.

Quester glanced over his shoulder as he climbed. He had a head start of sixty yards. But Lavochkin was as strong as an ox and, inch by inch, began to gain.

'Will it be enough?' Quester asked.

'I don't know,' Bren said. 'Maybe. Maybe not.'

Quester felt his heart pounding and his stomach churning with fear. The tension filtered through to his limbs, making them stiff and cumbersome.

'Keep going!' Bren's plea sounded like an order.

'I can't,' Quester said plaintively.

'You must.'

Quester looked back again. Lavochkin, breathing deeply and athletically, had closed the gap to fifty yards.

'He's coming,' Quester cried. 'He's too strong. He'll have me soon. I know it.'

'Keep going!' Bren barked. 'Don't look back. It wastes time and energy.'

They reached the steeper incline. Lavochkin found time to rest. He stood bolt upright, his hands on his hips, a short perpendicular figure on an angled white plain.

'Where are we going?' he shouted. 'Are you a Christian, Colonel? Do you want to be near Heaven when you die?'

Quester ignored him. He could see the snowbank ahead now. It was half an hour away at the current rate of ascent, but he could see it. It fed new blood to his legs.

It was not long before Lavochkin saw it, too.

'There, I told you that you could not go on for ever.

You are trapped, Colonel. Like a cat in a blind alley, with a Rottweiler dog at your heels.'

The sun disappeared. Billowing cloud blew in from nowhere, tumbling quickly down the mountainside until the air was thick with swirling mist. Quester looked back, but could no longer see the assassin. It did not trouble Lavochkin. He announced his presence by howling like a wolf. His pursuit was relentless.

Quester felt his feet slipping as the slope iced up.

'Dig in! Dig in!' Bren roared. 'Ram your toes into the snow.'

'I'm trying,' Quester stuttered. 'But it's impossible.'

'Nothing's impossible.'

'I'm slipping! Hold me!'

Quester felt his feet slip from underneath him and landed heavily on his face. He dug his fingers into the snow until they became claws, but there was nothing he could do. Slowly, inexorably, he began to slide down, gathering speed at a staggering rate until he thudded directly into Lavochkin, taking the assassin's legs away.

Lavochkin was caught by surprise. He tried to cling on to Quester and for one long, static-laden moment, the hunter and the hunted came face to face, each stunned by the suddenness with which it had happened. Then Lavochkin reeled off balance and plunged on to the snow, sliding away into the fog on his backside.

The collision broke Quester's fall and he staggered to his feet.

'Dig in!' Bren cried. 'There's still time.'

Quester punched his toes into the snow and began to climb again. Behind, he heard Lavochkin cursing and scrabbling in the snow. Then the controlled, regular, lung-expanding intakes of breath began again, and he knew the assassin was back on his trail.

It was nearly an hour before Quester reached the overhanging snowbank. All the time, he knew Lavochkin was closing, closing, closing – and he was near the end of his tether. Everything had gone. It had all drained away, as if someone had opened a tap on his ankle. Strength, fortitude, endurance. Every human quality he possessed.

'Except hope,' said Bren. 'Move fast, or that will vanish too.'

Quester tapped his breast pocket. The transmitter was there. A tiny package of microchip electronics. That was his hope. His final hope.

He staggered across the base of the snowbank, away from where he had planted the charges eighteen hours before. He turned to listen for the approach of Lavochkin. The cloud was lifting again. A shadow, head bowed as it traced Quester's footprints, loomed through the last creeping tentacles of mist.

'Come now, Colonel,' Lavochkin uttered impatiently. 'It is time for hand-to-hand fighting. Do you have the energy?'

'Now!' Bren shouted.

Quester did not react. He was transfixed by the sight and sound of Lavochkin. The Russian stopped fifteen yards from the snowbank. He put his hands on his hips and straightened his back, groaning deliberately to feign old age.

'Now!' Bren shouted again.

Lavochkin peered over to where Quester was standing. His expression was mellow, his smile content, but his eyes were still yellow and cold as ice. He shrugged his shoulders and shook his head as if there was something he could not understand.

'Why bother with all this climbing and such?' he said.

'We could have settled our business in the cottage, man to man.'

It was a question to which there was an answer, and Quester's eyes were drawn involuntarily to the frozen white cube that hid the radio receiver. Lavochkin tracked his gaze and saw it too. His smile vanished and was replaced by alarm. Every muscle in his face locked solid. He was alert, agile, ready for anything.

'What is it?' he snapped.

'Now!' Bren yelled frantically.

Quester's arm moved across his chest towards his breast pocket. But his hand was trembling and he could not flick up the flap.

Lavochkin glanced back at the white cube, then looked up at the snowbank towering above him. In an instant, he realized he had been lured into a trap, and with the split-second speed of the executioner that he was, he whipped a Makharov pistol from his pocket and pointed it at Quester.

'Take your hand away,' he ordered, taking a step forward.

Quester found himself obeying the command, though he could not explain why. Slowly, he moved his arm out from his chest until it was stretched in front of him.

Lavochkin took another pace forward behind the unwavering barrel of the Makharov.

'You see,' he said. 'You are not capable of killing. Few people are. You can't do it, but I can.'

'Hit it!' Bren pleaded.

'I will not kill you now,' Lavochkin said. 'It will be a wounding shot. There are things I must know before you die.'

'What things?' Quester uttered.

312

'Hit it now!' Bren cried despairingly. 'Dear God, this is the man who killed Lydia!'

Lydia . . .

The name shook Quester from his stupor. Lavochkin saw the change in him and took fresh aim, curling his finger firmly around the pistol's trigger. He took a third step towards his prey and said: 'You'll find out what things.'

'Lydia!'

Quester felt a burst of adrenalin released by Bren's fury and hatred. His teeth clenched, his body became as taut as stretched elastic and he emitted a primeval, agonized scream that tore through the still air like a knife through silk. Lavochkin fired. A bullet dug into Quester's left leg above the knee. As he fell, he made a fist and rammed it hard into his breast pocket.

The charges exploded with a strange, distorted report, muffled by the massive, absorptive snowbank above and around them. Quester was hit by shards of flying ice and was pinned to the ground. He heard a great wrenching sound, as if two giant fists were tearing a canvas sack to pieces. He looked up to see the tidal wave of snow moving. It slipped at first, as if someone had gently lifted it and put it on wheels. Then, with a numbing roar that crashed around the mountainside, it collapsed on to itself and burst outwards and downwards.

Lavochkin was caught by the full, brutal force of the avalanche. Quester heard a single scream of terror before the assassin was buried in the rushing snow and swept away to his fate.

The avalanche gained awesome speed and momentum in the space of seconds, sweeping all before it in a devastating surge of power, its sliding spearhead continually overtaken by the bulk behind it, its crest bouncing and spiralling through the air, the whole gathering thousands of tons of snow for its mighty cause as it hurtled down the mountain.

Quester hauled himself to his feet beside the gaping crater left in the snowbank. He watched the diminishing spectacle as it rolled away out of his sight, sniffed at the microscopic globules of ice left hanging in the air by the turmoil and shouted: 'Die, Stalin! At last, it's your turn.'

Holding the wound in his leg, he hobbled down the slope, following the channel of havoc carved out by the snow cascade. He slipped and fell often, but it did not matter. Nothing mattered now. It was all over.

The avalanche was arrested first by the gentler slope at the foot of the mountain, and finally by the first rows of pines.

Quester came across a sleeve of Lavochkin's greatcoat – somehow ripped off him and tossed to the surface of the solid white river. Quester sat down a few feet away and stared at it. Ragged, torn and tortured, it reminded him of himself.

The sun burst through what was left of the cloud as if to congratulate him on his survival. It was direct and uncannily warm – and soon the hoarfrost on the pines and maples began to melt. Large droplets of water gathered on the crystals, hanging precariously for a moment before falling to the ground with a heavy thud. Soon, the copse was alive with the sound of sun-powered rain. In such silent surroundings, it was like a thunderstorm.

Quester took it all in, but could not bring himself to smile. He had lost too much. Instead of contentment, he found himself thinking he was in the midst of another dream. In such a state, he barely noticed the hint of movement beneath the tattered sleeve.

It was real enough.

There it was again.

Beside the sleeve this time. A ripple just under the surface of the snow. A murmuring. A disturbance. Something that should not happen.

Within seconds, a human finger broke through, flicking from side to side and thrusting upwards, like the claw of a crab emerging from sand. It was followed by the back of a hand, turning, displaying its palm, padding the ground around it. Searching. Probing.

Quester was paralysed. He guessed what was happening, but could no more prevent it than move.

A shoulder pushed through the widening hole in the surface, loose threads hanging from the remains of the coat that covered it.

There was no stopping it now. Quester looked around, desperately searching for Bren. But there was no-one, not even in his mind. He was alone, facing the sight he dreaded more than any other.

A crown of fair hair, its spikes wet and flattened, emerged through the snow. Lavochkin gasped and gulped in air as if it was the last on Earth. As yet, he was a head with no body, turning to left and right as if on a plate. His eyes could not see Quester, yet a sudden roar of aggression revealed that he sensed his presence.

Quester knew he should force himself to his feet. He knew he should kick that evil head off its shoulders while he had the chance. But he had nothing left. No strength. No courage. No will.

Lavochkin heaved himself out of his tomb and turned to face the man who had entombed him. He was bleeding from both mouth and nose. His skin was purple and he could not stop coughing. He clutched at his stomach with

315

his left hand. There was no flippancy left on his face, not even arrogance. Just rage. Uncontrollable, demonic rage.

'Crushed, but not defeated,' he snarled. 'Buried, but not dead. You will not be so fortunate, Colonel.' He opened his greatcoat and took a long-bladed knife from a leather sheath stitched into the lining. 'I killed Beria with this!' he shouted. 'It's like the one I threw at my father all those years ago.'

Quester watched him come. Lavochkin was like a wounded bull. Snorting. Bellowing. Strong. Unstoppable. Quester prepared himself for death.

Lavochkin kicked Quester's chin as he sat, knocking him over on to his back. The assassin leaped on him, straddling his chest and pressing the tip of the knife against his throat.

'The choice is yours,' Lavochkin hissed. 'Tell me who ordered you to kill me at Yalta, and your death will be quick and clean. Stay silent and I will cut you to ribbons, but you will not immediately be granted the painless escape of death.'

He gave a slight push on the knife, so that Quester's skin was pierced.

'Come on now, tell me. Who were you working for? Was it the Nazis? The American secret service? The British? Who? Name names. Tell me their ranks. Was it someone just above you, or was it a leader? Perhaps it was even Hitler himself. Or Roosevelt. Or Churchill. Tell me!'

'So you can go on killing?' Quester asked. 'Where will it all end?'

Lavochkin slashed the knife across Quester's shoulder.

'You remember the Ardennes. White snow covered in red blood. That is how it will be here. Tell me!'

316

He cut Quester on the thigh. Quester winced with pain, but shook his head. Lavochkin became hysterical.

'Why do you think I have been so patient all these years? I have waited for this moment, when you would be forced to tell me who gave the orders. I shall have my revenge. My complete revenge!'

Lavochkin raised his arm in the air. Quester saw the ruby-tipped blade glinting in the sunlight, ready to plunge down into tendon and muscle.

There was a sharp crack in the distance, repeated as it echoed off the mountainside.

Quester did not see the bullet enter Lavochkin's head, but he saw it burst out, punching a hole the size of a golfball in the assassin's cheekbone. Lavochkin dropped the knife. It fell in a perfect line and dug into the outer flesh on Quester's neck, staying bolt upright as its tip was arrested by firm sinew.

Lavochkin lurched to one side and lost his balance. Quester caught a glimpse of him the instant before he thudded into the snow.

He was smiling.

Footsteps crunched through the snow away to Quester's left. Growing louder, coming closer. Quester dared not move in case the knife slipped and cut his jugular vein. A face came into view. Peering at him. Examining him to see if he was still alive. Silhouetted against the sun, it was hard to make out. But the silver crescent of hair was a clue.

'Do you know *why* Viktor Lavochkin wanted to kill you?' Rats took hold of the hilt of the blade and pulled it out with one firm, but delicate tug. Quester stared at the man from the Lubyanka. He did not know if he was friend of foe, but answered 'No' in any case.

Rats rubbed his chin as if in deep thought.

'There is no logic, never has been,' he said. 'The girl in Kazakhstan. The football player in Moscow. Your sweetheart in London. And many, many more.'

Rats saw Quester's bewilderment. He took a handkerchief from his pocket and dabbed at the bleeding wounds to offer some form of consolation.

'Oh yes, we have been watching him, letting him kill, trying to establish a pattern. Why do you think I allowed you to leave Moscow? I knew Lavochkin had followed you before and that he would follow you again.'

He helped Quester to his feet, shaking his head as he saw the rivulets of scarlet spilling from neck, shoulder, thigh and knee. Quester looked down at Lavochkin's spreadeagled corpse. Beyond it, tossed in the snow, was the laser-sighted Kalashnikov rifle which Rats had used to kill a comrade.

'Trying to establish a pattern, trying to find a reason,' Rats said. 'But there has been none. The only answer is that he was a killer, a psychopathic killer, an arbitrary killer. Choosing targets with a pin and then hunting them down for his own amusement.'

Quester started to say something, but stopped himself. Rats could not understand. No-one could understand.

'I had to end it,' Rats said. 'It was my duty. I was not joking at the Lubyanka when I said that Lavochkin scared us, too. I could not let a man like that rise to become leader of the Soviet Union. He was despised by most, feared by many. Some were even convinced that he thought of himself as a new Stalin.'

Rats bent to take hold of the body and said: 'We couldn't have that, now, could we?'

24

The car crash was not serious, but it triggered Siggi's labour pains. An ambulance took her and her husband, Gerd, to hospital in Martigny.

'When is the baby due?' the doctor asked.

'A month or so,' Gerd said.

'Where do you live?'

'Frankfurt. In a small flat.'

'What are you doing in Switzerland?'

'Touring. Last holiday together before having children. Friends told us it would be a good idea.'

'Do you want to be with her?'

'For the birth?'

'Yes – the baby is in the breech position and she will need a Caesarian. But what with the car crash and all, it will help her if you are there. It is not uncommon for fathers to be present at Caesarians nowadays.'

It was the most beautiful sight Gerd had witnessed. A perished walnut of an infant being tugged by the ankles directly from his mother's womb. The beginning of a new life.

After the child had been cleaned, after he had nestled against his mother's breast, he was given to his father.

'Hold him,' said Siggi. 'Hold your son.'

Gerd was overcome with emotion.

He thrust the tiny boy high in the air and said: 'This is your world, Josef. One day you will rule it.'

Acknowledgements

My grateful thanks to Jean Clarke, John Green, Jacqueline Ridge, Pratima Sarwate and Mark Sewell, who all helped me to hone the fine detail of this novel. And to the one and only Peter Smith for his invaluable support.